Stuart M. Kaminsky

Blood and Rubles

A Porfiry Petrovich Rostnikov Novel

WHEELER
PUBLISHING, INC.
ROCKLAND, MA

★ AN AMERICAN COMPANY ★

To Yukimasa and Setsuko Kusumoto,
with whom we share a true family

Published in Large Print by arrangement with
Ballantine Books, a division of Random House, Inc.
in the United States and Canada.

Wheeler Large Print Book Series.

Set in 16 pt. Plantin.

Library of Congress Cataloging-in-Publication Data

Kaminsky, Stuart M.
    Blood and rubles / Stuart Kaminsky.
        p. cm.-- (Wheeler large print book series)
    ISBN 1-56895-329-1 (hardcover)
        1. Rostnikov, Porfiry Petrovich (Fictitious character)—Fiction.
2. Police—Russia—Moscow—Fiction. 3. Moscow (Russia)—Fiction.
4. Large type books. I. Title. II. Series
[PS3561.A43B56   1996b]
813'.54—dc20   95-16365
                                                                      CIP

You'll remember me before you die! You think you've brought peace and quiet? You believe you'll live like squires from now on? Well, I see different things in store for you.
  –Taras Bulba, in *Taras Bulba* by Nikolai Gogol

Blood and Rubles

Chapter 1

A Day Not Unlike Other Days

Oleg Makmunov knew it was night. There was no sun. He knew he must be somewhere off of Gorky Street, for that was where he had started. The rest was a drunken blur. Even though he was dressed only in shoes, worn socks, threadbare pants, and a yellow and red American flannel shirt, Oleg Makmunov couldn't even have told a policeman if it was winter or summer.

Alexei Chazov and his two brothers had followed the drunkard for about five blocks. They had stayed back in the darkness, though it was unlikely the drunken man would see them unless they were in his face.

The street was narrow and empty. Well, not completely empty. The Chazovs had seen a young man and woman with their arms around each other in a doorway.

The drunkard had wandered far since he had been thrown out of the New Hampshire Café with its blaring American music. He had stumbled, seemingly without knowing it, in the general direction of the Strogino District, a neighborhood of cement tenements. When he entered the Strogino, the Chazovs spotted him.

The drunk stopped, but Alexei held his brothers back.

In front of them, sitting on a low stoop, a man smoked a pipe. The man seemed big, but it was hard to tell because most of the lights on the small street were out, and the ones that were on were dim.

Oleg slumped into a doorway and searched his pockets for the small bottle of vodka he had tucked away, but found nothing. Another search, this time for money, produced enough rubles to buy a small bottle should he stumble on someone who might have one to sell. He repocketed the money and tried to decide which way led back to Gorky Street. He guessed left and took his first few steps in that direction.

The big man on the stoop finished his pipe. He tapped the ashes out on the sidewalk, rose, turned, and went through the door behind him.

Now the Chazovs could move. As they neared the drunkard, Alexei supposed that the man was old, at least fifty.

In fact, Oleg was thirty-three. He had given up most of his teeth to drink and dissolute living. He was known to the down and the drunk as Smiling Oleg, not because he smiled so much but because he looked so incredibly funny when he smiled his near-toothless grin.

"One small step for Oleg," he said to the man who'd been smoking across the street, but now the man was nowhere to be seen. Oleg shrugged and took another step. "And one more step for the glorious future of Mother Russia."

Before he took another step, he tottered. Almost certainly he would fall to the pavement. It had happened to him before. And so many times he had rolled over on the street to look up at whoever had pushed him and saw no one. This time he did not fall.

He took another step and was shoved hard from behind. His hands went out to protect his battered face from smashing into the pavement. At that he was successful. He was aware of more than one person above him as he rolled over on his elbows and looked up with his loopy smile that usually brought a laugh. The three faces hovering over him did not laugh. Oleg was trying to rise when something hit him, something hard, something heavy, just above his left eye. It wasn't quite pain he felt but surprise. He slipped back down.

The second blow caught him flush in the face, and he was aware of his nose being smashed once again, probably along with his cheekbone. When something crushed his chest, cracking ribs, he found it very difficult to breathe.

He tried to speak when something cracked his skull, and he was vaguely aware that he must be dying. He made some attempt to breathe and think, but failed.

The three brothers continued picking up pieces of concrete and throwing them at the bloody mutilated head of Oleg Makmunov. When they were certain he was dead, the one who had jumped on his chest went through Oleg's pockets where he found his few rubles, two keys, a piece of smooth stone, the color of which they could not see, and a stub of a pencil.

It was enough. The Chazovs expected no more. They walked down the narrow street, saying nothing, in no great hurry.

Alexei Chazov was eleven. His brothers, Boris and Mark, were nine and seven.

Porvinovich stood in line reading a book at the Registration Chamber. The book was in Russian, a rather boring novel about a family that could not make a living in the new Moscow.

Making a living was not a problem for Alexei Porvinovich. He was a wealthy man with a weekly income, after payoffs to all including the tax police, of twenty-four million rubles a week, approximately twelve thousand dollars.

He owned three companies—a lamp factory, a cigarette factory, and a movie company. The lamps were flimsy things with green shades that sat on tables and would take no more than a 30-watt bulb. The cigarette factory was actually a packaging plant where the Turkish cigarettes Alexei bought for practically nothing were repackaged and sold at a profit of five hundred percent. The movie company was new. Alexei knew nothing about movies, but he had discovered that American, French, German, English, and Japanese producers wanted to make movies in Russia. Alexei's job, for a very high fee, was to get the foreign filmmakers through the new bureaucracy. Alexei was a master of *proizvol*, the exploitation of a system in confusion; the wielding of power to make rubles, and rubles to give power; the use of his power to further his own ends. He had been masterful at it when the bureaucrats were Communists, and he was an even greater master now that the bureaucrats were working for themselves. Capitalism had come with a typically Russian slant.

In addition to wealth, he had acquired a beautiful, intelligent wife who could speak five languages she had learned during her early years as a prostitute, and he supported his brother, who was little more than a *lokhl*, a simpleton.

The line moved up. Alexei could read the book no longer. He offered it to a lean, coughing man behind him. The man took it with no sign of thanks or gratitude. Alexei expected none.

Finally, it was Alexei's turn to sit in the metal folding chair across the desk from the man with many chins. Alexei had dressed for the occasion— a conservative definitely-not-new gray suit, a slightly rumpled white shirt open at the collar, a gray tie with little blue lightning bolts. He put his black vinyl briefcase on the desk and smiled wearily as he handed over the papers. The man took them in his swollen fingers.

"Let's see," the man said.

He was dressed more formally than Alexei, in the near-uniform of dark suit and dark tie at the tightly buttoned collar.

5

"*Protokal Sobradi* is in order, addresses are…Is this a seven?"

Alexei leaned over and confirmed that it was indeed a seven. The man nodded his head seriously, the opening move to inform Alexei that there would be a price to pay for this problem and others he would surely find.

"Your *ustav*, charter, seems to be correct. You are requesting a limited-liability charter. What will you be making or selling?"

"Books and other related items," said Alexei.

The other items included computers and apartment sublets.

The fat man did not pursue this. He turned the page to the financial statement, the heart of the matter.

"You have the twenty million rubles to start this venture?"

"As is stated on the forms, which are all certified," said Alexei. "All dues and charges have been paid, as the documents show."

"Good, good," the man said, moistening his finger and slowly turning the page to the landlord guaranty letters. "You will maintain your business at Forty-five Pushkin Lane?"

"I will," said Alexei.

The document before the fat man was signed by Alexei's wife, who was officially the owner of the office building where all of Alexei's businesses rented space.

Behind Alexei, the line waiting for permission to open a new business was long. Everyone waited patiently. They had waited patiently all their lives, and most of them fully expected that their requests to open businesses would be rejected and that they would be sent to some other office to have their documents "corrected."

"Temporary registration also in order," said the fat man, looking at the card before him.

It had cost Alexei five hundred thousand rubles to the lawyer appointed by the Registration Chamber to be sure the registration forms were in order so that he could be issued the card.

"Official police stamp," the man said. "Code number assigned by State Statistics Committee. The stamp is a bit underinked."

Alexei let out a small sigh.

"And your company stamp looks a bit too much like that of several others who have applied in the last month," the fat man said, shaking his head at the incompetence of those who did such things. "Signature card in order and notarized," he went on. "Three names. Partners?"

"Yes," Alexei said.

The fat man went to the next document.

"Bank account for the business seems to be fine." The fat man looked directly at Alexei for the first time.

"We are fortunate enough to have raised sufficient money for this venture," Alexei said softly.

"Good, good, good," said the fat man. "Let's see if we can move this along. Pension-fund papers are signed and stamped, and you have the form from the Tax Inspectorate."

The man flipped through the documents, once more shaking his head.

"I would like to issue you a permanent registration certificate," the man said, "but there are some minor discrepancies, words crossed out, stamps too faint. I would like to…" He shrugged his shoulders to show that he would like to help.

"I have one more document that might help," Alexei said, handing the fat man a small brown envelope.

The man opened the envelope and looked in, careful to keep anyone waiting in line or the registrar at the next desk from seeing. There were five one-hundred-dollar bills. The fat man slipped the envelope into the drawer of his desk and stamped the final certificate that would permit Alexei Porvinovich to open his new business. Alexei accepted the document, shook the man's flabby hand, and put all of his papers back in his briefcase.

Alexei relinquished the folding chair to the thin, nervous man who was next in line, the one to whom Alexei had given the book.

Success. It had taken only three weeks of waiting and bribing to get the document. He had two more envelopes in his briefcase, each with five hundred dollars. He had been prepared to give them all to the fat registrar. The man had sold his approval well below the going rate.

Swinging his briefcase, Alexei left the bureau building. Outside, he looked at the sky. It was early October. The first night frosts had already come, and soon the first snow would follow. Within a month the Moscow River would freeze and the city would be covered in snow. Good.

It was early, just before two in the afternoon, and Alexei decided to stop at the Grand Hotel for a drink and perhaps a sandwich before he went to his office.

He hurried down Nikloskaya Street—formerly Twenty-fifth of October Street—a street as old as the city of Moscow itself. The street was crowded with people. Alexei paused in front of the Old Printing House at Number 15. With its pale blue facade and neo-Gothic working of white stone, sundials, spires, and the prancing lion and unicorn above the main entrance, it was a building Alexei much admired. The first Russian book was printed there in 1564 by Ivan Fedorov. Alexei was confident that in time he would own this building.

He was looking up at the unicorn when the black Mercedes-Benz pulled up at the curb and two men stepped out of the car, both wearing ski masks and holding automatic weapons. People ran, fell to the ground, and screamed.

Alexei turned, saw the men, started to go to the ground, and then quickly realized that the weapons were aimed at him.

"In the car," one of the men ordered.

Alexei was stunned. A mistake was being made.

"I'm not—" he began but was cut off by the blow from a steel barrel against his face.

His cheekbone broke and he spat blood. The kidnapper repeated, "In the car."

Alexei staggered into the backseat of the car, followed by one of the masked men. The driver took off his mask as the car sped down the street, and his partner in the back- seat screamed, "What are you doing? You want him to recognize you?"

"I can't drive down the street wearing a mask," the driver answered reasonably.

The kidnapper in the backseat still wore his mask. He let out a grunt of nervous acceptance.

"Try not to bleed all over the car," he said, taking off his own mask and handing it to Alexei, "it's not mine."

Alexei took the mask and put it to his throbbing cheek. Then he looked up and recognized the man who had given him the mask. The man's hair was a wild frenzy and he was panting.

Alexei was certain that he was going to die very soon.

A few short blocks from the Neva River, not far from Saint Isaac's Square, a tall, lean man in black slacks, shoes, shirt, and jacket stood watching uniformed men pile efficiently out of two vans. At the side of the tall man—who some passersby thought resembled a vampire—stood a pretty, slightly plump young woman wearing an efficient gray suit. They were an odd and serious couple.

The men coming out of the vans carried standard-issue AK-47s and wore dark blue uniforms with helmets. Over their uniforms they wore bulletproof jackets that would have done little good against the automatic weapons that had been circulating in Moscow since well before the rise of Yeltsin's democracy.

A crowd was quickly gathering, most with nothing better to do, some with a curiosity that demanded satisfaction.

"Terrorists," one old babushka said with assurance to the plump, pretty woman. No one dared talk to the forbidding and somber Tatar.

The pretty woman, whose name was Elena Timofeyeva, nodded her head. This encouraged the babushka, who shifted a heavy cloth bag from her right hand to her left and said, "Afghans."

A murmur ran through the crowd, some accepting this conjecture, others declaring it garbage.

"Chechens. It was Chechens. I saw them," someone shouted.

There were now more than twenty uniformed men arranging themselves at even intervals in front of the ancient two-story wooden apartment building. They reminded Elena of the men she had once seen in an old American horror movie, *The Thing*, where the scientists circled a giant flying saucer buried beneath the ice.

There was no ice this morning, just the first cold nip of winter.

Elena had taken the number 3 bus down Nevsky Prospekt and walked another two blocks to get there. Deputy Inspector Emil Karpo, the gaunt man at her side, had arrived by metro at the Gostinniy Dvor stop.

Someone gave a sharp command and the uni-

11

formed men pulled out long lines of rope with grappling hooks.

Cameramen madly clicked away. Journalists frantically made notes in their pads.

"If they are trying to surprise the terrorists," grunted a one-legged old man with crutches and a two-day growth of white beard, "they are idiots."

"Not terrorists," said another man with a voice of weary knowledge. "Mafia."

"Mafia," ran voices through the crowd.

Elena Timofeyeva knew why the men in uniform were hurling their grappling lines to the roof of the two-story building, lines that were as likely to pull down the ancient bricks of the roof as to support the weight of overarmed men wearing supposedly bulletproof vests.

This was a show. Elena and Karpo had been assigned to the show as representatives of the Office of Special Investigation. They were to work, according to Colonel Snitkonoy, as liaison with the tax police, who were now scurrying up the sides of the building to the applause of the crowd. It was not the Moscow Circus, but it was quite a spectacle and cost nothing.

Karpo and Elena knew that there was no need for this show. The tax police could simply have knocked down the door. This was not a raid on a dangerous group or individual, but a follow-up on a tip from a reliable informant. The old man who owned the building had recently died. He had accumulated valuable jewelry and other items subject to taxation.

It was the job of the tax police to enforce the new tax laws that would bring in many billions of rubles from individual citizens, businesses, and foreigners doing business in a new but more than slightly frayed Russia. It was also the job of the tax police to strike fear into the people so that they would pay their taxes. Daytime raids featuring fully armed men were now common. The media were always informed when raids would take place. It was common now to see bewildered businessmen led out of their offices with their hands cuffed behind their backs.

A position in the tax police was much desired, for the tax police received not only their salaries but also a small percentage of what they recovered. Karpo doubted that such rampant capitalism had ever been practiced even in the United States.

The crowd had grown larger as the tax police officers scampered to the rooftop or crashed through windows on their way up the lines. As glass shattered and sprayed the crowd below, the onlookers jumped back and covered their heads.

Captain Sergei Valarov of the tax police, an ex-Soviet army officer, strode to Elena and Karpo and said, "The building is secure." Valarov looked like a captain—trim, efficient, with dark straight hair and the hint of a mustache.

No bullhorn had been brought forth to order the occupants out. No one had knocked on the door of the two-story house. It struck Elena that the front door might very well be open or that a knock might have resulted in a reluctant invitation from the building's occupant to come in.

"Thank you," said Emil Karpo. He followed the captain across the street and through the door of the house, which had been opened by one of the uniformed men who had scaled the building.

The crowd followed the captain, the vampire, and the young woman across the street, where they were stopped by two dozen uniformed police.

"As you know," the captain said as he strode past the saluting officer at the door, "we have been observing this house for some time."

Both Elena and Karpo were well aware of this.

"And," Captain Valarov added as he walked down a dark, narrow passageway with photographers behind him snapping and flashing madly, "we had reason to believe that a hoard of artifacts of historical significance was being kept by an old man named Dokorov. These artifacts—and we had reason to believe that it was a substantial collection—had never been taxed. In addition to which, some of them might be protected artworks. In that case they would belong to the state."

Both Karpo and Elena were certain that Captain Valarov had more than "reason to believe" the house was worth raiding. Otherwise he would not have been instructed to stage the elaborate invasion that would certainly be the highlight of the evening news on television.

The captain's step was certain. Elena, Karpo, and a select group of hand-chosen press representatives, some juggling video cameras, struggled through the narrow passageway for a better view.

What they saw through the next door was beyond what they had imagined, beyond what Valarov and probably his superiors had imagined. The interior of the house had been gutted. They stood in a large storage space with shelves piled almost two stories high, their upper reaches accessible only by the long ladder that leaned against the wall to their left.

Flashbulbs went wild. Captain Sergei Valarov stood flat-footed looking at the museum before him: rows of books, jewelry, a chandelier, paintings, serving dishes, wooden boxes marked MICROSCOPES, MANUSCRIPTS, and SMALL ICONS, and much more.

Karpo reached forward and touched the shoulder of the posing Valarov, who showed only the slightest trace of tightening in his cheeks to indicate that this was much more than he had expected to find inside the house.

"It might be best if the press were taken outside and told that you will be out in several minutes with a full report. Meanwhile I suggest you contact your superiors for instruction."

The captain nodded, blew out some air, and turned with the help of three of his men to urge the complaining crowd into the passageway. When they were gone, Karpo motioned to Elena, who closed the door. The two police officers were alone in the room.

"Notes," Karpo said, and Elena took out her

notebook and a white pen that had BARNES & NOBLE printed in red on its side.

He walked slowly down an aisle. The noise of demanding reporters could be heard beyond the closed door.

"Preliminary report," he said. "Random observations. Family painting of the Romanovs, official. If the date is to be believed, it is the last such portrait of the family. Shelves full of books are held in place by gold-and silver-framed icons."

He opened one book and went on. "First edition, Bible, dated 1639, signed 'To Ilya, Ivan Fyodorov.'"

Elena touched the book. She knew that Fedorov was the Russian Gutenberg. There appeared to be a dozen similar-looking volumes.

"There are hundreds of books," Elena could not stop herself from saying.

"Several thousand," Karpo amended, and opened a wooden box on the shelf before him.

Inside were tiny, fragile magnifying glasses, each in a separate compartment protected by cotton. Lying on top of the glasses was a yellowing page torn from a book. Karpo scanned the page and handed it to Elena, who read, "The microscope was invented by a Dutch oculist in the seventeenth century. It was a simple thing. He made each one himself. They worked surprisingly well. Most have disappeared into private collections or simply been lost. In 1923 a complete box of Leeuwenhoek microscopes was reportedly discovered in a pharmacy in Belgrade. The box had disappeared by the time the police arrived. The pharmacist was ordered to undergo psychiatric examination."

"And this....?" Elena began.

"...may well be that box," said Karpo, holding one of the glass and wire objects in his palm.

"This room," she said, looking around, "it must have more treasures than the Kremlin museum."

A mouse scampered across an old piece of paper somewhere in a dark corner.

"Not more, perhaps, but different," said Karpo.

"My God," said Elena.

Since Karpo believed in neither God nor blasphemy, he continued randomly selecting items, some of which he was unable to identify, but jewelry from the various courts of Russia was certain, including one very ancient ornate gold crown that, if Karpo read the worn inscription properly, had belonged to Ivan the Terrible.

"We will have to call in the experts on this," he finally said.

Elena put her notebook away and touched the crown of Ivan the Terrible. It was, like the room they were in, cool, damp, and smelled of mildew.

"Millions," she muttered. "Worth millions."

"In rubles," Karpo said, examining the portrait of a beautiful and quite regal woman, "billions upon billions."

"American dollars?" she asked.

Karpo looked around. "Beyond price. Billions."

"But who...?" Elena asked, just as a frail old woman in a badly worn dress stepped out from behind a set of shelves and said, "Get out."

"We are the police," said Elena.

The woman advanced on them. She was carrying what looked like a silver scepter embedded with red and green jewels.

"Out," she cried.

"Is all this yours?" asked Karpo.

"My brother's and before him my father's," the little woman said, holding up her scepter as if to strike. "All purchased honestly, piece by piece, from before the Revolution, until Pavel died."

"Your father died?" asked Elena.

"My brother, Pavel," the woman said. "Just last week. So now it is mine. All those…those parasites in the street who knew that my family collected, one of them went to the tax police." The woman spat dryly in the general direction of the front door. "Pavel never bothered anyone. He was a poor electrician for government cafeterias. We didn't live fancy. He loved…this."

The woman stood in front of Karpo, who did not blink, though the heavy scepter was waving before his eyes.

"There were people—speculators in homes, weapons, rare goods," said Karpo. "When the Revolution began, they bought these things for a few rubles from the members of the czar's court and from rich merchants fleeing the Soviet Union who couldn't carry everything they had stolen from the people. I have heard of such collections smuggled out of the country and sold to dealers, collectors, museums. I have never heard of one this size."

Unable to intimidate the pale man, the frail woman looked at Elena, who forced herself to wear a mask of determination. Defeated, the woman put the scepter on a nearby shelf.

"What were you going to do with all this?" Elena asked as the woman leaned back against a bookcase. Then, suddenly, the woman pushed away from the books and ran down an aisle screaming, "They are mine."

Elena started after the woman, but Karpo held out his hand to stop her.

"It is not the woman we want," he said, looking around the room.

Elena, too, looked around at the roomful of treasures. "This is wonderful," she said.

Karpo did not answer. The tax police were outside and would make their claims in the name of the new state. Karpo was certain that whoever controlled this cavern of riches would have enormous political power.

Karpo picked up a small icon. The dead Jesus, wearing a blanket that covered his head, was surrounded by his disciples, all of whom were wreathed, like Jesus, and clothed in what appeared to be ancient gold.

Valarov strode back into the huge room, his confidence returned, and announced to Elena and Karpo, "Experts will come in the morning to begin cataloging everything in this room. Meanwhile the old woman will be confined here with guards posted at the doors. I have been instructed to tell the press this much."

Karpo, now holding an ancient leather-bound book in his hands, nodded without looking at the captain. Valarov departed quickly, wondering if he might be entitled to a small percentage of what looked like the biggest tax recovery in the history of the tax police. Karpo closed the book gently and placed it back on the shelf, intending to return the next day.

But the next morning, when the three antique dealers and four professors from Moscow State University entered the room accompanied by Valarov and his men, they found it quite empty.

The man lay sprawled on his back over the front hood of the blue Lada, his arms extended out wide as if he had been frozen in the middle of a rather intricate Olympic high dive. At least that was Porfiry Petrovich Rostnikov's first impression, an impression dispelled by the fact that the man was fully clothed, certainly dead, and staring wide-eyed, open-mouthed, and upside down at him. The body on the car fascinated Rostnikov. The man's head was bald and covered with a minutely perfect tattoo of a flying eagle carrying something in its talons.

From the position of the body, the line of bloody holes in the man's black shirt, and the Kalashnikov automatic weapon lying on the ground a few feet away, Rostnikov concluded that he had probably been shot at close range on the sidewalk and blown backward over the hood of the Lada.

The Lada was the only car parked on the block.

Other cars had certainly been there, but in the four or five minutes it took for the police to arrive, their owners had hurried to move them before they could be impounded as evidence.

The body of another man, clothed in a leather jacket identical to that of the bald man, lay in the street on his face. There was no weapon near him.

The glass of a telephone kiosk on the sidewalk not far from the Lada was shattered, as were the windows of two small shops, a pharmacy and a café, on this side of the street, a few feet from the dead man on the car. Inside the pharmacy a woman was being treated for a gunshot wound to her right shoulder. She whimpered and looked around for a friend or relative. Her eyes met those of Rostnikov.

In the café there were three dead people: a foreign-looking little round man and a woman, who had been seated at the same table, and their waiter. In his right hand the dead man at the table clutched a Freedom Arms Casull .454, capable of bringing down an elk at one hundred yards.

Uniformed police had roped off the street for twenty yards in both directions, stopping afternoon traffic. Cars were backed up for half a block; their drivers, unaware of the slaughter in front of them, were angrily and uselessly honking their horns. Two men, one thin and marked by a large mole on his face and one quite old and marked by an apoplectic anger that might threaten his life, were being held back by two policemen across the street from Rostnikov and the man with the tattooed head.

"Who is that crippled lunatic staring at the dead man?" asked Irina Smetenova of no one in particular.

Irina, who had been standing in a long line waiting for bread at what might be a nearly sane price, had been present just after the shooting and well before the police drove up and began sending would-be looters scurrying away. Now she was surrounded by others, men in jackets and open collars, babushkas and businessmen, smartly dressed women carrying boxes of certainly expensive things, which they tried to hide in plain plastic bags marked PEPSI-COLA or ORANGINA.

No one answered Irina's question, though others had noticed the boxy man in a dark jacket, his weight decidedly on his right leg as he moved. Now the man was standing still, hands in pockets, while police hurried to cover bodies, find witnesses, seek evidence, and make phone calls. Irina shifted her heavy shopping bag from her right hand to her left and her little white dog from her left to her right.

Rostnikov, the crippled lunatic, had been a boy soldier who got his leg run over by a tank in 1941. The fool of a boy, whom the adult Rostnikov could not clearly remember, had stepped into a street in Rostov not much different from the one in which he stood now. The boy had stepped out of a doorway and, with a lucky grenade and a hail of bullets from the machine pistol he had taken from a dead German, had destroyed the tank. The cost had been a nearly destroyed left leg, which he would have to drag slowly and often painfully behind him throughout the rest of his life.

But that was not the event that caused the boy to become the man who now somewhat resembled the German tank he had destroyed. When he was a young policeman, he had caught a drunken thief named Gremko assaulting a young woman outside the Kursk railway terminal. The drunk had nearly killed Rostnikov with his bare hands, but a well-placed knee to the groin had turned the tables.

It was after that incident that Rostnikov began lifting weights, first in the hope of building the muscle that a policeman's life on the street seemed to require and later as a routine he could not and did not wish to break, a meditation of sweat and determination and—he had long ago admitted to himself without benefit of a state psychiatrist—a way to compensate for the nearly useless leg. A few years ago he had quietly entered the annual competition for men and women fifty and over in Sokolniki Recreation Park. He had easily won the competition and a gold-painted aluminum statue, which rested, the gilt already chipping in spite of his care, on a bookshelf in his living room. The June afternoon when he had been presented with the trophy by the great Alexeyev himself had been one of the great memories of Rostnikov's life.

Long before he was assigned as chief inspector in the Office of Special Investigation, he had earned a variety of nicknames including "the Refrigerator," "the Kiosk," and "the Washtub."

Behind Rostnikov, each body was being uncovered and photographed. Overworked police shouted at one another. The crowd warmed itself with speculation.

"Inspector," said someone at his side.

Rostnikov nodded, still fascinated by the tattoo.

"Inspector," Sergeant Popovich repeated, just a touch louder. Popovich had recently been promoted. He was thirty, had a child on the way, and hoped one day for yet another promotion. With a salary of less than ninety thousand rubles a month, about ninety dollars or less at current rates, it would have been impossible to feed his family if he, like most of the 100,000 police officers in Moscow who had the opportunity, did not take bribes ranging from sweet juices from street vendors to serious rubles from gangs large and small.

This time Rostnikov grunted. Popovich took this as a signal to report.

"Five dead. One, the pharmacist, injured. She saw nothing. Just heard guns going off. Appears to be a battle between two mafias."

"Witnesses?" asked Rostnikov.

"They don't want to admit it," said Popovich, "but..."

"Bring a witness over," said Rostnikov.

Popovich nodded and headed toward a police car whose lights were flashing across the street.

Rostnikov looked away from the upside-down dead man with the tattoo on his head and over at

24

the café whose windows had been blown out by gunfire. Cloth sheets covered the bodies of the man and woman that were still half-supported by the table. A wisp of the dead woman's hair showed from under the cloth. Rostnikov had recognized the woman. Perhaps he was wrong, but still he put off finding out.

"A witness, Chief Inspector," Popovich said.

Rostnikov barely heard, so intently was he re-examining the head of the dead man who looked at him upside down with eyes as defiant as they must have been in life.

"Popovich, what is your first name?"

"Vladimir. Vladimir Andreyevich Popovich."

"Vladimir Andreyevich," Rostnikov said, shifting his weight slightly to remind his left leg to retain some semblance of life. "Have you ever seen *Snegourotchka (The Snow Maiden)*?"

"I..." Popovich began in confusion.

"It's an opera by Rimsky-Korsakov, taken from a children's story," said Rostnikov. He looked toward the dead woman in the window of the café. "After finally succeeding, by the last act, in getting her beloved Miskar to fall in love with her, the Snow Maiden steps forward before dawn to receive the blessing of the czar. In her joy and happiness she has forgotten the warning of the fairies, and as the first rays of sun touch her beautiful face, she melts away forever, and Miskar in his anguish throws himself into the lake and drowns."

Popovich had heard of the chief inspector's

eccentricities, but telling fairy stories to a witness in the midst of this bloody madness went beyond eccentricity.

"You know what we must do, Vladimir?" Rostnikov said, putting his hand on the young policeman's shoulder.

"I believe I know the proper procedure."

"We must keep Miskar from drowning himself," Rostnikov said. He walked around the rear of the Lada and headed for the devastated café. He didn't bother to avoid stepping on the broken glass, though he did avoid the spatters of blood on the sidewalk in front of the shop.

"Witness," said Rostnikov, walking through the broken window of the café to the table where the dead man and woman sat under the cloth, their heads down as if they were taking a slight nap.

"I saw it all," said a man eagerly.

Rostnikov kept looking down at the dead couple.

"I saw it all," the man repeated eagerly. "I saw it. Lots of them saw it. The guy with the little table, the *Napyerstochnik*, the thimbler who plays that three-card game with the fools across the street. He saw it. He's out in the crowd somewhere, I think."

Rostnikov glanced at the talking man. He was skinny, wild-haired, wearing a coat too long for him and a look on his face of confident madness. He could have been thirty. He could have been fifty. He was certainly crazy.

"What did you see?" asked Rostnikov.

"Nazis," the man said, looking around to be sure no Nazis were listening. "Nazis," he repeated. "Dozens. Black pants. Brown shirts. Armbands with swastikas. They shot everyone and shouted, 'Heil Zhirinovsky, Heil Hitler.' They put out their hands in a Nazi salute like this, and then they all climbed into their SS armored cars and drove away. They didn't give a damn if anyone saw them."

"Thank you," said Rostnikov. "I assume Officer Popovich has your address. We will contact you."

"Just said 'Heil,'" the man repeated.

A uniformed officer came forward and led the man away.

"Other witnesses?" asked Rostnikov.

"Just getting them together," said Popovich. "Owner of this shop. Owner of the car on which the bald man is lying. A few people in the crowd who claim to have heard something."

"All old people," said Rostnikov, looking at the cloth covering the dead woman.

"Yes," said Popovich.

"The ones with lives left recognize a mafia killing and run. The old ones seeking attention stay," said Rostnikov. He pulled back the cloth and looked down at the face of the dead woman. Her eyes were closed. A very slight trickle of blood came from the left corner of her mouth. It was nearly dry. Rostnikov covered her again and closed his eyes for a long time.

Finally the chief inspector opened his eyes and turned to Popovich. "What do you conclude about this event?" he asked, rubbing his eyes as if he had just awakened from a short nap.

"Definitely mafias," Popovich said with relief now that he was on known territory. "Or perhaps a single mafia in some kind of internal battle."

"Why this conclusion?" Rostnikov asked, still rubbing his eyes.

"The dead man is covered with tattoos, which means he was probably in prison," said Popovich. "I don't know what the tattoos mean, but there is one that appears on both of the dead men. In the case of the man on the car, it is on his head. It is on the buttocks of the other one, the one in the street."

"You rolled him over and pulled down his pants?" asked Rostnikov, now looking at the sergeant with eyes rubbed red.

"He had fallen dead on his face," said Popovich. "His pants had slipped down. He had defecated on himself, but I could still see the eagle."

"What else?" asked Rostnikov.

"Else?"

"The eagle was carrying something in its claws. What was it?"

"It looked like a bomb of some sort."

"It was a bomb," Rostnikov said. "Did he have a weapon?"

"The eagle?"

"The dead man."

"No."

"I'm going to get myself a glass of tea. Would you like one?"

"No, Chief Inspector," said Popovich, though he would truly have welcomed something for his dry mouth.

"Bring in the witnesses one at a time," Rostnikov said. He moved toward the rear of the café, where there was a shining metal urn, its spigot slowly dripping tea into a saucer that had overflowed. "When you come back in, I'll have a glass of tea poured for you."

Unsure of what to do, Popovich saluted and stepped back out onto the street, where he waved at the two policemen who were detaining a group of men. He held up a single finger to indicate that he wanted one of the men sent over. One of the policemen ushered a thin man across the street. The crowd, assuming that the man was a suspect, began pelting him with a few bits of glass from the broken café window, the odd stone, and a piece or two of rotten fruit. Fortunately for the man, who was the owner of the Lada, and for the policeman who escorted him, the crowd found little to throw.

Chapter 2

Morning Meeting

The Gray Wolfhound entered the room and looked down at the four men seated behind the finely polished wooden table. "Reports today will be limited to direct criminal investigations in progress," he said. "I have an important meeting with the Minister of the Interior in twenty minutes."

Ever since the dissolution of Communism and the Soviet Union, the Gray Wolfhound had taken to wearing a green uniform of his own design. No one seemed to know or care if this act of creative military fashion was within the realm of protocol and law. But as the four men seated behind the table all knew but would admit to few, there was a kind of free-floating law in Russia—partly the remnants of Communism, partly an attempt to establish the semblance of a democratic process, and partly the whim of whoever was willing to act as if he knew what to do. The risk of taking this step forward was that it might well destroy one in the future. The political advantages of the move, on the other hand, were potentially great.

The Wolfhound's uniform was, as always, perfectly pressed, presumably by his adjutant, who lived with the colonel in a small but sufficient *dacha* not far from Moscow. The colonel's medals, his lone concession to the past, glittered on his chest. His mane of perfect white hair flowed back as if fashioned by a benevolent wind.

The senior staff meeting was being held, as always, in the colonel's office in Petrovka 38, the central headquarters of the various police districts reorganized in the last several years by an unknown Yeltsin associate. Today's meeting was out of the ordinary due to the presence of a solidly built man seated at the end of the conference table well apart from the others. He wore a blue suit and tie and had his curly black hair cut short. He looked decidedly athletic, and his age appeared to be somewhere between forty and fifty, though it was difficult for the colonel's staff to gauge the age of a black man. The need to do so had come up infrequently in their careers.

At the center of the table sat Pankov, the near-dwarf who served as the colonel's assistant. Pankov's primary function was to appear in public at the colonel's side, thus enhancing the image of the Wolfhound by comparison with the rumpled, unkempt, confused little Pankov.

To Pankov's right was Chief Inspector Porfiry Petrovich Rostnikov, who seemed to be taking notes on a large pad. Colonel Snitkonoy was well aware that the chief inspector was almost certainly drawing pictures of houses, people, books, flowers, statues, or even the window behind the colonel. The colonel had purposely sat the black man in the blue suit at the end of the table where he would not see such inattentive behavior.

To Pankov's left sat Major Gregorovich, a thick man in his late forties who survived by displaying absolute public loyalty to the Wolfhound on all issues while secretly reporting on the Office of Special Investigation to officers in other bureaus jealous of the increasing power of the Wolfhound's small but highly successful staff. Gregorovich, who had given up wearing any uniform other than a brown business suit, still held a faint hope that if the Wolfhound ever faltered, those to whom he had passed on information would wish

Gregorovich to take over the directorship. It would not simply be a reward. Gregorovich was too smart to settle for that. It would be the expedient, self-serving thing for them to do.

"Chief Inspector," the Wolfhound said. "Your report."

Rostnikov put down his pad, and though it was upside down and a dozen feet away, the Wolfhound could see that the drawing Rostnikov had been intent on was the face of a woman with billowing hair.

"Four new investigations begun," said Rostnikov. "Twelve ongoing, five closed with arrests."

"New investigations only," the Wolfhound said, looking at the clock.

Rostnikov seemed not to notice and went on. "Alexei Porvinovich. Owns several businesses, launders foreign money, and makes bribes to get permits. Suspected ties to several mafias, particularly the Afghan veterans. He was abducted on the street in a dark Mercedes-Benz by two men with automatic weapons. Both abductors wore ski masks. No body yet found. Wife reports ransom call. Three million American dollars."

"Three million…" Pankov said, and then shut up after a stern look from the colonel.

"Go on, Chief Inspector," said the Wolfhound.

"Another victim of an attack in the Strogino area," Rostnikov said. "Face and head crushed by pavement pieces, ribs broken, organs ruptured. This is the eleventh such killing in less than a year."

"If you think it is worth our attention," the Wolfhound said, "then assign someone."

"I will assign Inspectors Tkach and Zelach."

"Fine, fine, what else?" asked the Wolfhound.

"Liaison with tax police on information provided by paid informant who led them to a hoard of valuable artifacts. Inspectors Karpo and Timofeyeva report that sometime between the discovery of the items by the tax police and the next morning all of the articles were removed. The estimated value of the find, according to Inspector Karpo, may be in excess of one billion dollars."

"One bill—" Pankov started, and immediately shut up.

"We take these cases," said Colonel Snitkonoy. "Gentlemen, this presents the proper moment for me to introduce our guest, Mr. Craig Hamilton."

Rostnikov, Pankov, and Gregorovich now openly looked at the black man for the first time. Mr. Craig Hamilton looked at them, gave a small smile, and said in perfect and quite precise Russian, "It is a pleasure to meet you and an honor to be invited to your morning meeting."

The man learned his Russian in a good intensive language school, thought Rostnikov.

"Mr. Hamilton is with the American Federal Bureau of Investigation," said the colonel. "He is here to observe our methods, help if he can in ongoing investigations, and prepare a report for his own superiors and ours. Mr. Hamilton is an attorney and an accountant with thirteen years of investigative experience. I am assigning him to you, Inspector Rostnikov."

Rostnikov put the finishing touches on the drawing before him and put down his pencil.

"I will, with your approval, take the abduction myself and assign Elena Timofeyeva to the missing artifacts. Perhaps Agent Hamilton will be able to give us some assistance."

"I would prefer that you or Inspector Karpo handle the missing treasures," said the Wolfhound. "Inspector Elena Timofeyeva is lacking in experience."

"I have taken the liberty of assigning Inspector Karpo to the street killings yesterday," said Rostnikov.

"Five dead," said the Wolfhound, displaying to the FBI agent that he was fully knowledgeable about day-to-day criminal activity in his city.

"I will supervise Inspector Timofeyeva and conduct the investigation of the abduction with the assistance and advice of Agent Hamilton," said Rostnikov.

"Why assign Karpo to—?" the Wolfhound began.

"Inspector Karpo has a particular interest in the street killings," explained Rostnikov, "and I believe he will be zealous in his investigation."

"Particular interest?" asked the Wolfhound.

"A woman who was killed in the cross fire was a friend of Emil Karpo's, a particular friend. Her name was Mathilde Verson."

★ ★ ★

Sasha Tkach and Arkady Zelach sat in the small, drafty flat of Dmitra Klepikova, who wore a heavy blue man's sweater and slacks and hugged herself in a way that made Sasha wonder if she was ill. She had thin bones and was a woman who seemed to be taking the winter badly. Her skin was already dry, and her gray-white hair was cut very short. She was forty-eight years old but looked two decades older.

Dmitra had handed each of the policemen a cup of tea and then taken a seat between them. In this intimate semicircle Zelach was not at all comfortable.

Dmitra was the local *uchastovaya*. She was given her flat free of charge, for which privilege she was expected to know the neighborhood and its problems, to anticipate crimes, and to quickly identify those who had already committed crimes. Dmitra had a small desk in the corner of the room, and she rarely left her apartment. There were many people in the neighborhood, particularly old people, only too happy to come and chat in return for a cup of tea and a biscuit. Occasionally Dmitra made rounds so that she would be known around the neighborhood and given some respect—not as much as she had been given when she was a district Communist party supervisor, but sufficient respect to satisfy her.

She had never had a visit from criminal investigators before. In fact, she had never had a visit from any uniformed patrol at all. She had always gone to the run-down 108th Police District office to deliver her reports. In her three years as an *uchastovaya* she had seen Lieutenant Colonel Lorin, the head of the district of more than seventy thousand residents, only twice and had never exchanged a word with him.

"I can tell you who the local drunks are, who is likely to come home in a bad mood and beat his wife, who might break into an apartment," Dmitra said in a very high singsong voice that began to get on Sasha's nerves as soon as she spoke. The voice and the woman reminded him of his own mother. "But I can't tell you with certainty who killed Oleg Makmunov."

"You know the dead man's name," said Sasha.

"One of many. The police sometimes rousted him from doorways early in the morning. Another biscuit?"

Zelach nodded yes and Sasha answered, *"Da,"* throwing his head back to get the blond hair out of his eyes. It was a boyish act, one that contributed to his attractiveness to women, who wanted either to mother him or to smother him. At least that was the way Sasha now saw things. At thirty-one he was no longer a boy and his hair was growing subtly darker. At home he had a wife, two small children, and a mother who made shopkeepers cringe.

"The biscuits are from Poland," Dmitra said. She held out the small plate to the two policemen, each of whom took one small vanilla biscuit. Then she whispered, "Gift from a local vendor. The truth? Between us?"

"Between us," Sasha said, beginning to feel quite warm in the small apartment.

"I let her set up her table in front of the metro," Dmitra said, leaning forward. "She gives me a tin of biscuits here, a juice there. She has a prime location. You know how it is? You know what I get paid?"

Sasha was well aware of "how it is." His wife, Maya, worked, and his mother, who had had her own place for a while, had moved back in with them and was now contributing most of her salary as a government clerk to the household. With two small children it was still difficult, very difficult, but Sasha had never taken a gift from a criminal or a suspect.

"About the murdered man," Sasha said, giving a stern glance at Zelach, who reached for another biscuit on the small plate on the table in front of them.

"Who kills a drunk?" said Dmitra. Her shrug was a ripple of bony shoulders beneath her oversized sweater. "And especially a drunk like this Makmunov, who could barely put a few rubles together for a cheap bottle."

"Who?" asked Zelach, who had ignored Sasha's glance and devoured two more biscuits.

"Another drunk he got into a fight with," Dmitra guessed. "A creature of the night even lower than Oleg Makmunov."

"A creature of the night?" asked Zelach, his cheek full.

"Gang members wandering the streets, ready

to pick a fight and a drunk's pocket. Remember, we have no curfews any longer."

"A gang?" Sasha said.

"A gang of the very young," Dmitra said. "If they were older, they wouldn't be using pieces of concrete and their feet. They would have knives and guns."

"Wouldn't they simply be afraid to fire weapons?" asked Sasha. "Afraid to be heard?"

"Are we friends now?" Dmitra asked, leaning forward again and speaking softly.

"Well..." said Zelach.

"Fellow members of the law enforcement team, then," she said.

"Yes," said Sasha, looking directly at Zelach to keep him from answering.

Dmitra sat back with her tea, comfortable in the new camaraderie she had purchased with a few biscuits. "Response time on a gunshot in this area," she said, "is at least ten minutes from the time of the call, usually more like fifteen minutes. You could slaughter the entire Bolshoi Ballet on the Prospekt, quietly pick up the shell casings, and walk away singing those incomprehensible American songs. There are only one hundred and nine policemen in this district and five patrol cars. The police, I can tell you, are not anxious to go driving down a street where they might find themselves facing two or three men with submachine guns or those pistols that shoot through solid steel."

"Continue," said Sasha with an encouraging

smile, not his most winning smile, but certainly one that moved beyond mere politeness.

"Whoever killed Oleg Makmunov didn't have a gun," she said. "And what criminal doesn't have a gun?"

Sasha nodded for her to go on and she did.

"Almost any criminal today has a gun. Almost every civilian has a gun. Like Los Angeles. Only small children, at least most small children in this district, can't afford guns...yet."

"So you think this murder was committed by children?" asked Zelach, reaching for the biscuits. Sasha beat him to the plate, took one, and moved it out of Zelach's reach.

He underestimated Zelach's determination, however, and found the slouching man leaning far forward to get to the plate. Sasha put a hand on his partner's shoulder to move him back.

"Combined with the fact that there have been five similar killings within the past few months," Dmitra said, "and all within two square kilometers of where we are sitting—all were drunks out late—it fits the pattern."

Sasha had seen bands of poorly dressed children—three, six, ten at a time—hands in their pockets, smoking, looking around insolently, daring people to get in their way, begging, demanding. Some of the children were little more than babies, six, maybe seven, years old. Now, with winter coming, these children, many without homes, would be growing more desperate, needing money for clothes or for someplace to sleep.

"Where do you suggest we begin?" Sasha asked.

"Neighbors," Dmitra said confidently. "I'll give you names of people who live on the same street where our Oleg was murdered last night. You can tell them you talked to me, that you are friends of mine."

The prospect of two real detectives saying they were her friends had great appeal for Dmitra.

"I'll write their names and addresses for you." She fished a small pad from a great kangaroolike pocket in her sweater.

While she wrote, Zelach pleaded with his eyes for Sasha's permission to reach for another biscuit or two. Sasha ignored him and finished his tea.

"There," said Dmitra. She handed Sasha the list.

"Thank you," he said, glancing at the brief list of names. He took out his notebook and inserted the sheet of paper inside it for protection.

Then Sasha stood up. Zelach joined him and so did Dmitra.

"You hardly touched the biscuits," she said. "Here, let me give you each a box to take home."

"We..." Sasha began, but she had already hurried to a cupboard in the corner.

She was back almost instantly with two small blue cardboard boxes covered with Polish words. She held them out, and Zelach took his instantly. Sasha hesitated for an instant and then imagined the look on his daughter Pulcharia's face when he presented her with the biscuits. He took them, said "Thanks," and hurried Zelach out of the apartment.

"Let me know if I can help any further," Dmitra called down the hall as the policemen departed.

"We will," said Sasha.

When the thin woman had closed the door, Zelach grinned and held up his blue box from Poland. "You know what they call these in America?" he asked. "*Cookie*. My mother loves them."

Zelach lived with his old mother in a small apartment. For years he had taken care of her through her various maladies. When Zelach had been savagely beaten recently, she had pulled herself from her bed and taken care of her only child. It had made a new and healthier woman of her.

They hurried down the steps past the graffiti-filled walls and out into the street. Zelach was still grinning. He had plunged the package into the pocket of his jacket. He looked a bit odd to Sasha.

"Are you all right?"

"A bit dizzy," said Zelach. "Fine, just a bit dizzy. I have medicine for it at home, but sometimes I feel good and forget. I'll be fine."

So Sasha Tkach, his own biscuit box in his pocket, walked down the street, keeping an eye on his partner. *Just what every investigator needs,* he thought, *a partner who might suddenly pass out on him.*

Chapter 3

The Grieving Family

"Turn at the next corner," Rostnikov said in Russian. "Turn left. Cautiously. The street is narrow and the population surly at this hour."

The FBI agent turned the car to the left. The movement was smooth, and there were no pedestrians in sight for at least half a block.

"Why are they surly at this hour?" Hamilton asked without looking over at his passenger.

"Fear, hunger, political dissatisfaction, low-paying jobs, problems at home," said Rostnikov.

"Is it different at another hour?" Hamilton asked.

"Not really," said Rostnikov, looking out of the window. "Would you rather speak English?"

"Not particularly. I prefer the practice."

Rostnikov nodded in understanding. "You are a Negro," he said.

Hamilton smiled. "You noticed," he said.

"No," Rostnikov went on, trying to adjust his left leg into a less painful position. "I mean that it is unusual. The few dark-skinned people we see are from Africa or, sometimes, Cuba. Diplomats. You are the first American Negro I have met. But I wondered why they had decided to send you to Moscow. You stick out like a sore...tongue."

"Thumb," Hamilton corrected. "I speak Russian and know the culture and politics reasonably well."

Rostnikov nodded and said, "Public relations."

This time Hamilton smiled more broadly. "More than a bit of that too."

"Is this conversation making you uncomfortable?"

"No," said Hamilton.

"Good. Do you know Ed McBain?"

"Ed...Mystery writer?"

"Yes. Do you know him?"

"Personally, no. I haven't read anything by him either."

"Fine writer," said Rostnikov with a sigh. "I was wondering if you or any members of your staff might have one of his books with you that I might borrow."

"I'll ask," said Hamilton, slowing down so that an old man walking a dog could cross in front of them. The man and the dog moved very slowly. Hamilton had to stop.

"Most Moscow drivers would simply have slowed down a little and tried to miss them," said Rostnikov.

"The pedestrian does not have the right of way?"

"The pedestrian doesn't have much of anything," said Rostnikov. "There, the white building. Second one. Where the policeman is standing."

"At the meeting," Hamilton said, "you assigned a detective to a case involving the murder of someone he knew."

"Karpo," said Rostnikov. "He...they were very close."

"In the States we would be sure that a detective or agent was not assigned to a case involving someone he knew well," said Hamilton. "Objectivity breaks down."

"Perhaps," said Rostnikov. "But determination replaces it. When you meet Inspector Karpo, you will understand."

There were cars on the street, but parking was relatively easy. The cars tended to look new, American and French. This was a street of large apartments and wealthy people, many of whom, like Alexei Porvinovich, had become wealthy with the collapse of Communism and the rise of an insane free market. In front of the door a uniformed policeman with an automatic weapon looked at the pair getting out of the car and stood a little more erect.

"The hood ornament," said Rostnikov, easing himself slowly out of the car. "Can you remove it?"

"Don't know," said Hamilton, who was by now standing on the sidewalk. "It's an embassy vehicle."

"If it can be removed, remove it and lock it in the car—under the seat where it cannot be seen," said Rostnikov, locking his door and looking up at the building.

"But there's an armed policeman standing twenty feet away," said the FBI agent.

"The danger is not necessarily decreased by that fact," said Rostnikov.

Hamilton moved to the hood, unscrewed the shiny ornament, and looked at Rostnikov with his trophy in hand.

"Windscreen wipers," said Rostnikov, stepping up on the curb.

Hamilton removed the windshield wipers and looked at Rostnikov, who nodded.

"On the floor of the car," Rostnikov said. "If they see it on the seat, they might break the window."

"What if they steal the car?"

"Then it is gone forever," said Rostnikov. "Things disappear quickly and forever in today's Russia, not unlike yesterday's Russia. Tell me, in the United States would they call this a sky-scraper?"

Hamilton locked the car door and looked up at the twelve-story building before answering.

"Not even close."

The armed young man stepped in front of them at the door, and Rostnikov flipped open his wallet to show his identification. The armed young man looked quickly, nodded, and stepped out of the way. Hamilton and Rostnikov entered the small hallway of the building and found the door-bell marked PORVINOVICH. An answering ring popped open the inner door.

Again Hamilton smiled.

"May I ask what amuses you?" asked Rostnikov as they moved across the green-tiled floor of the empty lobby.

"That lock wouldn't keep out the most inept burglar."

"Nor would a better lock," said Rostnikov as they arrived at the elevator in the corner of the lobby. "The most inept burglar would simply break a pane of glass or kick in a panel. The door is designed to keep out the innocent and discourage the guilty. Tell me, what do you think of the actor Denzel Washington?"

They got into the elevator, and Rostnikov pushed a button.

"Because he's black?" asked Hamilton, his hands at his sides.

"Of course," said Rostnikov. "I have not seen him except in a tape of some movie called *The Mighty Flynn*."

"'Quinn,'" Hamilton corrected. "I hope that when I retire, Denzel Washington will star in the movie of my life."

"You expect such a movie to be made?"

"Never can tell," said Hamilton.

Rostnikov didn't smile. He liked this FBI man with a sense of humor.

The elevator hummed smoothly to a stop. Finding the apartment was no problem. Here another uniformed policeman, a little older than the one downstairs, faced them suspiciously, weapon ready.

"I'm Inspector Rostnikov," Rostnikov said. "This is American FBI agent Hamilton."

The policeman lowered his weapon and stepped back.

"Were you ordered here by your district commander?" Rostnikov asked.

"Yes, Inspector," said the policeman.

Rostnikov knocked at the door. "These must be important people," he said. "In an undermanned

46

district two officers are assigned to protect the apartment after the victim has been kidnapped."

"His wife and brother..." Hamilton said.

"If a plumber had been kidnapped," said Rostnikov softly so that the policeman standing guard would not hear him, "there would be no police—only perhaps a friend of his with a wrench and a bad temper, which might be more effective."

The door opened. The man who opened it resembled the file photograph Rostnikov had in his pocket. He wore dark slacks and a definitely disheveled white shirt, conservative blue tie, and a loose-fitting sport jacket.

"Inspector Rostnikov," said Rostnikov, without showing his ID. "And this is Agent Hamilton of the FBI. And you are the brother of Alexei Porvinovich."

"Yes, how did you know?" The man backed away to let them in.

"I am the Steve Carella of the Moscow police," said Rostnikov, looking around the apartment.

The room was large and modern, with white carpeting. The furniture was mostly white, with black enameled tables. There were two large paintings on the wall. One depicted a pale woman in a clinging black dress reclining on a red chaise longue while an attentive young man in a suit knelt before her, holding up a burning lighter for the indifferent woman, who held a cigarette and holder between two fingers of her left hand. The second painting seemed to have been done by the same artist. It, too, featured a pale woman, this time in white, surrounded by three attentive young men. The woman had her head back and was laughing insincerely. The paintings fascinated Rostnikov because of the woman who sat before him on one of the white chairs. She wore a black suit, and her cigarette, not in a holder, was already lit. She could have been the model for either of the women in the paintings.

"Madame Porvinovich," Rostnikov said.

"Anna Ivanovna Porvinovich," she said, her voice low. "I heard you introduce yourselves to Yevgeniy. Please sit. Yevgeniy will get you drinks if you—"

"Cold water would be fine with me," said Hamilton.

"Do you perhaps have a Pepsi-Cola?" asked Rostnikov, looking for the least uncomfortable chair.

"Yes," said Anna Porvinovich.

Behind them Yevgeniy left the room.

"I gather that you have not yet found Alexei," Anna Porvinovich said.

Rostnikov tried to keep his eyes from the paintings. "We have just begun to look," he said. "Shall we wait till his brother returns before…?"

"As you wish," Anna Porvinovich said. She put out her cigarette in an ornate glass ashtray, looked at Hamilton, and said, "You speak Russian?"

"Yes," he said. "Do you speak English?"

"No, but some French. I'm learning. Perhaps English would be more interesting," she said, her dark eyes examining the FBI agent.

"You do not seem particularly upset by the unfortunate disappearance of your husband," Hamilton said.

Yevgeniy returned with a tray on which there were three glasses. He placed the tray on the small table in front of Anna Porvinovich and sat next to her, handing out drinks. The possible widow had a sparkling mineral water with a slice of lime, a fruit Rostnikov rarely saw.

"People handle distress in different ways," she said. "I prefer to keep up appearances and my sense of dignity. Yevgeniy, as you can see, is a nervous wreck."

"My brother…" he began, and then trailed off.

Rostnikov took a sip of his Pepsi and nodded his approval. Hamilton didn't touch his ice water.

"You have received a ransom call," said Rostnikov.

"A call, yes," said Anna Porvinovich. "Yesterday. A man demanded three million American dollars by Friday or Alexei would be killed. Actually, he said Alexei would be beheaded and thrown in the street. He put Alexei on the phone. He said I should do as I was told. I said I would if it were possible and he would tell me how I was to get three million dollars. Alexei was understandably distraught. He said I knew how to get the money."

"Do you?" asked Hamilton.

Anna Ivanovna Porvinovich shrugged.

"Did the man who called have an accent?" asked Rostnikov.

She thought about this a moment and said, "No. But he did not sound well educated."

"Tell us what he said," said Rostnikov. He opened a notepad. Hamilton produced a small tape recorder.

Anna Porvinovich looked at the tape recorder and then back at Hamilton before going on. "'We have your husband. We want three million dollars American by Friday. We know you can get it. He told us you know where it is. Bring it in a suitcase to the art museum in Vladimir before noon tomorrow. Place the suitcase behind the bushes to the left of the entrance. Be sure no one is watching you. Then go into the museum and stay there for one hour.' Then he put Alexei on the phone, and Alexei said, 'Do what the man told you, Anna.' Then they hung up. That's all."

"How did your husband sound?" Rostnikov asked.

"Sound?"

"Was he frightened?"

"Resigned," she said. "I don't think Alexei believes he will live through this regardless of what Yevgeniy and I do, but I intend to deliver the money and hope for the best."

"We would like to wire your telephone in case they call back," Rostnikov said. He wondered if he could get a recording device through Pankov.

Anna Porvinovich shrugged and picked up her drink. She examined the rising bubbles for a moment and then drank, her eyes back on Hamilton.

"We would like to mark the bills and put a

homing device in the suitcase full of money," said Rostnikov.

"Whatever you like," she said. She put down her drink.

"You think he is dead?" asked Rostnikov, watching her face.

"No," said Yevgeniy vehemently.

"Yes," said Anna Porvinovich evenly. "In the United States," she said to Hamilton, "what would you do?"

"I would think that your husband is still alive and will remain so until they get the money and feel they are safe. Then they will kill him. Chief Inspector Rostnikov hopes to find them after they pick up the money and before they feel safe."

"Why won't they simply let him go?" asked Yevgeniy, holding his hands to his mouth.

Hamilton looked at Rostnikov, who nodded to him.

"Why risk it?" Hamilton said. "Mr. Porvinovich may know what his captors look like, or he may be able to recognize the place he's been taken to. It would be an unsafe risk to let him live."

Rostnikov shifted his leg and tried not to wince as he said, "Do you have any idea who might be behind this?"

"Alexei knows so many people," Anna Porvinovich said, reaching for a cigarette and looking at Hamilton.

She wants him to go down on one knee and light it for her, like the man in the painting, Rostnikov thought. Hamilton made no move while Anna

Porvinovich paused and then accepted a light from Yevgeniy, whose hand was shaking.

"Can you make a list of people whom Alexei Porvinovich knows—those with whom he does business, those he may have offended, anyone…?"

"I do not think Alexei would like you to have a list of his business associates," Anna answered. "But…all right. You will have such a list in an hour."

"And you, Yevgeniy," Rostnikov said. "Can you help make this list for us?"

"Yes," he said. "If there's any chance we can save Alexei, I will do whatever is necessary."

"Do either of you like to dance?" Rostnikov asked.

"Do we…" Yevgeniy began, confused.

"I like to dance," Anna said. "And Yevgeniy is a hippo on the dance floor. I have more than once had the misfortune of having him step on me."

Yevgeniy shook his head.

"Alexei, does he dance?" asked Rostnikov.

"A little," she said. "Does it matter?"

"Perhaps, perhaps not. Do you read?"

This time Anna looked just the slightest bit annoyed. "Yes, I can read and I do read. I am currently reading a book in French. The newly discovered Jules Verne novel. But—"

"Are you enjoying it?" Rostnikov interrupted.

"Not very much."

"Then why read it?" Rostnikov asked.

"When I begin a book, I always finish it. When I go to a play or a movie, I always sit through it. I do not leave anything unfinished."

"I understand," said Rostnikov. "And you, Yevgeniy?"

"I don't think this will help my brother."

"Humor me," said Rostnikov.

"I am not reading a book. I don't read many books. I am a businessman."

"What do you do with your time besides work?" asked Rostnikov.

Anna now looked at Rostnikov as if he were a madman. "Go to museums, clubs," she answered. "Read an occasional book. Hold an occasional tea. Time passes. I find things with which to fill it."

"Yevgeniy?"

"I am in business with my brother. That leaves me little free time. I normally spend it with my family."

"Family?"

"Wife, mother-in-law, daughter, dachshund."

"How old is your daughter?"

"Sixteen," he answered with restrained anger.

Rostnikov rose, finished the Pepsi in his hand, and placed his drink on the table. Hamilton got up. Yevgeniy got up. Anna Porvinovich remained seated.

"I've seen that pose," Rostnikov said, looking up at the painting.

"I wish I had lived in the late twenties or early thirties, in France or America, or even England."

"I quite agree," said Rostnikov, moving to the door with Hamilton. Yevgeniy, anticipating the move, had hurried ahead of them to open it.

"We will send someone back to install the telephone recording device," said Rostnikov.

And then the two men were in the hall walking to the elevator.

"What do you think, Agent Hamilton?" Rostnikov asked in a whisper.

Hamilton answered in English. "Anna Porvinovich gave me a clear invitation to return for more than talk of her kidnapped husband. I don't know if she was serious or if she does that in the hope of manipulating all men."

"She is a beautiful woman," said Rostnikov in English. "Do you think she had her husband kidnapped?"

"Possibly," Hamilton said. "But if she did, her act is all wrong. She should be playing the distraught wife and she seems too smart not to know it."

"I agree," said Rostnikov. They both entered the elevator, and Hamilton pushed the ground-floor button.

"With what?" Hamilton asked.

"That she may have been responsible for her husband's kidnapping and that she is very smart. Why would we suspect a woman who is not playing the role of the grieving wife? Why would we not assume that she is likely to be innocent of wrongdoing precisely because she is calm and carrying on a possibly innocent flirtation with an FBI agent?"

"You are too convoluted in your thinking," Hamilton said.

The elevator stopped and the two men walked out into the lobby.

"It is my heritage," said Rostnikov, limping to-ward the door beyond which the armed soldier stood. "Over eight hundred years of trying to out-wit authorities who can do what they want to you makes a people suspicious of authority and turns many of them into good and devious actors."

They were on the street now. The policeman was standing erect instead of slouching.

"Your name?" Rostnikov asked.

"Officer Boris Guyon."

"Boris Guyon," he said. "Do you like to dance?"

"I...do not know how to dance well, but what I can do I like...have liked."

"Thank you," said Rostnikov.

He and the FBI agent walked to the car, where Hamilton paused and said, "Are we going any-where else where I have to take off the hood or-nament and the windshield wipers?"

"Yes," said Rostnikov.

Hamilton waited till they were both in the car before he said, "Why all these questions about dancing?"

"It is not dancing that is important," said Rostnikov. "It is getting to know people. If you talk to them about crime, they have prepared answers, wary answers. If you talk to them about what they read, drink, do, you often discover quite a bit about who you are dealing with. And if you ask them mad questions, they are often caught off guard and reveal something of their true selves."

Hamilton pulled into the nearly empty street

and said, "Did you find out anything about Yevgeniy and Anna with your questions?"

"Quite a bit," said Rostnikov. "Are you aware that we are speaking English?"

"Yes," said Hamilton.

"Do you remember when we began speaking English?"

"In the corridor outside the apartment," Hamilton answered in Russian.

"Why?"

"I didn't want them to know what we were saying," said Hamilton, now clearly determined to speak Russian.

"No," said Rostnikov. "The door was closed and we were speaking softly."

"Your theory?"

"The woman had made you nervous and you were looking for something that would make you feel more comfortable—your own language," said Rostnikov. "Turn right at the next corner."

"Yes, the woman made me feel nervous, and the fact that Yevgeniy Porvinovich kept touching the gun under his jacket as if he might pull it out and start shooting if someone said a wrong word."

"That too," agreed Rostnikov. "So what would you do next?"

"Go to the telephone company and see if Anna Porvinovich really received a phone call yesterday," said Hamilton. "No call and we go back and confront her."

"I think you will find that the call was made," said Rostnikov. "I could be wrong, but Anna

Porvinovich is, as we said, very smart. I'm hungry. You?"

"I'm hungry."

"Then park right over there, near where those two people are talking. The building behind them is where I live."

"The photographs," said the man in the blue smock. He was looking at Karpo over his glasses and holding out a set of full-color photographs. "They're all of the man with the tattoos. The other victims are nowhere near as interesting."

Emil Karpo took the photographs and looked at each one slowly.

One of the "not so interesting" dead was Mathilde Verson.

The man in the blue smock was Paulinin, who presided over a morbid flea market in his laboratory two floors below street level in Petrovka Headquarters. Paulinin had a mass of wild gray-black hair on an oversized head. He watched Karpo's face as the policeman went through each photograph of the naked body of the man whom Rostnikov had found sprawled on the hood of a car twenty feet from where Mathilde Verson had been shot while drinking tea. Karpo had already seen photographs of Mathilde and had looked at her body. He had resisted the urge to touch her flowing red hair and had tried instead to create a mental picture of her that would stay with him till he died.

For more than four years Mathilde Verson, who

had made her primary living as a prostitute, met Karpo in her room each week for an hour, for which he dutifully paid in clean bills laid neatly on her dresser. But gradually, somehow, the relationship changed. The ghost of a man who showed no emotion had been a challenge to her. She had tried to bring him out, had started to understand him. They had become friends and then real lovers, and no more money was exchanged. Mathilde had been the more present of the two, for Karpo had spent a lifetime withholding himself.

It was three bullets from the weapon near the tattooed man that had killed Mathilde.

Karpo's hands moved slowly, his eyes stayed fixed. He had lost all meaning in his life. He had devoted himself to Communism and its eventual triumph. Karpo knew that there were corrupt leaders, that some, such as Brezhnev, might even have been both corrupt and stupid, but since the day he had been taken by his father to a party rally as a small boy, he had been won over to the cause. So, with the help of his steelworker father's connections, he joined the police force as soon as he was old enough. Karpo's mission was to let no crime against the state or its members go unpunished. He had put in sixteen-hour days and rarely took a day off. He lived alone in a small room, no larger than a monk's chambers, where he slept on a bed in the corner. The rest of his meager furnishings consisted of two straight-backed wooden chairs, a desk, and a bookcase, which ran along one wall up to the ceiling. The only author represented in the several hundred identical black books was Emil Karpo. These books held his notes on all of his cases, with a special section for those that had not yet been solved. It was the unsolved cases that had occupied Karpo's attention most of the time he spent in the apartment.

All of his clothing, and there wasn't much of it, had been black until Mathilde had bought him a tie, a blue French tie with a small flower in the middle. Karpo had worn the tie twice before. He was wearing it today.

The Soviet Union had collapsed. Communism had almost disappeared. Crime, which once could be contained within the pages of his neatly kept notes, was now overwhelming. He would need a library the size of a football field to keep track of the anarchy that had clutched Moscow. Karpo had lost his mother when he was born. He had no sisters or brothers, aunts or uncles. His father had died four years ago, and now Mathilde. What had attracted her, she who was so full of life, so willing to laugh, so beautiful, to the dour, pale, humorless man Karpo saw in the mirror? That was the question he had asked both her and himself ever since they had been drawn together. And now she was gone.

"Well?" Paulinin prompted after a fruitless search for something among the mountain of piled-up books and the jars containing specimens of human organs, appendages, and even a man's head. There were items of clothing on a rack in a corner, arranged in no particular way. Knives, wrenches, a hammer, saws, a pair of false teeth, plaster casts of footprints and handprints littered a table that ran the length of one wall. The other tables were similarly cluttered with boxes, large and small, and various objects including the metal handrail from a Moscow city bus stained with blood.

"Well?" Paulinin repeated, folding his hands for an instant on a mass of reports and papers on his desk and then rubbing his palms together.

Emil Karpo's opinion of him was the only one Paulinin valued. This little man saw no one socially, lived alone, and slept at his desk as often as he went back to his apartment, which was in as much disarray as his office. He cared little who ran the government. Paulinin cared nothing about politics, which was one of the reasons he worked alone in a converted storeroom and was given almost no funding.

No one, however, ever considered getting rid of the nearly mad man in the blue smock, for it was generally acknowledged that Paulinin was an encyclopedia and a near-genius at examining forensic evidence.

"I have a surprise," Paulinin said, trying to pry his visitor's eyes from the photographs. Karpo was always quiet and correct, always spoke little, but today was different—today he was nearly a robot.

The police inspector continued to look at the photographs slowly, carefully. Finally he looked up, and Paulinin handed him a two-cup beaker of tea. Karpo took it and drank some of the brown, tepid fluid. It tasted of something sharp and bitter, the residue of some experiment that Paulinin had failed to remove completely from the beaker before brewing his tea.

"What do you make of it?" Paulinin asked, taking a sip of his own tea from a black cup on which was written in English PENSACOLA EYE AND EAR CLINIC.

Karpo looked down again at the photographs of the man who had killed Mathilde. The man was literally covered with tattoos—head, neck, arms, fingers, back, front, legs and toes, even his penis. The tattoos were colorful, vivid, and extremely well done. The subjects seemed random. On his right forearm a series of church domes, on his chest just below the collarbone a fiery eight-pointed star. The tattoo on his back depicted a rearing horse mounted by a man with a death's-head, who in turn held a bearded man by the hair and appeared to be about to behead him.

Karpo turned to the photos of the nude body of the man who had died in the street. He, too, was covered in tattoos.

"Prison tattoos," said Karpo.

"And?" Paulinin prompted.

Karpo knew a little about prison tattoos. He knew that professional criminals spent much of their time inflicting themselves with the tattoos when they were in prison, giving themselves some distinction from the other prisoners.

"Your tattooed men carried no wallets, no identification. There was a rubber band in the pocket of the bald one, a thick one. I would guess he was carrying a great deal of money and that it was taken from him before the police arrived. More likely, it was taken by the first officer at the scene."

Karpo said nothing. He took out his notebook and began to write.

"All but one of your dead men's tattoos are in code. This corpse," he said, pointing to the bald man, "had been a *pakhan*, a prison boss, a member of the *vory v zakone*. The eight-pointed star makes that clear."

"The eight church domes?" Paulinin asked.

"Each dome represents a completed sentence."

"Good, good," said Paulinin, gulping down his tea. "You paused at the death's-head. A creature from medieval folk tales told by the Bogatyrs, a violent, crusading breed. It indicates that our corpse was a murderer. No drug tattoos. None that look forced on him by other inmates to mark him for crimes such as heroin addiction, crimes against children, submission. Your man has no facial tattoos and no sign that he ever had one and had it removed. In fact, he had no tattoos removed and has continued to shave his head prison-style. He was proud of his record."

"And?"

Paulinin put his cup down. "His name is Mikhail Sivak. He was last imprisoned in Correctional Labor Colony Nineteen, maximum security, just outside of Perm. Your people will discover all this through his fingerprints perhaps, but it will take them days, perhaps a week or more if they even bother."

Paulinin shook his head fiercely. His hair bounced.

"The newest tattoos on Mikhail Sivak are definitely in the style of Correctional Labor Colony Nineteen. I have seen them before. As for knowing his name, did you notice that his eyes are open in all the photographs?"

Karpo nodded.

"Those dolts at the hospital couldn't tell you his name, though it was written right on him."

"In prison code?" Karpo guessed.

"No," said Paulinin. "I looked at the corpse when they were done with him. I closed his eyes. On one lid was written 'Do not wake me.' On the other was his name, Mikhail Sivak. The other one had no name tattooed on his body."

"This eagle on his right buttock, the one carrying the bomb?" Karpo asked.

Paulinin was up now, lifting bottles, opening boxes—searching for something.

"The bomb and eagle is recent," Paulinin said. "It suggests that he now deals in powerful weapons. The artist who did this tattoo was especially precise, definitely an artist. The bomb is an exact replica of a hydrogen bomb. I expect I'll be seeing more of these in the future."

"You said you had a surprise for me," said Karpo. "Was that it, the trade in nuclear weapons?"

"No…here," said Paulinin, finding what he was looking for. "I knew it couldn't be far."

He held up something that looked like a small painting, a replica of the eagle and bomb that was tattooed on the head of Mikhail Sivak. The painting was sandwiched inside two sheets of glass. Paulinin handed the treasure to Karpo.

"I took it from his body," said Paulinin. "Scalped him like one of those American Indians. Such art deserves to be preserved."

"May I keep this?" Karpo asked.

"A gift from me," said Paulinin with some pride.

The pressed, colorful skin of Mikhail Sivak fit tightly into Karpo's jacket pocket.

"Questions," said Karpo.

Paulinin waved an arm to show that he was prepared.

"What can you tell me about the dead man at the table with the woman?"

Paulinin paused in his fussing over the box from which he had taken the patch of Mikhail Sivak's skin. "The bullets from his weapon killed the two tattooed men in the street. He must have been a good shot to use a handgun against people who knew how to use automatic weapons. Our man with the four-fifty-four Casull was, as you know from looking at his wallet, a German. Heinz Dieter Kirst. He and the woman were both killed by the same weapon, instantly. The bald man must have been firing after he died. The man and woman were killed by a dead man."

Paulinin pointed to a spot on his right temple to indicate where the bullet had entered and exited the German.

"The dead waiter was named Waclaw Wypich," Paulinin said. "A Pole who—"

"I know," said Karpo.

The other two, the ones without identification, wore blue Adidas sweat suits and leather jackets. Both had light-colored, recently barbered hair. Both appeared to be in their late twenties or early thirties.

"Can you tell me anything about the German?"

"Interesting question," said Paulinin, holding up half a cookie he had unearthed from his boxes. It was wrapped in a see-through bag. Karpo showed no interest in the cookie, so Paulinin opened the bag and began eating it as he continued. "Judging from the fact that he was carrying a gun and knew how to use it, I would say that the tattoos had come to kill him, and he half expected it. My guess is that the woman, whom I examined, was a prostitute, and the German was negotiating with her."

Karpo had already come to this conclusion. What he hadn't been prepared for was Paulinin's simple statement that he had examined Mathilde's dead body.

"Treachery," said Paulinin, taking a bite of his cookie after dipping it into his tea. He did not notice that Karpo had closed his eyes. "Who knows? German promises something and then fails to deliver. Our tattooed mafia think the German has betrayed them or made a deal for whatever he is selling or buying with someone else. Who knows? That's your job."

Karpo opened his eyes.

"Yes," he said.

"What am I?" asked Paulinin, wiping the crumbs off his hands on his smock. "A grub of a scientist with almost no budget and certainly no bloated reputation like Rostov or Kelenin or…or any of them. They fired their automatic weapons at Kirst, not concerned about who else might get shot. Kirst fired back, killing them. A pair of innocent bystanders got in the way. Someone was waiting for our killers to do the job. When they were both killed, whoever was waiting saw no reason to stay, and off he went."

To illustrate the car's driving away, Paulinin rolled what was left of his cookie across the papers on his desk.

Karpo looked down at the rolling cookie. Paulinin was simply talking now, presenting nothing Karpo himself hadn't immediately determined at the crime scene. He willed himself to see Mathilde's face, but he could not.

Paulinin sat down at his desk and popped the rest of the cookie into his mouth. "And now?" he said.

"We are most likely dealing with a mafia of ex-prisoners who are dealing in the sale of nuclear weapons to foreigners. I will find the leader of this mafia. I will find whoever ordered these murders."

And when I find him, Karpo thought, *I will kill him.*

"I brought American peanut-butter sandwiches

for lunch," said Paulinin, moving to a refrigerator behind his desk.

He opened the door to the refrigerator. Karpo could see jars of specimens and a lone cloth bag. Paulinin pulled out the bag, closed the refrigerator door, and turned to Karpo.

"Plenty for both of us," said Paulinin. "And I have Pepsi-Colas."

"Yes," said Karpo.

Paulinin smiled and handed a sandwich wrapped in frequently used aluminum foil to Karpo, who hoped that the food would ease his growing nausea.

Chapter 4

Money, Money, Money

Besides the storeroom of treasures, the kitchen was the largest room in Ivan Dokorov's house. It now held sixteen people, two of them women. The two women were Elena Timofeyeva and Natalya Valorovna Dokorova, the sister of the deceased man who had amassed the now-missing treasure.

The men crowded around the old woman, who sat at the kitchen table, hands folded, a distinct look of determination on her face. She did not move her head but turned her eyes in the direction of whoever spoke the loudest.

"How long had your brother been accumulating his collection?" someone shouted.

Natalya shrugged.

This was no criminal investigation. It was a madhouse in which no one knew who was in charge.

There were representatives from two separate police districts, both of which claimed, under Yeltsin's redistricting plan, that they were responsible for the investigation. There were three members of the tax police, none in uniform, claiming loudly that this was a tax case. There were members of the State Security Department, which had gone through so many changes that even they were not sure of their jurisdiction, but they were certain that they were the elite in the room. The State Security Department was a child of the former KGB, the *Komitet Gosudarstavennoy Bezopasnosti*, or Committee for State Security. Following the coup that brought democracy, capitalism, and an explosion of crime and corruption the Second Directorate of the KGB, the section responsible for counterintelligence, had been merged with the Sixth Directorate, which was responsible for economic crimes. The new department, reporting directly to the presidium and the president, was to focus on fraud and corruption. All these agencies wanted to be in on the treasure hunt.

"Is there some way out of this building other than through the front door and the rear door?" came another voice.

Natalya shook her head.

Elena had tried, without success, to push forward through the crowd of elbows and suited men.

Now she stood with her back to the sink wondering what temporary disease had so deranged Rostnikov and Colonel Snitkonoy that they had assigned her to this important case.

"Who do you think took the collection?"

Another shrug.

"How could they get past guards on both doors?" boomed another voice.

Natalya's hands were folded on the table, her gray hair tied in a bun. *Let her hair down*, Elena thought, *and it would touch the floor.*

"Everything in this house, everything my brother left, is mine," she said evenly. "You have no right to be here. You have a duty to recover that which was stolen from me during the night and return it to me."

"How could all of the things in that gigantic room have been taken during the night without your hearing it?"

"I sleep the sleep of the dead," said Natalya Dokorova.

"It would have taken most of the night to remove it all," shouted a man.

Natalya shrugged.

Elena leaned back against the sink. The huge elbow of a sweating man shot back and barely missed her face. The least experienced member of the department, Elena had been assigned to what appeared to be a very important case. And Karpo, whose very presence would draw attention and respect, had been taken off this case and assigned to a street-gang killing. Karpo had a sense of the inventory and extent of the treasure. Karpo knew the value of each item. But Karpo was out working on common street gangs.

"We will need a list of everyone who knew of this collection," came a voice.

Natalya didn't answer. Through a break in the male bodies her eyes met Elena's, and Elena read into that look a plea for help. Maybe Elena was mistaken. She looked again, but the gap between the two women had been filled again by the men.

The room was hot in spite of the cooling weather. Too many bodies in too little space. About half of the men were smoking.

"What did your brother plan to do with his collection?"

"Nothing. He wanted to have it nearby. He wanted to save books, icons, and paintings that the Communists wanted to destroy after the Revolution."

There was a brief moment of silence. No one in the room was openly Communist, and very few would have acknowledged that they had ever belonged to the party.

"Did he have partners? Who are they?"

"We lived alone and had no friends. Ivan worked. He saved. He bought."

"Relatives?"

Natalya shook her head.

The men in the room were growing restless. They pushed for position, muttering threats and insults. They all knew that they were in competition for evidence, clues, and leads in the now nearly empty treasure room. But if there were leads, they had long since trampled them. They had contaminated the scene, and Elena admitted to herself that her own department had also done so with a pair of evidence specialists borrowed from the Petrovka forensics laboratory.

"How could—?" a man with a gruff voice began.

"No more," Natalya Dokorova interrupted. "No more."

"Then," said a man up front, "we will have to take you with us for further questioning."

There was a fresh rumble of argument among the men.

"You will have to?" one man shouted. "It is we with whom she will come."

"I have committed no crime. There is no crime here except the theft of my legacy," Natalya said.

"There is more than a little doubt that the property belongs to you," shouted a man close to Elena. "We will have to determine if the items have been stolen by your brother or by someone who sold them to your brother."

"Decide who will arrest me and for what crime," Natalya said, standing slowly. "Or leave my house."

"We are here to help retrieve the items," a new voice called out with a fresh plan. "When we find the items, if they are judged to be yours, they will be returned to you. Surely you want to cooperate with us."

"If and when I understand who you are," said Natalya, "I will answer your questions. I am not defying the law. I am attempting to cooperate with it. Now, you will all leave, or one of you will have to arrest me."

More talking, more shouts, debates, tempers rising. Elena's eyes and those of the old woman met again for an instant.

An older man, probably the oldest in the room judging by his white hair and weary face, finally said, "We will meet with our superiors and determine jurisdiction, and some of us will return. Those of us who do return will want answers, and you shall either give those answers or face arrest."

Natalya did not respond. Reluctantly the men began to file out of the kitchen, down the short corridor, and out the front door. Pressed at the edge of the crowd, Elena waited, and found herself the last one to leave. A hand on her shoulder stopped her. She turned and faced Natalya Dokorova as the last man to depart turned back and witnessed the two women standing beside each other. But in an instant he had turned his head again and was gone.

Natalya stepped into the hall to be sure the men had departed.

"Cannibals," said Natalya. "And they've made my kitchen stink. Let's go into the parlor."

Elena followed the old woman into a modest living room with two windows. The thick drapes had been closed either to keep out the sun or to protect its occupant from the eyes of reporters and the curious.

"I have some questions to ask you," Natalya

said, sitting down on a straight-back chair and pointing to an identical one for Elena. Elena sat.

"Are you married?"

"No," said Elena, smoothing down her straight skirt and trying to get reasonably comfortable.

"You live alone?"

"With my aunt. She's ill. She used to be a procurator."

"That's more than I wanted to know."

Elena didn't speak.

"You were with that vampire yesterday," Natalya said.

"Inspector Karpo, yes," replied Elena.

"I'm glad he is not back," said Natalya. "He recognized my brother's accomplishment, but he did not seem to appreciate it."

"Inspector Karpo is not an emotional man," said Elena.

The old woman nodded in understanding.

"If they find my brother's collection, will you see to it that I get it back?"

"I don't know," said Elena. "That is up to my superiors. And those above them. I'm sorry."

"Do you think there is any chance that the collection will be returned to me if they find it, any chance at all? Please, the truth."

"No," said Elena.

"They will steal it," she said, suddenly sitting erect, her arms tight on the arms of her chair. "These piranha ready to devour the carcass of a fatted calf. This 'state' of chaos. They will sell it to the Japanese and the Americans

73

and will throw the money away on economic plans that don't work."

Elena said nothing.

"The creature you were with yesterday. This…"

"Karpo."

"He knew the real value of my brother's collection, not just its worth in rubles."

"Yes," said Elena.

"And you?" Natalya asked.

"I'm sorry," she said. "I am in awe of your brother's collection. I recognize that it is special, something awesome."

"Awesome, yes," said Natalya, savoring the word. "Those men who tromped through here and asked me stupid questions, they know nothing of what my brother has done."

Elena agreed that this was probably true, but she remained silent.

"Are you comfortable?" Natalya asked.

"The chair is exceptionally comfortable," said Elena.

"A woman's chair," Natalya said with satisfaction, running her hands over the carved wood of the arms of her chair. "They were made for Catherine the Great. What do you think of that?"

Elena looked at the dark, smooth carved arms, and finally said, "A sense of history… awe."

"I'll help you," the old woman said. "As much as I can."

At that moment Elena Timofeyeva knew why Rostnikov had assigned her to the theft. He couldn't have anticipated that Natalya Dokorova would seek her out, but he must have believed that the old woman would be more likely to confide in Elena than in any man, including himself.

"Then let's begin," said Elena, removing a notebook from the red bag she carried.

"Shall I make tea?" Natalya asked.

"That would be nice," said Elena.

In Alexei's dream he had been looking out a window in the old printing house at 15 Nikloskaya. He had a sense that he was looking from his office building. Below on the sidewalk a man paused to look up at him. The man's hands were in the pockets of his lightweight coat. The eyes of the two men met, and Alexei knew he was looking down at himself. Suddenly a car stopped behind the man on the street. People hurried by, other cars passed. Two men emerged from the stopped car, their faces covered with black ski masks.

Alexci tried to shout a warning to himself. The two men in ski masks were carrying weapons. The Alexei who stood on the street did not seem to understand. The Alexei in the window pointed, gesturing in helpless desperation while his doppelgänger was hauled into the backseat of the waiting car.

Alexei Porvinovich opened his eyes. He was sweating. He dimly remembered where he was and was surprised that his hands were now unbound and that he could wipe his own forehead with a warm palm. Pain throbbed in his cheek and he could feel the swelling.

He looked up at a familiar face in an unfamiliar room.

The man with the familiar face was Artiom Solovyov, big, broad, clean-shaven, forty-three years old, and very tough-looking. He had been a boxer in the 1968 Olympics, but that had been in a much lower weight class than he would now occupy.

Alexei knew a great deal more about Artiom Solovyov as well.

"Rules," said Artiom. He drank some hot liquid from a large mug. "You understand me?"

Alexei nodded.

"Good," said Solovyov nervously.

His captor still wore the black uniform.

Alexei had a question. He almost asked it and then stopped himself. "Why am I still alive?" he almost said, but then his sense of survival and hope took over and he said nothing.

"You see the carpet?" Artiom said without looking down.

Alexei looked. It was not a bad Persian, he couldn't help thinking. A bit worn, but at least eighty years old.

"Answer," Artiom demanded.

"I see the carpet," Alexei croaked, feeling the dryness in his throat, the pain in his cheek. He could hear his speech slurring from the damage to his face. In addition Alexei's eye was beginning to swell and close.

"If you step past the middle of the carpet, my friend at the door will shoot you," Artiom went on after another sip.

Alexei looked across the large living room. On a chair at the door a thin man in black sat with a handgun in his lap, a very large handgun. The man in the chair wore a black ski mask, which struck Alexei as pointless and probably uncomfortable. Alexei's eyes scanned the rest of the room. His area of the rug included a pair of chairs, the badly worn sofa on which he now lay, a pair of closed windows, and a small table, on which was a pile of what looked like old magazines.

"My friend will watch you for a certain period and will be relieved. A series of friends will watch you until our business is done. Do not talk to my friends. Do not make them shoot you. Would you like some tea?"

"Yes," said Alexei, who was now sitting up and was making an effort to stop the room from vibrating.

Artiom shook his large head as if to indicate that it was a reasonable request. He moved across the room to a table in the corner where a bright green plug-in water heater bubbled away. The table was definitely not on Alexei's side of the room.

"Sugar?" Artiom asked.

Alexei was looking at the armed man at the door.

"What? Sugar? Yes."

"Lumps," said Artiom. "I have regular English lumps. How many?"

"Two," said Alexei.

"Two," Artiom repeated, dropping in the two lumps and stirring with a spoon, which he placed back on a white napkin on the table.

"Thank you," said Alexei as he took the hot cup. It felt good. It felt more than good, and it tasted strong and sweet, though it hurt to open his mouth.

Artiom sat across from him and watched him drink.

"You have a question you don't want to ask?" Artiom said.

"Why don't you keep me tied to a chair or—"

"We want you to be reasonably comfortable. We are not going to torture you. We are not political terrorists. But that was not the question you were thinking of."

Alexei shrugged and drank.

"You were thinking," Artiom asked, "'Why don't they kill me?' Am I not right?"

Alexei shrugged again.

"You know who I am. You can identify me. I can shoot you and still ask for the ransom, but you know and I know that your wife is too smart to take my word that you are alive. You will talk to her on the phone. You will tell her or your brother that you are well and unharmed."

"And when you get your money, if you get it?" Alexei asked, drinking more tea.

It was Artiom's turn to shrug.

"We will see," he said with a smile. "Are you almost awake now? You have your senses?"

"Almost," said Alexei.

"Good," said Artiom with a smile. "Then make your offer. Not the details. I'm sure you haven't worked them out yet, but the general offer."

"What do you plan to ask for? How much?" asked Alexei.

"Three million American. Nice round number," said Artiom. He had finished his tea and now crossed the room for a refill.

"I'll give you two million and a promise that the police will not look for you," said Alexei. "Providing we can work out a way for me to be sure I will be set free alive."

Artiom had crossed the room again to Alexei's side. He looked at the man seated at the door. The seated man's eyes rolled to Artiom, but revealed nothing behind his mask. Artiom settled into the same chair he had left, thought for an instant, and said, "You know who I am. You will tell the police."

"No," said Alexei.

"Why not?" asked Artiom.

"Because the two million will be to perform a job, a quite illegal job, and I will put it in writing that I am paying you for that job. You will hold the document for protection."

"You are thinking quickly, Alexei Porvinovich," said Artiom. "I can't think this quickly."

"It is how I have stayed alive and gotten wealthy," said Alexei.

"The document, the job…?"

"I will hire you to murder my wife and brother," Alexei said. "If I try to betray you, you can go to the authorities yourself. You kill them and I write the document."

"Why do you want to…?"

"Because my wife and brother planned this," Alexei said, the pain surging sharply. "Didn't they?"

Artiom was reasonably clever but had lived by his rugged looks and his strong body. Alexei was already far ahead of him.

"I'll think about it," said Artiom, getting up. "You hungry?"

"No," said Alexei as he examined the leaves at the bottom of his cup. "Of course the plan needs refining—many details need to be worked out."

Artiom said nothing.

The plan had been to demand the ransom. Alexei's wife and brother would gather it and get it to Artiom. The police would know all about it. Alexei Porvinovich would be found dead on the street.

For this Artiom would keep the money and continue his affair with Alexei's wife. But the plan had troubled him from the first. Anna's interest in him was waning. Artiom knew this, knew that he was just a novelty for her, knew that another novelty would appear. He wasn't even certain that she would let him survive to be a possible witness against her.

But then again, Alexei Porvinovich, who sat before him clutching a tea mug, was certainly not to be trusted either.

This had all been a mistake. Anna had insisted that it had to be done quickly. She had given him a genuine Rolex and an hour of passion in his bedroom.

Artiom was not smart, but he was not a fool. When he worked honestly, he repaired automobiles. The man at the door was a half-wit named Boris who worked with him on cars. Boris was a genius with cars. Boris would also do whatever Artiom told him, including murder. Artiom had met Anna and Alexei when they brought in their Buick to be repaired. The next day Anna had come alone to pick up the car and Artiom.

Artiom's wife had left him almost a year ago and taken their son, Kolya, with her. She had had enough of his women, his gambling, his indifference, and his outbursts of rage and brutality. She lived now with another man whom she said was her cousin from Sverdlovsk. She called Artiom often, demanding money. He would send what he could when he could.

Artiom had never before committed a major crime. He had been in jail for two weeks for hitting a policeman when he was drunk, and he had been questioned about a stolen car on which he had worked, but they had let him off on that one.

And now he was a kidnapper, and people were offering him millions to murder each other, people he did not trust.

"Work on your plan, Porvinovich," Artiom said. "When I come back, we will make a call to your family. You will cooperate and you will tell me more about your plan."

Alexei Porvinovich nodded. His legs were weak. His stomach was still upset, but he had something to scheme about now and he was a champion schemer. If he played it carefully, there was just a chance that he could survive.

Artiom moved to the man at the door, who slid over to let him pass.

"I am in pain," Alexei said.

"Toilet is through that door on your side of the rug," Artiom said. "Tell my man you have to use it and go in. There are no windows. There may be something you can use in the cabinet. You will have two minutes each time you use the toilet. You will be allowed three visits to the washroom each day. I've brought you newspapers and magazines."

"I'll need paper and a pen to write drafts of our agreement."

"I'll bring them," Artiom said, thinking that it would not hurt to keep his captive hopeful.

When Artiom left, Alexei looked at the seated man in the ski mask. "Boris, I wish to go to the washroom."

Alexei was sure that the seated man was Artiom's assistant, a creature even more slow-witted than his boss.

The man did not answer. Alexei knew that Artiom was his wife's lover. He knew that his brother Yevgeniy, though barely capable of an erection, had also been lured into Anna's bed. There was hardly a man of their acquaintance whom Anna had not seduced or tried to seduce, particularly the odd or different man—the mechanic, the apparently sexless Moscow University history professor they had met at a party. Anna knew her husband was aware of most of the names on her long list, but the names were not important to Alexei. Neither, he was beginning to think, was Anna.

The idea of getting his captor to murder Anna and Yevgeniy had come to him in an instant. Anna had to have planned all this. Yevgeniy had to know. They planned to kill him and make it look like a botched kidnapping.

Alexei did not feel safe. Far from it. Nothing was certain, but he had dealt masterfully with bureaucrats all of his life. He had dealt masterfully and patiently. He smiled at the man at the door. He doubted if the man even recognized that the broken, purple face had smiled.

Chapter 5

The Silence of Children

Rostnikov's wife opened the door to their small apartment on Krasikov Street when she heard her husband's key in the lock.

She was wearing a black dress with an artificial pearl necklace. Her still-red hair was cut short, and she looked, thought Rostnikov, quite beautiful. She had lost a great deal of weight during a long bout with a brain tumor. Her recovery had been slow, but now, with her moments of dizziness fewer, she had gone back to her job at the music store and lately seemed even radiant.

"This is Craig Hamilton," Rostnikov said.

Sarah took the black man's extended hand.

"Pleasure to meet you," Hamilton said.

"Does Emil know?" Sarah asked, closing the door behind the two men. "About Mathilde?"

"I have assigned him to the case," said Rostnikov.

"The officer whose friend died in the street killing?" Hamilton asked.

"Yes," said Rostnikov.

"In the United States, if an officer is involved with a victim, we rarely assign him or her to the case," said Hamilton. "Too close. Too emotional."

"In Karpo's case," said Rostnikov, moving toward the cubbyhole near the window that served as a kitchen and pantry, "emotion will not be a visible factor. But he will be on the killers like a piranha on the carcass of a dying cow."

Sarah was bustling to a wardrobe in the corner. She took out a lightweight dark overcoat and said, "I'm late. The girls are at school. There's some bread and herring and a little rice pudding." She picked up a small handbag from the sofa. "And bring Emil Karpo here tonight. Order him to come."

She hurried over to Rostnikov, her heels clicking on the tile floor. Rostnikov and their son, Iosef, had done the tiling themselves after a lucky purchase on the black market several months ago. Sarah gave her husband a kiss on the cheek as he searched the cupboard. He turned and hugged her, lifting her easily from the floor.

"If you feel dizzy..." he said.

"I will sit down," she said.

He put her down, and she hurried to the door, pausing to take Craig Hamilton's hand again and say, "It was nice to meet you. May we meet again soon."

And she was off.

"Lovely lady," said Hamilton, following Rostnikov into the kitchen alcove. "Didn't even ask who I was."

"She knows I'll tell her later," Rostnikov said, rummaging for something. He found it and said, "Yah."

He turned triumphantly with a tall jar of French strawberry preserves. "Coffee, bread and jam or bread and herring?"

"The bread and jam," Hamilton said, sitting at the small table not far from the window.

"So, what do you think?" asked Rostnikov as he prepared the meal.

"Think?"

"About the apartment." Still focused on the components of the meal before him, Rostnikov absently waved the knife in his hand.

Hamilton had taken in the room without looking around. Now he looked. A faded, flower-patterned sofa was positioned between two solid-colored peach wingback chairs that almost coordinated with the sofa. A bookcase lined an entire wall, its shelves filled with not only books but old LP records and what looked like small dumbbells. There was a large painting on the wall with a woman in the foreground, her back to the viewer, her red hair and green dress billowing forward as she held her left hand up to keep the hair from her face. She looked out along a vast green field toward a house in the distance, a modest farmhouse with a small barn. The sun was going down behind the barn. Hamilton assumed that the painting was of Rostnikov's wife or that he had bought it because it resembled her.

"The painting was a gift from Mathilde Verson," said Rostnikov. "That is Mathilde in the painting, a self-portrait in a way, a birthday gift from one redhead to another. Mathilde gave it to Sarah when my wife was recovering from surgery."

"Mathilde Verson was an artist?" Hamilton asked.

Rostnikov looked at the American and smiled.

"What's funny?" asked Hamilton.

"You know that Mathilde was a prostitute. I'm sure you read all the reports."

"She was a talented painter," said Hamilton, looking at the painting. "Did she do any other work like this?"

"As far as I know, this is the only painting she had done in more than twenty years. As a young girl she studied art briefly."

"And Karpo was...?"

"It is my hope that her death does not destroy him. As long as he is seeking her killers, he will function. Later, who knows." Rostnikov looked over at the American. "Real coffee," he asked, "or decaffeinated?"

"Real," said Hamilton. "And black."

"You know Dinah Washington?" asked Rostnikov.

"Personally? No. I think she's dead."

"Pity," said Rostnikov, setting the small table. "She makes me weep. 'Nothing Ever Changes My Love for You.' Wonderful song."

"I'm not terribly familiar with her work," Hamilton admitted.

Rostnikov paused, a jar of herring in one hand, a half loaf of bread in the other.

"She is the most famous singer in America," Rostnikov said.

"No," Hamilton corrected. "She is not even well known."

Rostnikov pondered this for a moment, shook his head, and continued serving. When the water had boiled, he made the instant coffee.

"Black," said Rostnikov, setting the cup in front of Hamilton.

"For me, sugar, cream, anything," said Rostnikov, sitting awkwardly. "I don't like this fake coffee."

Hamilton nodded. He had a grinder at home in his apartment in Bethesda. His selection of coffee beans was large, and ranged from the standard to the exotic, all purchased from a nearby shop that dealt exclusively in coffee and coffee products. Craig Hamilton was an early riser. He always had coffee ready for his wife and breakfast plates set out before he woke her and his daughters.

"We are settled now?" Rostnikov asked, adjusting his leg and cutting off a thick slice of dark bread for his guest.

Hamilton nodded.

"Then," said Rostnikov, "tell me what it was that you put under the coffee table in the Porvinovich apartment."

Hamilton had been sure no one had seen him make the move.

"Voice-activated recorder," he said. "Six-hour capacity. When we go back, we can retrieve it."

"And you were going to tell me about this?" asked Rostnikov, carefully making a lopsided herring sandwich.

"If there was anything on the tape that would either implicate or clear them," said Hamilton, drinking his coffee.

"So small." Rostnikov shook his head. "It was so small. We have nothing like that. I mean the police. Internal Security has. They have devices that can hear through walls, as I am sure you do. I do have a recorder taping all phone calls to the Porvinovich apartment, however."

Hamilton hungrily chewed the rough bread.

"It is possible that in six hours of tape we will be lucky," said Rostnikov. "On the other hand, we may hear conversations about Madame Porvinovich's wardrobe."

Hamilton smiled, and Rostnikov rose, still working on his herring sandwich. The phone was across the room, on a shelf of the bookcase. He checked his notebook and called the Porvinovich apartment. Yevgeniy answered with a tentative "Yes?"

"Is Mrs. Porvinovich there? This is Inspector Rostnikov."

"Yes…" He paused.

Rostnikov could tell he was putting his hand over the speaker. Rostnikov knew that he was asking her what to do.

"This is Anna Porvinovich," she said with irritation.

"This is Inspector Rostnikov. I have good news. We have a definite lead on the people who kidnapped your husband. We expect even better news, possibly his very location, within the hour. As soon as we know just a bit more, we will come and see you."

"Very good," she said evenly.

"That is how we view it," said Rostnikov. "Ah, my other phone is ringing. It may be that information about your husband. Please excuse me."

With that, Rostnikov hung up and started back to the table.

"Now she will either discuss the situation with the brother," he said, "or…"

"She will call the kidnappers," Hamilton said, wondering whether it was polite to ask for more bread and jam.

Rostnikov recognized the signs of the FBI agent's unsatisfied appetite and sliced another piece of bread, then pushed the jam in his direction. He would, as soon as possible, make a stop to see Luba Lasuria, an old woman from Armenia whom he had once kept out of jail. Luba lived a short walk away on Garibaldi Street, a few doors from the Ceremuski Cinema. Luba was an extremely successful dealer in blackmarket food. She never revealed her source, but it was said to be three nephews who regularly crossed over into France and Germany by paying bribes to border guards. The three nephews would return with suitcases full of food that could be sold for ten times what they'd paid for it.

When they had finished the meal and cleaned up the dishes, Rostnikov returned to the phone and made a call while Hamilton openly examined the books that lined the wall. There were books on art and music, a few on Russian history, a great many well-worn mystery paperbacks by Ed McBain, Susan Dunlap, John Lutz, Lawrence Block, Marcia Muller, Bill Pronzini, and many others. A far smaller number of books—in both Russian and English—dealt with plumbing.

"Report," Rostnikov said to the person on the phone. Then he listened, watching the American move to the small assortment of dumbbells and metal weights in the corner of the bookcase. Still listening to the person on the other end, Rostnikov opened the lower shelf of the bookcase to reveal far more weights, lifting bars, seventy-pound dumbbells, and a portable weight bench with a well-worn gray plastic covering.

"Good," Rostnikov finally said, and hung up the phone. "You lift weights?"

"Machines," Hamilton said.

"You lift machines?"

"I use weight machines, and I run on a track."

"I've seen those weight machines," Rostnikov said. "In the Olympic gym where the great ones train. I think I prefer the old iron. Let's go."

"Where are we going?" asked Hamilton.

"To an automobile repair shop," said Rostnikov. "Anna Porvinovich just placed a call to an automobile repair shop and asked for an Artiom Solovyov. Between us, we will soon have all her secrets, including the answer to the question 'Why does the woman whose husband has been kidnapped call an automobile repairman moments after being told that the criminals are on the verge of being caught?'"

"I can think of many reasons," said Hamilton, following Rostnikov to the front door. "But only one of them particularly appeals to me."

"Come, let us have a pleasant talk with this Artiom Solovyov," said Rostnikov.

They were almost out of the door when Hamilton could not resist asking, "Why do you have all those plumbing books?"

"Do you meditate?" Rostnikov asked, stepping into the hall.

"No," said Hamilton.

"Do you do anything to take brief vacations from reality?" Rostnikov closed the door to the apartment.

"Jigsaw puzzles," Hamilton confessed. "All black, all white, three-dimensional, thousands of pieces."

"Your meditation," Rostnikov said. "Plumbing is mine."

★ ★ ★

The old man held up his cane, pointed it at the two detectives like a gun, and said, "Boom, boom, boom." Then he tucked the cane back under his arm and smiled with satisfaction.

"You are saying that Oleg Makmunov was shot and killed in the doorway across the street?" asked Sasha.

The old man nodded sagely and said, "Tall man, loud gun. All the rest around here will be afraid to tell you, but I saw it all."

The old man was wearing a postman's cap and a coat too warm for the weather. He needed to decide whether to shave or grow a beard. Beards had not returned to fashion yet except among some highly successful businessmen and mafia leaders.

"You saw a man shoot down a drunk last night in that doorway?" Sasha asked, pointing to the doorway. The crushed body of Oleg Makmunov had been removed hours ago.

The old man on crutches shook his head firmly. People passed. A few older ones with string bags or a small child in tow glanced at the three men and moved on.

"It was Zorotich," said the old man firmly.

"Someone named Zorotich shot the man in the doorway over there?" asked Sasha.

Zelach was somewhat bewildered by the exchange since he knew that Makmunov had been beaten and kicked to death, not shot.

"Svet Zorotich shot him," the old man said decisively. "With an American tommy gun, an old one with one of those cans wrapped around it."

"Where can we find this Zorotich?" Sasha asked politely.

"Right up there," the old man said, pointing above him with his crutch and almost knocking off his postman's cap. "He lives right over me, makes noise all night. I heard him go out, saw what he did. I'll say so before any judge, any judge."

"Thank you," said Sasha, brushing back his hair, putting away his notebook, and shaking the old man's trembling hand.

"Others around here are afraid to talk." The old man looked up and down the street with contempt. "But someone's got to stop this lunatic. Am I right?"

"You are right," said Sasha, moving past the old man and motioning for Zelach to follow.

Sasha entered the building and started up the stairs with Zelach behind him. Outside, the old man watched them for a moment, then looked up and down the street, wondering which way to hobble.

"What are we doing, Sasha?" Zelach asked, panting as he climbed the narrow, dark stairway.

"We are going to talk to Mad Dog Zorotich," Sasha answered. "He mows people down in the street for daring to look at him or utter his name in vain."

"Seriously, Sasha."

"It can't hurt," said Sasha, walking down a

narrow corridor. There were only six apartments on each floor. It wasn't hard to find Zorotich's. His name was finely scripted on a white card pasted to the door.

Sasha knocked. No answer came from within. He knocked again, this time more loudly. Still no answer. He motioned for Zelach to move away. Zelach did what he was told, but Sasha remained in front of the door, motioning for Zelach to continue down the stairs. Zelach dutifully obeyed, proceeding out the door. Sasha put his ear to the door just above the finely lettered name. He heard a shuffling movement and then he said, "We know you are in there, Zorotich. Open the door, or my partner will break it down."

"No," came a voice inside. "You've come to kill me and take my apartment, like Illyna last month."

Sasha removed his identification card from his wallet and slid it under the door.

"You see my card?" he said.

More shuffling, a move toward the door.

"It could be a fake. You people can make good fakes."

"It's not fake. I'm a policeman. Your neighbor downstairs said—"

"The fake cripple? There's nothing wrong with him. He can walk as well as you or me. He's crazy. He wants sympathy, a pension."

"Last night, late, someone was killed across the street. Did you see anything, hear anything?"

The man inside laughed bitterly. Zelach was now coming slowly and carefully up the stairs, calculatedly making a good amount of noise. Sasha waved him to the door.

"So," said the man inside with a sigh, "if I don't let you in, you break down the door and kill me. If I open the door, maybe you just kill me. How do I know you are policemen?"

"Do you have a phone?"

"Ha," the old man laughed.

"My ID, common sense. We are not thieves. We are not some mafia wanting to steal your apartment."

A series of locks and chains went into action, and the door came open to reveal a man. He was tall, thin, and quite old and he wore dark trousers, a blue shirt, and a dark sweater vest. At the man's side was a large white dog.

"Well, if you're going to kill me, do it. Just let Petya go."

The old man in the doorway, Svet Zorotich, was obviously quite blind. His eyes were a clouded white and his gaze missed both detectives.

"I'm still alive," the man said, "so you must be the police or thieves or both. As you will see, there is very little in here worth stealing."

Sasha looked around. The man was right. A bed in the corner. Two chairs at a small table. A cupboard. A chair against another wall. A radio on a small table near the chair.

"Obviously," Zorotich said, "I did not see anything last night, nor anything since 1971."

"Sorry," said Zelach.

"Since you're here," he said, "maybe you can

get that damn cripple to turn down his television at night and go to sleep at a reasonable hour."

"We'll tell him," said Sasha. "Sorry we bothered you."

"You're not going to ask me, are you?" the old man said. "Hear that, Petya? They want to know what we saw, not what we heard."

The dog was alert now.

"What did you hear?" asked Sasha, certain that the man was going to blame his downstairs neighbor for the murder.

"Voices, outside," said the man. "I had the radio turned down out of consideration for my neighbors, a consideration they do not choose to extend to me."

"Voices?" Sasha prompted.

With the help of the dog the man found his way to the chair near the wall and next to the table.

"I turned off the radio like this," he said, demonstrating his action. "And I heard him talking to himself on the street, the drunk. Then they came. I could hear them talking to him. I could hear them crushing him with rocks that scraped the sidewalk when they missed."

"Do you know who they were?" asked Sasha.

The old man shrugged and reached down to pet his white dog. The dog moved closer to the man.

"I recognized their voices," he said. "They don't live far away. I've heard them in the street at night."

"Who are they?"

"Who knows?" asked the man.

"If we find them, could you identify their voices?" asked Sasha.

"Yes."

"Would you?"

"I don't know. I think so. One of them was named Mark. They used his name. And they live near here."

"Anything else you can tell us about these men?" asked Sasha.

"Men? Who said 'men'? Not me. They were boys, little boys, children. I knew they were killing and I was afraid to go to the window and shout down, afraid they would come up for me and kill me. So I said and did nothing."

"But you've told us now," said Sasha.

"I'm a veteran, you know," old Zorotich said. "Pension. Terrible pension. Can't live on it. Got a niece who helps me out as much as she can. Anything else?"

Sasha looked at Zelach, then said, "Nothing I can think of."

Once the policemen were out the door, Sasha said seriously, "He did it, Zelach. The tommy gun was hidden in his closet. He is only pretending to be blind."

"Then why didn't we arrest him?" asked a perplexed Zelach.

They were almost to the foot of the stairs. Sasha stopped and turned to Zelach. "Svet Zorotich is really blind."

"I thought so," said Zelach.

"Now we are searching for three children who

live in this neighborhood. One of them is named Mark."

"That shouldn't be so hard," said Zelach.

"It shouldn't?" said Sasha with less certainty than his partner.

When they stepped out onto the sidewalk, they were immediately confronted by the old man in the postman's cap.

"Did he confess? Why aren't you dragging him away?"

"He is blind," said Zelach.

The old man on the crutches looked skyward for help in enduring such fools as these.

"He is pretending to be blind to collect his pension," the old man said.

"I don't think so," said Sasha.

"Then Zorotich had that dog lead him down with the tommy gun and he shot the man, blind or not. Shot him and took his money. A blind man could do that. I saw him."

"You were mistaken," said Sasha. "Do you know any small boys in this neighborhood? Two, three, four of them. One of them is named Mark."

The old man suddenly looked terrified.

"No," he said, hurrying down the street, almost falling. "I know nothing."

Zelach turned to Sasha and said softly, "It may not be so easy."

Karpo walked through the hall of the Khovrino Municipal Police Station half listening to the uniformed sergeant who had been assigned to him.

The police station had been built in 1946 as a school. Now it was falling apart, as were most of the district stations, which occupied whatever space had been found for them—old apartment buildings, taxi garages, large shops. One district station had once been a toy store. Some of the walls of the former toy store were still covered with fading cartoon drawings of Donald Duck, Elmer Fudd, Casper the Friendly Ghost, and Yogi Bear.

But it was the Khovrino where Karpo found himself through a combination of determination and good luck.

Beneath his feet were cracked floor tiles. Above him the ceiling was a trail of exposed electrical wires. The wallpaper was peeling badly, and many of the light fixtures had no bulbs.

"Here," said a somber young sergeant with a mustache, indicating a door on their right. There was a thick plate of scratched glass at eye level. Karpo looked in.

Inside were six men. There were six cots lining the walls. Three of the men were seated on the floor playing some kind of card game. One of the prisoners was lying on a cot reading the newspaper, *Moskovskiy Komsomolets*. He was the only prisoner who wore leg chains. The other two men in the room were looking out the barred window on the wall opposite the door. One of the men was talking heatedly.

"This is where we keep the toughest," said the sergeant. "Murder suspects, strong-arm robbers. We've got two other lockups."

Karpo knew all this. He continued looking into the cell, showing no sign that he had heard what the sergeant said.

"Your man, Voshenko, is the one looking at the newspaper."

Karpo looked at the man lying on the cot. The man seemed to sense his gaze and looked up from his newspaper at the gaunt specter at the cell door. Their eyes locked, and neither man wavered.

"Voshenko's been in for twenty days. We expect to charge him with murder soon and to transfer him to a prison to await trial," the sergeant said.

The man on the cot smiled at Karpo. It was not a pleasant smile.

"Is the interrogation room empty?" Karpo asked.

"Yes, I think so," said the sergeant, looking into the gloom farther down the hall. "The light is not on."

"Can you bring Voshenko to me there?"

"Yes, but…"

The sergeant had been told by the colonel who was chief of the district to do whatever the strange-looking detective from Petrovka wanted, and to do it without question. The sergeant unlocked the door. The men playing cards and the two men at the window looked at him as he stepped into the cell, his hand on his pistol. The black-clad vampire had disappeared. The sergeant was about to speak Voshenko's name, but the prisoner had already put down the newspaper and was standing. He was a huge man, dressed like the others in a badly faded blue two-piece uniform. Voshenko's face was dark, ugly, and freshly shaved. He got up slowly and stepped past the sergeant, who, even though the prisoner was shackled, backed away to give him room.

"Down the hall. To the right," the sergeant said, stepping into the hall and closing the cell door, which clanged and echoed in the corridors of darkness.

Voshenko, six feet six, close to three hundred pounds, filled the narrow hallway built for children. He shambled forward, his leg chains rattling.

"Stop. There," called the sergeant from a safe dozen feet behind, his weapon now out of the holster.

Voshenko had been brought in drunk after having killed two people, a man and a woman, in a bar on Kachalova Prospekt. He claimed there had been a fight. No witness stepped forward. Both victims had broken necks. Less than a week after entering the police-station lockup, another prisoner in the same cell as Voshenko had been found one morning with his neck broken. Voshenko denied the killing but admitted readily that the dead man had repeatedly looked at him even after having been told to stop. It was then that he had been shackled. There was no room in the three cells of the station house to place him in complete isolation, and there was no point in asking any of the other stations to take him. No one wanted another mouth to feed on an already meager budget.

Voshenko looked back over his shoulder at the sergeant, who took a step back before he could stop himself. Voshenko smiled and stepped into the interrogation room. The sergeant moved forward cautiously behind him. When he got to the door, he could see that Karpo was already seated behind the small metal table facing Voshenko, who moved to the chair across from the pale policeman.

The sergeant was about to close the door and stand ready, weapon in hand, while the strange inspector from Petrovka questioned the giant. The sergeant believed there was no chance Voshenko would even yield his name.

"Wait outside," said Karpo. "Down the corridor, next to the cell. I'll call you when I want you to return."

"I don't think..." the sergeant began, and then remembered his orders.

What would happen to him if Voshenko broke the neck of this lean ghost? Would the sergeant be held responsible? Yes, without doubt, and he might well find himself in one of the cells. But he did as he was told, locking the interrogation-room door firmly behind him.

Karpo and Voshenko looked at each other without blinking and without speaking. Finally Voshenko looked away as if in boredom.

"Do you know who I am?" Karpo asked.

"The Tatar, the Ghost, the Vampire," said Voshenko. "Karpo."

"Do you know why I am here?"

Voshenko shrugged. He looked at the peeling, once-white walls.

"I called many stations and several prisons asking if they had any prisoners with a specific tattoo," said Karpo.

Voshenko folded his hands in front of him. They were large with long fingers. On each finger, just above the knuckle, was a minute tattoo of an animal, but only the head of the animal.

"When you were brought here, you were photographed," Karpo said, his own hands flat on the table.

Voshenko did not remember. He had been too drunk. But he knew of the procedure.

"One of the officers on duty looked through the photographs of all tattooed prisoners," said Karpo. "He found the tatoo I was looking for on you."

Voshenko smiled and shook his head. He started to rise, but there was no response from the man who remained seated in front of him. Voshenko lifted his shirt. He was covered with tattoos, almost as many as the man who had been shot outside the café where Mathilde had been murdered.

"None of those," said Karpo. "An eagle with a bomb in its claws. It is on your right buttock. You need not display it."

Voshenko hovered over the detective, looking down at him, his fingers spread now within inches of Karpo's.

"I do not wish to kill you," Karpo said calmly. "I have questions to ask you. But I can find another prisoner somewhere with this tattoo. Please sit."

Voshenko did not move.

"Sit," said Karpo calmly. "Or I shall hurt you very badly."

Voshenko laughed. Karpo did not. Down the corridor the sergeant heard the laughter and wondered, but did not move. Voshenko sat.

"What does that tattoo mean?" Karpo asked.

Voshenko shrugged, clasped his hands together, and shrugged once more.

"Answer, Prisoner Voshenko. Or I have no use for you."

Voshenko looked at the man. He could easily reach across the table and have the man's neck before the detective could pull a weapon. Perhaps he would choose to end the interrogation in that manner. But for now he was curious.

"It is a patriotic work," said Voshenko. "The strength of the nation, now lost by weaklings."

"It is the sign of a mafia that deals in nuclear material," said Karpo.

Voshenko's bushy eyebrows went up slightly and then back down again. "If so, it is a coincidence," he said. "For me it is a patriotic picture."

"Stanislav Voshenko, there was an attack by members of your mafia, the assassination of a German businessman named Heinz Dieter Kirst. Why did your people want to kill him?"

Voshenko shrugged and said, "I don't know any Germans and I don't belong to a mafia."

"I wish to know where I can find the leader of your group," Karpo persisted.

"I belong to no group," Voshenko said, placing his hands flat on the table again, ready.

"No more lies," Karpo demanded.

Voshenko lunged across the table. One hand slammed down on Karpo's hand. The other hand went around Karpo's throat. Voshenko looked at his victim with a mad grin of satisfaction, but the pale face of the policeman showed no fear or pain. Voshenko lost his grin and continued closing his thumb and finger, cutting off the air. He had done it many times, always without concern for the consequences. And this time he had nothing to lose. They would never let him out anyway. They would give him a quick trial and shoot him against a wall. But until that moment he would brag that he had killed a policeman.

And then Voshenko felt a sudden pain, an electric shock in his left hand. He pulled it back as if he had been bitten. He held his grip on Karpo's neck as he painfully lifted his left hand. His thumb hung loosely and his hand was rapidly swelling.

In the instant that the prisoner looked away, Karpo grabbed the massive thumb that was pressing his windpipe and jerked it back hard. Voshenko sat back and tried to pull his hand from Karpo's grasp, but the policeman held fast. Voshenko reached up with his left hand, but with his thumb broken it was useless.

"And when I break your other thumb, you will be unable to attack or defend yourself," said Karpo. "I think your cellmates might find that interesting."

"They are cowards," said Voshenko, clenching back the pain. "Break the thumb. Then kill me. If you don't, I will find and kill you the first chance I get. Today. Tomorrow. In a year."

"I will find your leader, and when I do I will inform him that it was you who betrayed him."

"He won't believe you," said Voshenko, still trying to free his hand. "You don't have the power to free me."

"I will see to it that the moment I learn the name of your leader, you will be set free," said Karpo. "It can be done. Will your leader believe that the police just let you walk out the door?"

Voshenko tried to laugh, but it had none of the crazed power of his earlier laughter. He shook his head to indicate that he would not speak. Karpo bent the thumb back even farther.

"Then I shall break this thumb too," said Karpo.

"Why does it mean so much to you?" growled Voshenko, now sweating and breathing heavily.

"Talk now or you will have no thumbs," said Karpo.

Voshenko knew that he meant it.

Chapter 6

Moonlight on the Golden Spire

It took less than an hour on the phone back at Petrovka for Rostnikov to find the first garage where there was a mechanic named Artiom. He had continued to call garages and had located two more Artioms.

"We'll start with these three," Rostnikov said, standing slowly.

His desk was in the corner of a large office that had been divided into four cubbyholes with low fiberboard walls over which one could both look at and hear one's neighbors. Each little section had a desk, a phone, and two chairs. There was no uniformity to the furniture. It was whatever Pankov had been able to scrounge, beg, and steal from other offices in Petrovka. There was a cubbyhole office for Rostnikov and one each for Emil Karpo, Sasha Tkach, and Elena Timofeyeva. The only sign of Rostnikov's superiority was that his cubicle was the one with the window. When he had been a chief inspector with the procurator general's office several flights down, he had had his own office. It had also been small, however, and his window had looked out not at the outside world but at a line of desks of those of lesser rank. He had not liked that office. He definitely preferred his present cubbyhole. From the sixth floor of Petrovka he could look down into the rapidly decaying courtyard and guard gate, where two armed officers stood, one of them smoking, an act that would have meant his job a year before. Now no one except the corrupt, the desperate, the stupid, and the psychotic seemed to want the low-paying, dangerous, and despised job of being a police officer.

"Rostnikov?" Hamilton said.

"Yes?" Rostnikov had paused to look out the window.

"The Artioms," Hamilton reminded him.

"Of course," said Rostnikov. "Look at this."

Hamilton moved to join Rostnikov at the window and look down at the guards and the courtyard.

"The changing weather and a lack of interest," Rostnikov observed. "Only one bush still blooming and flowering. Do you know the name of that bush?"

"No," said Hamilton, locating the bush.

Rostnikov took his notebook from his pocket and made a crude drawing of the shrub and its flowers, then scrawled a description of it. He put the notebook back in his pocket and asked, "Do we start with the three Artioms or with the wife?"

"We Americans would do both at the same time," said Hamilton.

"We are a small department. To do that, I would have to remove one of my associates from the case he or she is working on," said Rostnikov. "Or I would have to ask permission to assign an investigator from one of the other departments, and it's likely that that investigator would be chosen for his or her dependability to report back to an officer within his or her own department. Should anything be uncovered that might lead to an arrest, that department would rush in, make the arrest, and get the credit."

"Tricky," said Hamilton.

"It has been like that for almost six hundred years," said Rostnikov. "When the first little huts went up to form a village where the Kremlin now stands, the Russian people began to develop a society of distrust, corruption, and subservience. Then came the czars, then the Communists, and now the frightened confusion until a new authority is firmly in command. Russians are not built for capitalism. It has turned them into victims, cowards, and criminals."

Rostnikov reluctantly left the window, walked out of his cubicle, and headed toward the door to the office.

"You care about the credit?" asked Hamilton, following.

"The survival of our department depends upon Colonel Snitkonoy's outstanding record for taking on the most difficult cases and handling them to everyone's reluctant satisfaction," said Rostnikov. "You have two children?"

"Yes," said Hamilton.

They passed a few people, a woman and two men, in the hall. One of the men nodded at Rostnikov. He nodded back. Rostnikov and Hamilton stopped in front of the elevator.

"You have photographs?" asked Rostnikov.

Hamilton reached into his back pocket, removed his wallet, opened it, and handed it to Rostnikov.

"Good," said Rostnikov as he took in the picture of a boy around twelve with his arm around a younger girl, who had a tooth missing in the middle of her mouth. Both were smiling. "The girl looks like you. The boy?"

"Like his mother," Hamilton said.

Rostnikov looked at the floor indicator over the elevator. It seemed to be stuck on the first floor.

"I think it is broken again," Rostnikov said. "We will have to walk down. Beautiful children."

Hamilton started to put his wallet back in his pocket. Rostnikov caught his hand.

"In the front pocket," he said. "It is not so stylish, but more difficult for pickpockets."

Hamilton smiled.

"I'm an FBI agent."

"Yeltsin's pocket has been picked in a crowd of people cheering as if he were a god," said Rostnikov, heading for the stairway.

The trip six floors down the stairway was slow and painful for Porfiry Petrovich. Hamilton had placed his wallet in his right front pocket. It made an awkward bulge. He would have to remember to remove it and put it in his rear pocket before he went back to the FBI's temporary offices in the U.S. Embassy building.

People shuffled past them in both directions when they hit the wide, bare lobby. A helmeted and armed duo of guards near the door glanced at them, and a uniformed woman at a small desk where people were checked in and out looked up at the well-dressed black man.

"They don't know what to make of me," Hamilton said as they moved into the courtyard of Petrovka. The wind was brisk and chilly.

"They probably think you are a rich African or American businessman setting up bribes for protection," said Rostnikov, who moved very slowly now.

"You want to rest?" asked Hamilton.

"The day moves on and we have Artioms to meet," said Rostnikov in English. "That is a reasonable approximation of your Robert Frost?"

"Very close. We have Artioms to meet," Hamilton replied.

"And late-flowering bushes that shall reveal their names," added Rostnikov, moving through the wrought-iron gates where a car, a Buick, sat waiting.

Rostnikov nodded at the car. Hamilton returned the nod. Hamilton opened the front door and held it open while Rostnikov slid in. Hamilton got in the backseat.

There had been seven Chazov brothers in all: the oldest, Yakov, was probably around thirty and had left the one-room apartment three years earlier. It was not really an apartment but the end of a second-floor hallway in a converted office building. A flimsy wall and door had been put up by the Communist party—appointed carpenters, who didn't know what they were doing.

Elvira Chazova, who was forty-one going on seventy, had worked with her sons to steal bricks and wood and a new door to reinforce the front entrance. Two decades ago, after being almost beaten to death by Elvira and her then ten-year-old son, her first husband had crawled out of the apartment and never returned. Elvira had heard that Yakov, recently returned from prison after serving a long sentence for robbery with force, was now living in the streets with friends. At present Elvira had three sons living with her, plus a baby and another on the way. Government investigators, frowning on the number of children, had threatened her, but had in the end given her a meager subsidy, which was supplemented by whatever her children could bring in. Sometimes the boys posed as ragged Gypsies and begged in subway stations. Their favorite hangout was Pushkin Square in the little park in front of McDonald's. On three occasions the boys had followed drunks from the Pushkin Square underpass, beaten them, and taken their money. Twice they had stolen bottles of liquor from the Night Flight disco near the square.

Elvira herself had sat cross-legged with a tin cup beside her in the subways and in doorways where foreigners would see her. She held her latest baby on her lap and rocked him, looking as pathetic as she could and thanking each donor aloud while cursing each one who gave her nothing.

The youngest three boys, who had never seen their older half brother, Yakov, were the children of a brutish ex-soldier named Leon. The boys feared nothing but their mother's displeasure and the threat that their father might return. But Leon, who had never given Elvira his true last name, had packed his few belongings one day and headed west.

So now Elvira Chazova—her hair white and stringy, most of her teeth long gone, her face wrinkled and beaten by days in the sun and diseases of the dampness—had to make do with a meaningless government subsidy and what could be scrounged and stolen. The boys begged, but they were a sorry lot, thin, sharp-featured like their father, and with their father's perpetual surly challenge on their faces. They were much more successful at stealing, roaming the streets at night, finding stray drunks, late-night hotel prostitutes, and restaurant workers heading home after long days. They chose their victims carefully. A man might appear to be prosperous, but if he looked to be more than the three boys could handle, they passed him by. They had actually gone by tram as far as the town of Oryol to find drunks for the taking. For when they brought their earnings home, they were praised by their mother.

There was only one window in the apartment, at the end of what used to be the corridor. A curtain had been put up to create a bit of privacy for Elvira. The boys slept on cots in a small space beyond the curtain. On the other side of them was another curtain, which established another space before the door to the apartment, which held two stolen sofas and four chairs plus a television that sometimes worked, a table, and a small refrigerator. There was no sink. There was no toilet. One of the old offices at the far end of the corridor served as a kind of communal room for those who lived on the floor and the one above. It had a sink and a filthy toilet.

Occasionally a lost child or adult would wander into the communal room and curl up to sleep. If the Chazovs found such a person, he or she was lucky to escape with little more than a split head and a broken limb.

At night and during the day the black-and-white television set droned on, losing both the top and bottom of its picture to blackness. Elvira was expecting her latest baby soon. Its father was a half-mad fool named Kirsov, who claimed to be in a Georgian mafia but who was in fact kept around by one of the mafia's minor members to run risks such as delivering messages to rival gangs. About three months ago Kirsov had tempted his luck one too many times and had been shot and dumped in the Moscow River with his eyes plucked out, a warning to the Georgians, who ignored it.

This murder of Kirsov had been further proof to Elvira that one could only survive by violence and that one had to be cautious when choosing one's victims and friends. "Family," she had frequently told Alexei, Boris, and Mark. "That is all you can count on."

Were the boys a bit brighter, they might have noticed that their family had hardly been a model of reliability: Their older half brothers as well as their father had fled as soon as they could; their own father had gone west; and their mother's latest friend had had his eyes plucked out, leaving her with another baby.

Elvira hoped the child in her belly would be a girl. Girls were much more likely to be given money by people, particularly foreigners. Besides, Elvira had always wanted a girl. Not that she hadn't loved her boys. She had, each one of them. The baby was always lavished with love, coddled, allowed to sleep next to his mother till he was six or even seven. But then Elvira would begin to lose interest in the child, except as potential income. When asked, she'd fiercely proclaim her love, but in truth she often felt more comfortable when they were in the streets.

Elvira heard a knock at the door and knew it was an official knock, not the kind made by a timid neighbor. She rose from her chair in front of the television, where she had been watching an old movie about a pretty blond woman with a beautiful apartment and lots of men friends. The woman had a white living room right down to the telephone.

The one-year-old, Ludmilla, was angry because the knocking had startled her and made her drop the empty tin can in her hand. The baby inside Elvira was kicking. Elvira held Ludmilla back with one hand and made her way to the door, shouting, "Who is it?"

"Police," said Sasha Tkach.

"I've done nothing," she said.

"We want to talk," said Sasha pleasantly.

"About what?" she asked.

"We will tell you when we come in," said Sasha.

It was not the first time the police had come. And it had always been the same thing. She had told the same lies, and eventually, when they saw there was no money in this and probably not even a reasonable arrest, the police had left, talking about the filth of Elvira Chazova's home.

"All right. All right," she said, opening the many bolts on the door and leaving the heavy chain in place as she peeked at the nice-looking young man and the slouching hulk behind him.

The young man held up an identification card, but Elvira didn't bother to try to read it. Her eyes were not good for reading and her reading skills were minimal anyway. Besides, a police identification card could be forged. She knew two people who could do it for her for the price of a half-dozen eggs.

She unchained the door and stepped back to let the two men in. "I'm pregnant," she said, moving to her chair and not offering a seat to the policemen.

"Congratulations," said Zelach.

Neither policeman sat. It was not a place they wished to stay long.

"You have three sons," said Sasha, "one of whom is named Mark?"

"My youngest boy. My baby boy. He is only five."

She was lying by two years, but it made no difference. She could see by the young policeman's face that he had already decided to doubt whatever she might say.

"Your three sons," Sasha went on, "where were they last night?"

The one-year-old had decided to hold on to her mother's dress and produce a red-faced scream, which Elvira ignored.

"Here," she said.

The television droned on. The child screamed. The blond woman on the screen laughed. Zelach glanced at the television and then back at the screaming child.

"What time did they come home?" shouted Sasha Tkach, his hands at his sides and looking very official.

"Just before the first news on television," Elvira said, holding her large stomach. "I don't like them out at night anymore. Too dangerous since the new life. Too dangerous for little boys."

"May we talk to the boys?" Sasha asked.

"Now?" she said.

"Now," said Sasha.

The woman looked at the other policeman. He bore a faint resemblance to her second husband but without the angry look.

"They are out," she said. "In school."

"They are not in school," shouted Sasha, searching for something in his pocket. "We have checked with the school. They have not been going to school."

"Lots of children don't go to school anymore," she said defensively, "except when they hear that free food is being given."

She glanced at the television screen, where an older man in a tuxedo was lighting a cigar and looking at the blonde, who smiled coyly.

"True," agreed Sasha, finding a small sweet he had stashed deep inside his pocket for his daughter, Pulcharia. "But it is your children we are interested in."

"Why?" she asked.

"We have questions," said Sasha, handing the sweet to the red-faced, screaming child, who immediately became silent.

"Questions?" asked Elvira.

"About something that happened last night," said Sasha.

"They were here last night. All night. I told you. We are a poor family. They are out begging. That's what this new government, this new democracy, has done to us. We have to send our children out begging like Gypsies."

"Your children begged even before the new government," Sasha said, though he did not know this as a fact any more than he knew that the boys had not been in school.

"And so did I," Elvira said, touching her hand to her breast. "I have always had a big family and worthless husbands. I've had a big burden. I have the luck of a Siberian."

"And you are to be much admired and appreciated," Sasha said without expression. He looked at the little girl, who sucked at the candy and regarded him with hostile curiosity. "I would like to talk to your sons."

"They are not here," Elvira repeated.

Sasha nodded. Zelach moved past the woman and pushed back the first curtain to reveal a space with three unmade cots and clothes in piles. Zelach moved through this space and pushed back the second curtain to reveal a small bed and an old dresser near the window.

"I told you they weren't here," Elvira said, almost weeping now.

Zelach looked back. Sasha nodded and Zelach began to go through the dresser.

"This is wrong," the woman said. "I'm a mother. I'm pregnant. This could upset me, make me lose my baby, get my little one frightened again. It will be your fault."

Sasha glanced at the television again. A maid and a butler were talking. Zelach pushed each drawer back carefully, checked the bed, and then moved into the boys' space, going through their clothing and the contents of several cardboard cartons under each cot.

Elvira sat in silent indignation, rubbing her stomach and glaring at the young policeman. It didn't seem to bother him. Zelach returned and shook his head. Nothing.

"Satisfied?" she said.

"No," said Sasha. "We will return."

"When?" she asked.

The young man didn't answer. He headed for the door with the other policeman behind him.

"If you were a parent," Elvira said, following them, "you wouldn't do this to a loving mother."

The policemen left. The door locked behind them.

Elvira pushed her daughter away and ran back through the apartment, opened the window, and touched the wooden sill to be sure it hadn't been moved. There was a space, a narrow space, beneath the sill. Everything that was not cash or could be immediately converted to cash but was thin enough to fit was in a bag in the narrow space. Other things the boys brought home—wallets particularly—were thrown out immediately blocks away. Whatever cash the boys brought in was kept in a pouch she wore on a belt under her clothes. She slept in the belt, certain that the boys did not know it existed. She was wrong.

These two policemen were not the first who had come to harass her, but the young one was the first who looked as if he really cared about her answers. He said he would be back, she was sure he would be back. She had a sudden chill. The changing weather, the fear for herself and her children? She went back into the front of the apartment to watch the rich people in a movie from long ago. The baby began to cry. She had finished her candy.

"What did you get?" Sasha asked when they were back on the street in front of the crumbling building.

"A photograph of a soccer player, Belitnikov," said Zelach. "A flashlight. An empty yogurt carton. I was careful."

They had partial fingerprints from the belt of the dead man, Oleg Makmunov. The fingerprints were small. They might match others taken from the Chazov apartment. If they were inconclusive, Sasha and Zelach would take turns watching the apartment till the boys returned. Then they would bring them in for fingerprinting. Even if the fingerprints did not match, they would tell the boys that they did. Normally it was not difficult to get children to turn against one another.

Sasha felt lucky. This was only the second Mark they had tracked down and he was certain this was the right one. But he also felt depressed. The Chazov boys were only eleven, nine, and seven. The young child he had just seen was just a few years younger than his daughter, Pulcharia. He had a sudden vision of his daughter lying with her head crushed by a rock. He pushed the image away, but it mocked him by coming back even clearer.

"What's wrong, Sasha?" Zelach asked.

"Nothing," he said.

"You work here alone?" asked Rostnikov as he looked around the dark garage, which was about the size of a tennis court.

Three cars were parked in the rear. It was difficult to make out exactly what they were because there were only two lights in the garage, both dim, and two windows, both dirty. But Rostnikov and Hamilton could make out piles of automobile parts. In the middle of the floor was a black BMW hoisted on wooden blocks with four fully extended bumper jacks firmly locked on the undercarriage.

"No," said Artiom Solovyov, wiping his hands. "I have an assistant."

The man looked a bit like an ape with a handsome battered face and dark hair in need of a cut. He wore a pair of dark slacks and a long-sleeved white shirt with vertical blue stripes.

"Where is he?" asked Rostnikov.

"Where is he? Boris is home. He is ill," said Artiom with a sigh, looking around. "And all this work."

"So you have to do it yourself?" asked Hamilton.

Artiom had tried not to look at the tall black man next to the policeman. The black man had dark, disbelieving eyes.

"What choice have I?" asked Artiom with a shrug.

"Then why aren't you in work clothes? Why aren't you covered in grime?" asked Rostnikov.

Artiom Solovyov now looked from man to man in front of him. They had said they had some routine questions about a crime and that he might know the victim. Artiom had emerged from his tiny office with its thin waffle-metal walls. He had smiled and said he had never been involved with something exciting like this before and had pledged his cooperation. But the questions were getting too uncomfortable.

"I just arrived, right before you," Artiom said. "I was doing some paperwork and—"

"The full name and address of your mechanic," said Rostnikov.

"Ah...I don't think I have his address. He just moved. His name is Boris, Boris Ivanov."

"Shouldn't be hard to find," said Hamilton. "How many Boris Ivanovs are there in Moscow?"

"Probably close to two thousand," said Rostnikov. And then to Artiom, "Alexei Porvinovich."

Artiom blinked and didn't answer.

"You know a man named Alexei Porvinovich."

Fight the panic. How did they find him so quickly? How did they find him at all? They couldn't have too much on him since they weren't simply grabbing him right away and hauling him off to the local police station for a "conversation." Artiom had been the victim of such "conversations" in the past. More than once he had been pulled in to the local station, each time by the same cop, who suggested that Artiom's garage was a refuge for stolen cars. Each time, Artiom had denied it. Each time, he had been hauled in, placed in a small room, and beaten by the policeman. The last time this happened, Artiom lost part of his hearing in his left ear. He never got it back. The irony was that Artiom did not deal in stolen automobiles. He had insisted, sworn, and endured beatings, but finally he had agreed to pay the policeman a manageable amount each month. The irony had mounted when a local mafia of Chechens also visited him. Artiom had agreed instantly to pay them. If he had not, he was sure, he would have had more than a minor hearing loss. Were he not paying the policeman and the Chechen mafia, he would now have more money. And without the payments and Anna Porvinovich's demands for him at the oddest of times, he would probably not have considered kidnapping Alexei Porvinovich. And now he had to cope with these two new policemen who knew something.

"Porvinovich," Artiom repeated, looking up at the rusting ceiling and touching his chin as if deep in thought. "Porvinovich. I think I have a customer with that name. I can check my books."

"You don't remember for certain?" the black man asked.

"I have a thriving business. Lots of customers. Some come only once. Some come twice. Some keep coming back."

"This is the Alexei Porvinovich whose home you called less than an hour ago," said Rostnikov.

"I made a long list of calls," Artiom said with a shrug, hoping he was not sweating. He sweated easily. It was something Anna said she liked about him. "You know, with my mechanic out, everything will be running late and—"

"You remember the call?" the black man asked. "You spoke to Mrs. Porvinovich. You've met her. You could hardly forget her."

"Porvinovich," Artiom pondered. "Ah, yes, that one. A beauty. Not my type."

"What is your type?" asked Rostnikov.

"Big. Blond. Loud. Not too smart," he said with a grin.

"Just the opposite of Mrs. Porvinovich," said the black man.

"I suppose," said Artiom.

"So?" said Rostnikov. "You called her."

"Yes, ah, yes. Now I remember," he said, hit-

124

ting his forehead with the palm of his right hand. "They were scheduled to bring in their car, a black Buick. I said I couldn't take care of it. She seemed quite upset that she couldn't make a new appointment."

"Mrs. Porvinovich does not strike me as the kind of woman who, if she were upset, would allow herself to display it to a mechanic," said the black man.

"I'm perceptive," Artiom almost pleaded. "It's a gift and a curse from my mother. She was perceptive too. Could see right through to people's souls." With this, he laid a palm across his chest in a suggestion of where one's soul might be found.

"What am I feeling?" asked the black man.

"I never got your name," said Artiom, extending his hand.

"Craig Hamilton," said the black man, taking Artiom's quite moist hand. "What am I feeling?" he repeated.

"I'm sorry. My intuition is hindered by a lack of familiarity with Africans."

"Then what am *I* thinking?" asked Rostnikov.

"That I know something or am guilty of something," said Artiom. "But I tell you, I promise you, I pledge to you: You are wrong. If you'll just tell me what you want, I—"

"You kidnapped Alexei Porvinovich," said Rostnikov. "You and your assistant, Boris. If you have killed Porvinovich, you shall be tried and executed, as you well know. If he is alive, life will be hard, but you will at least exist. Look at this bush."

125

Rostnikov pulled a notebook from his pocket and opened it to the page with the flowering bush he had sketched earlier.

Artiom looked at the picture. It was not at all badly rendered. "Yes?" asked he.

"Do you know what kind of bush it is?"

"No," said Artiom. "I know nothing of plants. I know cars."

"If you have killed Porvinovich," said Rostnikov, taking another look at the picture of the bush and returning it to his pocket, "then you will never see a flowering bush again."

"I did not kidnap Alexei Porvinovich," Artiom cried with sincerity. "I'm an honest businessman. Ask Sergeant Boronov. I run an honest business."

"And you go to bed with Anna Porvinovich," said Rostnikov.

"And with her brother," added Hamilton.

Artiom's sincerity turned to anger.

"What are you saying? That I'm a homosexual? I am not."

"Then," said Rostnikov, "you have had sex only with Mrs. Porvinovich?"

"I haven't had sex with anybody," Artiom protested, both hands moving up and down.

"You are celibate?" said Hamilton.

"I didn't say....What do you want?"

"Porvinovich, now, uninjured," said Rostnikov.

"I didn't kidnap him," Artiom cried. He clasped his hands together and said, "As God is my judge, I have kidnapped no one."

"How long have you believed in God?" asked Rostnikov.

Artiom shrugged again. "All my life," he said. "What's God got to—"

"We are leaving," said Rostnikov. "You will deliver Alexei Porvinovich before this day ends."

"I…" Artiom began, but saw that nothing he could say would convince these two. "It has come to my attention from a source I cannot reveal that this Alexei Porvinovich has been engaged in illegal activities."

"I thought you couldn't remember him?" asked Hamilton, who was following Rostnikov toward the door of the garage.

"I didn't want to get involved in anything," Artiom said, now sweating profusely and not trying to hide it. "But if someone were to find this Porvinovich and turn him loose and they had information about important criminal activities by this Porvinovich…?"

"It would be interesting," said Rostnikov, limping toward the door. "We might be appreciative of such information."

"How appreciative?" asked Artiom.

"That would depend on the information," said Rostnikov. "And the evidence. Call Petrovka, ask for me. Let us say in four hours."

Rostnikov pulled out his pad of paper, wrote down his own name and phone number, and handed it to Artiom, who took it and followed the two men through the door into the chilly gray day.

"I don't know anything," he said.

"Four hours," Rostnikov repeated, continuing to walk away, his back to Artiom Solovyov. "That should be plenty of time."

Artiom gave up, went back into the garage, and slammed the door. Rostnikov continued to walk toward the dark car parked at the end of the street.

"We were lucky," said Hamilton softly.

"He is an amateur in love with a professional," said Rostnikov. "An affair made in hell."

"She would have had Porvinovich killed," said Hamilton.

"I'm certain."

"So am I," said Hamilton. "You think he'll let Porvinovich go and give you something dirty on him?"

"Yes," said Rostnikov, opening the front passenger door of the car. "He has heard tales of Russian prisons." He sat and closed the door while Hamilton went around the car and got into the driver's seat.

"Should we call someone to follow him?" asked Hamilton, starting the engine.

"It will take too long," said Rostnikov.

"We could follow him ourselves," Hamilton suggested.

"I have a bad leg and you have a black face," said Rostnikov. "He would have to be an even bigger fool than he is not to spot us. I think he will give us our kidnap victim if he is still alive."

Chapter 7

Flowers

They sat, as they had planned to, inside the Saint Petersburg Café, formerly the Café of the October Revolution. Normally they would have met at a café less than a half mile away, but that was where Mathilde Verson had been killed.

They had pulled two rectangular wooden tables together. Rostnikov sat at one end of the improvised table, Craig Hamilton at the other. Rostnikov always sat where he could see everyone's faces without any painful movement of his leg. On his left were Sasha Tkach and Zelach. On his right were Emil Karpo and Elena Timofeyeva. In front of each person was a cup of coffee or tea and two thin wafers that the management called imported biscotti but that Tkach described as sugar-plaster sandwiches.

Several months earlier they had begun meeting informally at a café. There were two major reasons for this. First, the Gray Wolfhound, Pankov, and Major Gregorovich were not present. Second, it was unlikely that anyone had bugged the café, whereas it was highly likely that the Wolfhound's office was bugged and almost certain that Major Gregorovich was passing information on to people who might be appreciative when the proper time came.

"Pulcharia said what?" Elena asked.

"'Grandmother gives me a *gahlahvnahya bol*,' a headache," answered Tkach, looking, with a proud smile, around the table. "Three years old, not even three."

He shook his head. The others were appreciatively silent.

"'*Gahlahvnahya bol,*'" Tkach repeated almost to himself.

"And how is your aunt?" Rostnikov asked.

"Anna Timofeyeva has good days and bad," said Elena, a bit self-consciously.

"She is a bad cook, a stubborn woman, and was the best procurator in all of Russia," Rostnikov said.

"'No foundation up and down the line,'" Zelach said.

Everyone looked at him. Zelach did not attend all of these sessions, and when he did, he seldom spoke unless directly addressed.

"William Saroyan," said Hamilton.

All heads turned to him except for that of Emil Karpo. They had not wanted to be so rude as to examine the black FBI agent who spoke perfect Russian and sat erect in an impeccably pressed blue suit.

"A play, *The Time of Your Life*," explained Hamilton. "It's a favorite of mine. One of the characters keeps repeating that line."

"*Arkady Sergeyevich Zelach,*" Rostnikov said with deep interest. "You read American plays?"

Zelach shrugged and didn't meet Rostnikov's eyes.

"When I was recovering, I read what was in the apartment," he said. "My father's old books."

Sasha Tkach took some tea. It was strong but not particularly good. Zelach had spent a long convalescence after he had been shot, a near-fatal shooting that, with good reason, Sasha felt responsible for. Zelach had many months of reading behind him.

"We will speak freely in front of Agent Hamilton," said Rostnikov, looking around the table. "First we all wish to extend our sympathy to and support for Emil Karpo for the loss of Mathilde Verson, a loss that is also ours."

Karpo said nothing. His head moved slightly to acknowledge the words of condolence.

Later, when he could get Karpo alone, Porfiry Petrovich would invite him for dinner as Sarah had suggested. If necessary, he would order him to come for dinner. Sarah might get him to talk or at least to listen. And normally Karpo appeared to like the company and questions of the girls. But that would be later. Sarah would want a gathering soon of the entire group so that there could be some kind of formal toast, a farewell to Mathilde.

"If there will be a funeral...?" Rostnikov began.

"I've spoken to her sister," said Karpo. "When the autopsy is complete, her body will be cremated and her ashes taken to the sea. I would prefer that this end the discussion."

With Karpo it was difficult to determine if he was showing signs of cracking. The blank look remained the same as always. When Tkach had suffered a breakdown, it had been easy to spot—increasing irritability, abnormal defensiveness, and a self-pity that easily turned to anger. But Karpo displayed nothing.

"First order of business," Rostnikov went on. "Does anyone know what this is?"

He grunted and pulled his drawing of the bush in the Petrovka yard from his pocket and passed it around. When it came back to Rostnikov, Karpo said, "It is a vinarium, also called a sure bush or a Russian angel."

"It endures," said Rostnikov, looking at Karpo, who met his eyes.

"'No foundation up and down the line,'" Karpo said. "'Nothing endures.'"

Karpo had lost himself to Communism and the Revolution. He had believed in it religiously, recognized the faults of those given the task of making it a success, sought to cleanse society of those who would break the law or try to erode the Revolution. That was all gone now. Mathilde was gone. There was no foundation. There was only unfinished business.

"Elena," Rostnikov said, turning his eyes from those of Karpo. Whether or not Emil Karpo was going to break would be impossible to determine. Karpo's expression never changed. It always amazed Rostnikov that children loved Karpo; they ran to him and took his hand. Pulcharia Tkach always jumped into his arms, and he held her firmly and spoke to her as an adult, which may well have been where the child picked up her precocious vocabulary.

Mathilde Verson had begun, after more than five years, to bring a sense of life to Karpo, had managed to keep him from falling apart when the Soviet Union fractured. Now she was gone.

"Elena?" Rostnikov repeated. "The electrician's treasure?"

Elena looked at Hamilton, who had finished his tea and was attempting to eat one of the wafers.

"It all disappeared," she said. "Every piece. During the night. Natalya Dokorova claims to have burned everything—books, paintings, furniture. There were guards at both doors of the Dokorov house who confirmed that she had a fire going all night."

"Guards?" asked Rostnikov.

"Teams from different units," said Elena. "Even so, I checked. No hidden rooms, no secret level below the floor."

"Walls?" said Hamilton.

"Checked them," Elena said. "And the roof. Getting them up to the roof would have been more than Natalya Dokorova could have done, and landing a helicopter without being heard or seen would have been impossible."

"And the old woman claims to have burned everything?" asked Rostnikov.

"Everything. She stayed up all night determined that if she could not keep what her brother had left her, she would not let the government take it."

"She destroyed everything?" said Rostnikov. "Did you find ashes?"

"Some," said Elena.

"Many of the items in the collection could not

be burned," said Karpo. "And I do not believe, given the magnitude of the collection, that she could have burned it all in one night."

The little finger of Karpo's left hand was splinted and taped. Everyone was curious. No one asked.

"That is what she told me," Elena answered, glancing at the American.

"And you believe her?" asked Tkach.

"I…no. But if she'll talk, I think it will be to me. She seems to like talking to me."

"Do you like her?" asked Rostnikov.

"Yes."

"Perhaps I'll talk to her later in the office," said Rostnikov. "Perhaps if I can get our colonel to pull some strings, I will talk to the guards on both doors."

"Tomorrow?" asked Elena, making a note.

"Today, five, no…six for your Natalya Dokorova. Same time for the guards, if it can be arranged," said Rostnikov. "Emil."

"We may be dealing with a mafia that is stealing nuclear weaponry or the means of making it," said Karpo.

All heads turned to him.

"The members of the mafia are all former convicts," Karpo went on. "Each bears the prison tattoo of an eagle clutching a large bomb. The tattoos are generally on their buttocks or back. Two of these men were killed in the street battle this morning. I found another convict with a tattoo and interviewed him. In spite of my most zealous interrogation and persuasion, I was unable to get him to reveal more about his gang than that they are called the *Zveri*, the Beasts. He seemed particularly proud of that."

There had been a message on Rostnikov's desk when he and Hamilton had stopped by the office. He had called the major in charge of the district station where Karpo had interrogated the giant, Stanislav Voshenko. The major was an old acquaintance of Rostnikov's. The major thought it would be nice to have Rostnikov owe him a favor. Rostnikov made the call and discovered that Karpo had broken both of the prisoner's thumbs and was methodically twisting Voshenko's ear, which was beginning to tear, when the policeman in charge of the lockup had finally responded to Voshenko's shouts of pain and anger.

"I will report this possible breach of national security to Colonel Snitkonoy," said Rostnikov. "However, until we have some evidence that these people actually have nuclear weapons or access to them, we shall continue our investigation. Do you have a plan?"

"Yes," said Karpo.

"Would you like to share it with us?"

It was clear that Karpo wanted to say no, but he answered, "I will interview members of Voshenko's family and continue the search for others with the tattoo," he said.

"You wish assistance?" asked Rostnikov.

"Alone," said Karpo.

Rostnikov nodded.

"Sasha?"

"There are desperate people in Moscow living like animals," said Sasha as he brushed aside his hair and caught the eyes of Elena Timofeyeva, who was paying particular attention. "There are small children murdering people for a few kopecks."

They knew all this, and Sasha was quite aware that they did, but no one stopped him or spoke.

"Progress?" asked Rostnikov.

"Several possibilities," said Sasha. "I don't think it will take more than a few days to find our children who murder."

"In Buenos Aires," said Zelach softly, "there are policemen who go out and murder the homeless children. I read it in the newspapers."

"In the United States?" asked Rostnikov.

"There are children who commit crimes," Hamilton said slowly. "As yet there are no bands of homeless children murdering in the street, at least not on a statistically meaningful level."

"Statistically meaningful level?" Sasha asked, looking at the American.

"I have children," said Hamilton calmly in precise Russian. "I have a family. I have seen murdered children and children who have murdered. I deal in kidnappings and serial killings. Like you I can still see the faces of the killers of babies and the babies who kill. Statistics are not the enemy. They are a means of determining where we should put our efforts."

Sasha folded his hands.

"So," said Rostnikov, looking down at the tea leaves in his empty cup. "Agent Hamilton and I

136

hope to free a kidnap victim, Alexei Porvinovich, shortly and take his kidnappers into custody. Anyone need anything, want anything, have anything else to say?"

All eyes with the exception of Zelach's met those of Rostnikov. Rostnikov assumed the slouching man with his mouth partly open was pondering some passage from the playwright Saroyan or the philosophy of Camus. The effort seemed to be straining the poor man's brain. He would have to ask Hamilton, given his limited exposure to the members of Rostnikov's team, which one he felt most likely to crack. It was a near certainty in a world gone mad that the police who dealt with the madness would also go mad. Rostnikov would vote for Zelach. He would have bet an extra dozen seventy-five-pound curls tonight that everyone else around the table would vote for Karpo.

"Then I do," said Rostnikov, nodding at the waiter, who was only too glad to cooperate with the police.

The waiter brought a tray of wineglasses and a bottle of red wine. He poured the wine and handed the glasses to the people around the table. When he had finished, Rostnikov raised his glass and said, "To the memory of Mathilde Verson. Her laugh will be remembered. Phrases, words, and the touch of her hand will be upon us when we least expect them. We drink to her with love."

They all touched glasses. Karpo showed no emotion but drank deeply from the glass though he had never been known to drink anything alcoholic.

They finished their drinks, and all except Rostnikov and Hamilton left the café after stopping to pay for whatever they had consumed.

"The slouching one," Hamilton asked before Rostnikov could ask his question.

Rostnikov smiled.

"What about him?" asked Rostnikov.

"Most likely to crack," said Hamilton. "That's what you were going to ask me, I think. I watched your eyes, your body language."

"Body language?" Rostnikov repeated.

"Am I wrong?" asked Hamilton.

"No," said Rostnikov. "And you, you were thinking about your children, worrying about them, wondering how quickly you could get to a phone without appearing to be concerned. Am I right?"

It was Hamilton's turn to smile.

"Body language?" he asked.

"No," said Rostnikov. "You are the very model of perfect posture and professionalism. But your eyes fell most frequently on Sasha, and it was that in part that made him respond. Ironic that your empathy with Sasha should be misread by him as cold indifference."

"Perhaps he has a lot to learn," said Hamilton in English.

"He is young," said Rostnikov, also in English. "I should read this Saroyan?"

"He is quirky and haunting," said Hamilton.

"An Armenian," said Rostnikov. "As a people they are quirky and haunting."

"Allow me to pay for your tea and wafers," said Hamilton, rising.

Rostnikov nodded his acceptance of the offer and slowly, painfully, rose from his chair and silently spoke to his twisted leg to soothe it.

"And now?" asked Hamilton.

"I get the Wolfhound to pull those strings we discussed. Perhaps we will pay an unexpected visit on the wife and brother of Alexei Porvinovich."

It was early afternoon when they left the café. The sky was gray. A chill wind was blowing.

"I like Moscow like this," Rostnikov said, hands plunged into his coat pocket, old fur hat pulled down on his forehead.

"Reminds me of Chicago," said Hamilton.

"You are from Chicago?" asked Rostnikov.

"Yes," said Hamilton. "West Side."

"A difficult neighborhood?" asked Rostnikov in English.

"A very difficult neighborhood. I didn't like weather like this. It made people irritable knowing the hard winter was coming."

"Odd," said Rostnikov as they walked. "Almost all Russians love the winter. We long for the snow, the clean cold."

Hamilton shrugged and went back to Russian. "Shall we pull some strings and save the world?"

"I'll consider the day well spent if we save a life," responded Rostnikov.

Hamilton looked at the limping man at his side and knew that he was telling the truth.

★ ★ ★

"You are the sister of Stanislav Voshenko?" Karpo asked the woman who sat at a table in McDonald's on Pushkin Square eating some meat on a bun.

The woman was young, no more than twenty-five. Her face was plain but clean and the McDonald's uniform she wore, complete with little cap that covered most of her short, dark hair, gave her an aura of neatness she shared with the other two similarly uniformed young women at her table. The place was crowded, and people with trays jostled one another. Outside, there was only a short line to get in. It was nearly three in the afternoon. It should have been busier.

"I am Katerina Voshenko," the young woman said.

Karpo showed his identification card.

One of the uniformed girls with Katerina stood up, gobbled down the last of whatever she was eating, and left quickly, making her way through the crowd. Someone jostled Karpo and said something in a foreign language.

Karpo sat in the vacant seat. He was, as always, in black. He wore a jacket, no coat, and a look of unblinking determination that made the young woman think this policeman might be more than a bit mad.

"Most of the people who come here are tourists or visiting businessmen," Katerina Voshenko said, picking up a long, limp french fry.

Karpo looked at the other young woman at the table, a pretty blond girl with good teeth. She tried to avoid his eyes but failed. Her right cheek was filled with whatever she was eating.

"Back to work," the blonde said through a mouthful of food.

The girl gathered her food and a plastic cup with a straw in it and plunged into the crowd of people carrying food trays and looking for tables.

"Smells like another country," Karpo said.

Katerina Voshenko shrugged and said, "America. I'm used to it. Ever have a burger?"

"I came here once."

The woman looked at the pale, straight-backed man before her and wondered what would bring a man like this to stand in line to buy a Big Mac and fries.

"Alone?"

"With a friend," he said.

"A woman?" asked Katerina as she downed a fry and selected another.

A lone man in a dark business suit spotted the empty seat at their table, took two steps toward it, hesitated when his eyes met Karpo's, and lost the spot to a very big young man in a leather jacket and an almost shaved head.

"You are Stanislav Voshenko's sister?" Karpo repeated.

"No," the young woman said, chewing on a french fry. "I'm his daughter. He had one sister, my aunt, who raised me. I do not see my father often. He denies that he has a child."

The girl looked at the young man with the nearly shaved head. He looked back, his mouth turning just a bit in what was probably his best attempt at a smile.

"Your father is in prison," said Karpo, his voice penetrating the noise of the crowd.

"I'm not surprised," she said. "He hurts people. He kills people. He killed my mother. Beat her. She was small. I watched sometimes. And then…" She shrugged and stuffed another fry in her mouth. "One day she was dead. I'm not surprised."

"When did you last see him?" asked Karpo.

"*Kahk dyihlah?* How's it going?" asked the large young man who was now sharing their table. He had a thin face, poor teeth, and wore a tight blue T-shirt under his leather jacket, showing lean muscle.

"*Khurahshoh, spahseebuh.* Fine, thanks," said Katerina with a smile.

"Go away," said Karpo, turning to the young man.

"What?"

"Go away now," said Karpo.

The young man grinned, avoided the eyes of the gaunt vampire, and went on eating. Karpo reached over, took the sandwich from the young man, and placed it on the tray. The man started to rise. A few people were looking. Most of those nearby managed to ignore the confrontation or pretended to do so. The young man stood to his full height and looked down at Karpo with both fists clenched.

"Your food grows cold," Karpo said. "Take it elsewhere, or you will find yourself humiliated."

The man cocked his shaved head to one side

like a parrot and saw determination and maybe even madness in the eyes of the lean ghost. He had friends to meet, cars to steal. He gathered his food and stalked into the crowd, bruising ribs and arms and even sending a tray flying.

"When did you last see your father?" Karpo went on.

A woman in a fake-fur jacket took the vacated seat. She was about seventy and looked as if she had a great deal of experience at minding her own business.

"I saw him at my aunt's apartment," Katerina said, looking in the direction the young man had gone. "A few weeks, maybe a month ago. He needed a place to sleep. He was drunk. Said he couldn't go to his own apartment, not that night. He has done this before, and my mother's sister has never been able to say no."

"Your father has a tattoo," Karpo said. "An eagle with a bomb in its claws."

The girl nodded. She was running out of french fries and had only a bit of Coca-Cola left in her cup.

"He showed it to us. He took off all his clothes and showed it to us," she said. "Then he talked. He sat there with nothing on. Before, when I was little, he was full of hair, a great bear. Now he is shaven to show his tattoos. He is proud of them, especially the one with the eagle and the bomb."

"What did he say about it?"

"I don't remember," the young woman said, looking again to where the leather-coated young man had gone. "Something about being an eagle and swooping down for a bomb full of gold. He was drunk."

"He looks a little like your father," Karpo said.

"Who?"

"The young man in the leather jacket."

"No," she said. "A little, maybe."

"Your father has friends," Karpo said.

"People who are like him," she said. "Who in his right mind would want my father as a friend? I've got to get back to work."

She began to gather the cup and paper.

"Names," Karpo said. "Did he ever mention the names of any of his friends?"

"He was very drunk," she said. "Kept saying that he was a personal friend of Kuzen's, that Kuzen was an eagle, that he had been in Kuzen's apartment on Kalinin and at his dacha more than once for dinner."

"Did he give Kuzen's first name?" Karpo asked as the young woman started to rise.

"Igor," she said with certainty. "Is my father in prison for killing someone?"

"Yes," said Karpo.

Katerina Voshenko rose from her chair and looked blankly at the passing people and at the long counter behind which she would soon be standing.

"Will he ever get out?"

"I don't think so," said Karpo.

The girl nodded her head.

"Igor Kuzen," Karpo said. "Did your father say anything more about him?"

As Katerina stood there, Karpo could see a hint of her father in her pose.

"He said Igor Kuzen is a famous scientist. But my father was drunk. He is a liar."

"Could he have made up this Igor Kuzen?" Karpo asked, rising from his chair.

A pair of men eyed the soon-to-be-vacant spaces but did not advance.

"My father has no imagination," she said. "It is one of the things I inherited from him, that and some of my looks. The uniform helps overcome that. Sometimes it turns a man on. Some men like to say they went to bed with a girl who works at McDonald's."

Her eyes sought the young man in the leather jacket. When she turned back to the ghostly detective, he had disappeared. The two businessmen took the empty seats and she hurried to dump her garbage and get back to work. Then she saw the young man move toward her through the crowd. He was smiling. She smiled back and checked her watch. She had about a minute left before she'd have to resume her shift. She pushed back the thought that this young man did remind her of her father, then she allowed herself to consider it. She did not like what she saw, but that did not stop her from smiling at the young man who stood before her, wiping his hands on his work jeans.

★ ★ ★

"You will be all right?" Sasha asked as they stood looking across at the battered apartment building.

People came and went. Mostly old people, but also a few young boys.

Sasha had listened at the Chazovs' door and heard nothing. Now they had stood in this doorway for over an hour. No boys fitting the description they had of the three Chazovs had come either in or out. There had been no usable fingerprints on the items Zelach had taken from the apartment. Now they had to do this the hard way—the usual way.

"I'll be fine," said Zelach.

They had decided to watch the apartment building in shifts. It was certainly possible that the Chazov boys would come through some rear entrance, but eventually they would use the front door.

The night was growing cold. A wind wailed down the corridor of beaten tenements.

Zelach had volunteered for the first shift so that Sasha could have dinner with his family and get two or three hours' sleep. Sasha had promised to call Zelach's mother or, rather, to call the apartment of the man from the Water Bureau, who lived down the hall and had a phone. The man was proud of his phone and had made it clear that having a policeman in the building was something he appreciated.

Sasha tried the door behind them. The cold would keep Zelach awake for a few hours, but then it would dull him into frozen lethargy. The door was locked. He had no problem opening it with his pocketknife and an identification card. He entered and motioned for Zelach to follow.

They were in a small, far-from-clean hallway with a narrow band of concrete steps leading upward.

Sasha knocked on the door to his left and waited. He knocked again. No answer. Then they moved across the hall, heard a voice behind the door, and knocked.

"Who?" asked a woman.

"Police," said Sasha.

"Police, there are all kinds of police," she said. "All kinds of people who say they are the police."

"We are the police," Sasha said, looking at Zelach, who stood patiently.

"What do you want?" the woman asked.

"To talk to you without shouting," said Sasha.

"Talk about what?" she said.

"You will find out when you open the door."

"I'm not that curious," the woman said.

"Then you will find out when we break the door down," said Sasha.

"I'm calling the police now," the woman said with more determination and less fear than Sasha would have expected. He was reasonably certain that she had no phone.

The door was heavy, and time was passing. Sasha looked back toward the front door of the building and hoped that the Chazovs didn't coincidentally arrive in the minutes they were wasting. Sasha had no intention of trying to knock down the woman's door. It would be easier to move up one flight and try another door. But it would have to be done quickly.

He took a step back from the door and was about to head for the wooden stairs when the door opened and he found himself facing a woman and a rifle. The rifle was large. The woman was small, and she seemed to be about fifty years old.

"Show me," she said.

Sasha and Zelach took out their identification cards.

"Proves nothing," she said. "Come in. Remember, I can shoot this."

"We will find it difficult to forget," said Sasha, stepping in. Zelach stepped in beside him.

Sasha looked at the windows of the apartment. They were barred. Through the bars Sasha could see the front entrance of the Chazovs' apartment building.

"May I close the door?" Sasha asked.

The woman considered and looked at Zelach. Something about the way the woman looked at his partner reminded Sasha of the way his mother looked at Pulcharia when she was doing something Lydia thought was particularly cute.

"Close it," she said, "Softly."

Zelach closed the door. The apartment was really only a single room, with a bed in one corner covered with a colorful quilt. A small alcove had been converted into a kind of kitchen. There were two standing portable closets and a trio of matching cushioned chairs covered in a well-worn green material. A small table with two chairs stood next to the bed. The rest of the room was taken up by cheap bookcases of various sizes and shapes. One particularly impressive floor-to-ceiling bookcase was jammed with books.

"What do you want?" the woman asked.

"To sit at your window," said Sasha, looking out the glass. "We are waiting for some suspects to enter that building across the street."

The rifle was obviously getting heavy. She hoisted it up.

"The Tivonovs?" she said. "Short, fat man and a woman who looks like his twin?"

Sasha did not answer.

"The boys," she ventured again. "Tried to get in here once. I keep the shades down when it gets dark, but I sit by the window and read and watch when I can."

Still Sasha didn't answer her question but said instead, "We would simply like to take turns sitting at your window. We will require nothing of you but your silence. You can go on with your routine."

"What if they don't come back till night? What if they don't come back for days?" she asked.

The rifle was now definitely aimed at the floor in front of Sasha. There was little chance that she could raise it and fire before he could step forward and take it from her hands.

"My partner will begin the watch. I will relieve him at midnight. You may sleep while I watch."

"Someone tried to rape me once," she said, looking with suspicion at the two men.

"I'm sorry," said Sasha, feeling a rush of impatience he recognized as dangerous. "We will not harm you. When we are finished, we will give you a letter of commendation for your cooperation. The name of a chief inspector will be on the letter. You can say that you have a friend in the police who is a chief inspector."

"In this neighborhood," she said, moving to the door and leaning the rifle against the bookcase, "such a letter could get me killed. No letter."

"No letter," Sasha agreed.

"Money," the woman said.

"Perhaps a little, after we catch them."

"How little?" the woman said, facing the young detective.

"I don't know."

"American dollars," she said. "Five American dollars."

"I can't get five American dollars," said Sasha, glancing out the window again. "I'll get what I can in rubles."

The woman shook her head and said, "I have a choice?"

"No," said Sasha.

"You want tea?" she asked.

"I am leaving," said Sasha. "You don't have a phone. Where is the nearest phone?"

"Two blocks that way. In front of what used to be a hotel. It still works. You want to know why?"

"Why?" asked Sasha wearily.

"Because the drug dealers use it and they'll kill anyone who breaks it," she said. "If it weren't for the drug dealers, this neighborhood would be a hell. It takes the police more than half an hour sometimes to answer a complaint in this neighborhood. You call one of the drug dealers and they take care of things fast. They don't want the police around."

"I would like some tea," Zelach said, moving to the window.

"You have the appreciation of the Moscow police," Sasha said to the woman, who had moved to her alcove to prepare the tea.

"I'm the widow of a policeman," she said. "You people appreciated him so much that now I have a pension so small, I can barely stay alive on it and I have to live in this prison. You have families?"

"My partner lives with his mother," said Sasha. "I have a...This is not relevant."

"To me it is," said the woman. "And to your family. What happens to your wife if you get shot down dead in the street? I'll tell you what happens. She gets a pension too small to live on."

Zelach was standing at the window.

"Sit down," the woman said.

Zelach sat, still wearing his coat.

"I will return at midnight if they haven't come back by then," Sasha said.

The woman shook her head and said, "I get little company. Having a man sitting at my window may not be such a bad thing."

Sasha left, closing the apartment door behind him. Zelach knew the routine. If the boys returned, he was to call Sasha at home and

151

do nothing till Sasha arrived, nothing but watch the door.

Sasha's jacket was a bit too light for the weather. His heavy coat was not yet needed. He walked through the chill toward the nearest metro station. People moved in both directions. Sasha scanned faces for a trio of young boys as he moved.

He was now in a decidedly bad mood. He imagined himself on a hospital stretcher, his dead body flat, Maya looking down at him, wondering how she could manage without his salary. It was a good thing that he did not see the Chazov boys before he got to the metro station. He was certain that had he seen them, he would have done something quite foolish and possibly dangerous.

Alexei Porvinovich paced his designated side of the room considering something quite foolish and possibly dangerous. He had paced for hours. Artiom Solovyov had not returned. Alexei had leafed through the magazines that had been left for him. He had glanced at the lean masked man with the automatic weapon. The lean man sat watching Alexei and not speaking.

The pain in his face had been reduced to a constant tender throbbing, but his face in the mirror looked as if he had contracted some horrific, disfiguring disease.

Before doing something foolish and possibly dangerous Alexei decided upon a plan. He had made a near fortune being patient and dealing with bureaucrats at all levels. Some had been smart or at least cunning. A number had been fools. Usually the fools were much more difficult to deal with, and the man in the chair across the room certainly looked like a fool.

"You can remove the mask," said Alexei. "It must be very warm."

The man did not answer.

"Your name is Boris," said Alexei, finding it difficult to speak through his pain. "You work for Solovyov. I've seen you many times. I can identify you with or without the mask."

Boris considered this and looked at the door, wondering what Artiom would say if he returned and found him without the mask. But Porvinovich was right. What difference could it make? And the mask was driving Boris mad. He pulled it off and placed it nearby on the floor. He brushed back his hair, which resisted and turned him into a wild-haired clown with a gun.

"What do you know of me?" Alexei asked him.

Boris didn't answer, but he did look at his prisoner. It was a small step.

"I am very rich," Alexei said. "You know that. That is why you've joined Solovyov in this."

Boris said nothing but watched Alexei, who had stopped pacing and now sat in a chair, which he turned to face the man with the weapon. Alexei would have liked to put on his business face, a resigned, understanding smile, but he knew it would look grotesque. Instead he sat casually, one leg crossed over the other. A cigarette would be a wonderful prop now, especially if he could pluck it casually from the silver case he normally kept in his pocket. Unfortunately, the case had been taken from him.

"How rich do you think I am?" Alexei said softly, the voice of a conspirator.

The man with the gun did something that may have been a shrug.

"How much is Solovyov paying you for helping him, Boris?"

Boris did not respond.

"A few thousand rubles? More? Maybe he promised you millions," said Alexei casually. "I have that, and what does it hurt him to promise you anything?"

He had the attention of the man with the gun, though he had still not gotten a word from him.

"He will have to kill me, Boris," said Alexei. "I know who he is. I know who you are. Would I go to the police with this information? Never. I don't want the police to start looking into my businesses. No, I would go to a man I know, a man so much worse than you and your friend that any comparison would be comic. This man, to whom I would pay a great deal of money, would gather his friends and they would find you. They would find you, cut off your heads, and bring them to me."

The man on the chair had opened his mouth slightly, using what imagination he had to conjure the image of someone awkwardly chopping his head from his body.

"But," said Alexei, "that will not happen,

because Solovyov must kill me. I know that. You know that. Am I right?"

Boris did not answer.

"I'm right," said Alexei with a resigned sigh. "He will kill me and then he will kill you, Boris."

The man in the chair looked as if he was going to speak and then thought better of it.

"He will kill you because you will know that he is a kidnapper and a murderer," said Alexei. "He will kill you because he thinks you are too stupid to keep your mouth shut. He will kill you because if you are dead, he need not pay you or worry about you. It takes only a small brain, perhaps the size of a crow, to know that what I'm saying is true."

"I'm not stupid," said the man with the gun.

Alexei shrugged and looked at a neutral wall.

"I have thought about these things"—Boris was lying—"I know how to take care of myself."

"How?" said Alexei, turning back to his captor.

"I know how to be careful," the man said. "Artiom is my friend. He wouldn't hurt me."

"The woman might tell him to," Alexei said. "Does he talk about her? Don't you know he'll do whatever she tells him? Don't you know that he is only a little smarter than you?"

The man in the chair blinked and put one hand to his forehead.

"No more talking," the man said.

"Of course," Alexei said. "You need to think. But you had better think quickly. Once Artiom comes back, it may be too late."

Boris stood up, gun in hand.

"No more talking," he said.

Alexei held up his hands and said, "Fine. No more talking. There are ways out of this for you, but if you say no more talking—"

"What ways out?" demanded the man.

"You take me away from this apartment, some-place where I can make a call to that friend I told you about." Alexei was whispering rapidly. "My friend finds Artiom and kills him. You still have me. I call my brother and tell him to deliver a sizable sum of money to a place of your choice. It will be a great deal of money for you. A small amount to me."

"And then you have me killed," the man said.

"Why?" asked Alexei, showing the empty palms of his hands. "You know what will save you? Your stupidity and in-significance. You aren't worth my time. I have others to deal with, others who set this up with your friend, Artiom, who plans to kill you."

"Where could I take you?" asked the man softly.

Alexei forced himself not to smile, though he doubted if a smile could be recognized on his purple, broken face.

"I know of such a place," he said. "An apart-ment I keep for a young lady. You understand. She is in the countryside now visiting her grand-parents."

"I..." the man began.

"You'll have to decide now," said Alexei. "If Artiom comes through that door before we leave, we are both dead men."

The man with the gun was pacing the floor now. It was Alexei who was sitting.

"I don't know," Boris said, running his hand over his head. "I can't think it through."

"It is really very simple and clear," said Alexei. "We leave here and live, and you walk about safely with more money than you had been promised by Artiom, far more. You can either leave Moscow or stay. Artiom Solovyov will no longer be among the living."

The man with the gun kept pacing, but Alexei sat back, relaxed. He knew that if Solovyov did not enter the room in the next few minutes, Boris would give in. Alexei knew that if time was just a bit kind to him, he would succeed.

Natalya Dokorova wore a plain black mourning dress with long sleeves. It was not new. Rostnikov suspected that the old woman wore black even when she had not lost a relative. The Wolfhound had left early for a reception for the French ambassador, and Rostnikov had bullied Pankov into letting him use the colonel's office for the interrogations.

"I will take full responsibility," Rostnikov had told the little man. "Why don't you try to find the colonel? I'll be happy to explain the situation to him."

"He did not want to be disturbed unless it was an emergency," Pankov said.

"Does sitting at the table in his office constitute an emergency?" Rostnikov asked.

Pankov sat thinking. "First thing in the morning," he said, "you must be here to tell the colonel what you have done and that you did not listen to me when I told you not to do this."

"First thing in the morning," Rostnikov had said.

And now they sat around the table. Rostnikov on one side. Craig Hamilton on his left. Elena Timofeyeva on his right. Across from them sat Natalya Dokorova. The tribunal had begun.

"First," Rostnikov said, "I am sorry for the loss of your brother."

Natalya nodded.

"Second," Rostnikov went on, "I am responsible for recovering the items that were stolen from your house."

"They are mine," she said, back straight, looking at Elena.

"That is an issue that can be addressed when we have the items," said Rostnikov. "First we find them. Then we discuss who owns them. That, however, is not a decision for me to make. I have something for you."

Rostnikov leaned over. When he sat upright, there was a flower in his hand. He looked at it for a moment and then reached over and handed it to Natalya Dokorova, who took it and sat back in total confusion. Rostnikov could see from the bewildered look on her face that no one had ever given her a flower before. She placed it on her lap with her right hand over it as if to keep it from fleeing.

"I burned everything," said Natalya Dokorova.

"No," said Rostnikov, "you did not."

"I..." she began, but Rostnikov raised a hand to silence her.

"Guards from two different jurisdictions on each of the doors," Rostnikov said. "Ground floor is solid. Insufficient space in the walls to hide much. Distance to the buildings on either side too far to run a ladder or a plank, and even if it could be done, the noise would clearly draw the attention of the guards. Someone suggested a helicopter on the roof. Too much noise. Conclusion?"

Natalya sat silently now, clutching her flower.

"Show her," said Rostnikov with a sigh.

Elena reached under the table and came up with a piece of dark wood. She placed the piece of wood carefully on the table so as not to scratch its surface. Natalya looked at the wood.

"Can you tell us what this is?"

"It looks like the leg of a chair," she said. "Or a table."

"Found in your garbage," Rostnikov said. "A number of pieces of burned furniture were found in your garbage and the closets of your house. Why are you burning and hiding broken furniture? The furniture in your closets and garbage has no great value."

"I am eccentric," the old woman said.

Rostnikov nodded at Elena, who said, "Natalya, you spent the night burning cheap furniture to give the impression that you were destroying your brother's collection. I don't believe you could destroy any of the items your brother had collected.

You told me that the chairs in your parlor once belonged to Catherine the Great. We think that every item in your home, every painting, every table is an antique of great worth, and it is only the cheap, everyday furniture you have destroyed."

Natalya said nothing.

"The jewelry, books, paintings, that's a different story," said Rostnikov. "Would you like to tell us what you did with them?"

"I burned them."

"No," Rostnikov repeated softly.

Natalya said nothing.

"They will cheat you, Natalya Dokorova," said Rostnikov.

"No one will cheat me," she said firmly.

"You mean if someone cheated you, you would simply tell us who it was or threaten to do so," said Rostnikov. "If I were your accomplice and I were a criminal, I would offer you very little, far less than you expected but enough so that you would take it. I would be sure that you had no choice but to accept my offer."

Natalya was silent again, twirling the stem of the flower between her fingers.

"But you see, Natalya," Rostnikov went on, "we think that whoever might make you such an offer would be greatly miscalculating your determination, your belief in your entitlement. I believe you would turn him or her in."

The old woman looked at the chief inspector with clear determination.

"Put the flower in cool water by a window

facing east if possible," said Rostnikov. "It will last longer."

"You are finished with me?" Natalya said with some confusion.

Rostnikov nodded, and she stood up, clutching the stem of her flower in her right fist. Elena also stood and moved to the door.

Rostnikov, in English, asked the FBI man something about a man named Ed McBain. What it was he asked was beyond Natalya's limited English. Elena opened the door leading into the reception room and found herself looking at four men. For an instant she didn't recognize them. They wore casual clothes, not the uniforms they had worn the other night.

They all looked at her, but she did not let her eyes meet any of theirs.

Elena closed the door and turned to Rostnikov and Hamilton, who stopped speaking and listened as she said, "Orlov and Terhekin."

"They were...?" Rostnikov asked.

"Back door," said Elena. "May I ask a question?"

"Yes," said Rostnikov, trying to move his leg into a more tolerable position.

"Why did you give her the flower?"

"Because she needed it," said Rostnikov.

Chapter 8

Night and Tides

"It is beyond my comprehension," said the tall, well-built young man.

His name was Sergei Orlov. He was a sergeant in the tax police. He had a small blond mustache that did nothing to hide his extremely boyish looks. He sat with his back straight in the chair before Rostnikov, Hamilton, and Elena Timofeyeva. His eyes met those of whoever questioned him, and he answered in a voice that was controlled and a bit high.

At his side sat Officer Konstantin Terhekin, a member of the District 9 police department. He looked even younger than Orlov and not nearly as confident. His light blue eyes strayed from those questioning him. He was a bit on the portly side and sat not quite as rigidly as Orlov.

"Then you and Officer Terhekin did not allow the items to be removed through the back door of the Dokorov house?" asked Rostnikov.

"Absolutely not," said Orlov.

"Terhekin?"

"Absolutely not," Terhekin answered without looking directly at anyone across the table.

"And you had not met each other till the night of this incident?" Rostnikov continued.

"No," said Orlov.

Terhekin nodded his agreement.

"What did you talk about that long night?"

"Talk about?" Orlov repeated.

"Yes."

"We did very little talking," said Orlov. "I did mention that I had a brother who had been captured by the Chechens a few months ago, and he said something about being in Afghanistan."

"That would take a minute or two," said Rostnikov. "The rest of the night you just stood quietly. Is that right, Officer Terhekin?"

"*Da*," said the plump young man. He changed his position slightly in the wooden chair.

"And in the silence of the night you heard nothing inside the house. No movement. Nothing."

"We heard the old woman moving around," said Orlov. "Then we smelled something burning."

"Burning? And you didn't rush in to see what it might be?" asked Rostnikov.

"It was a cold night," said Orlov. "We assumed..."

"Do you believe in magic?" asked Rostnikov.

"No," said both men.

"In miracles?"

"No," said both men.

"I confess," said Rostnikov, shifting his chair back in the hope of restoring minimal feeling to his left leg, "I believe in something like magic. I've seen it performed by a shaman in Siberia. But in this case I agree with you. No miracles. Officer Timofeyeva?"

Elena sat up just a bit straighter and looked down at her notes. Both men would normally be expected to look at the pretty, full-figured young woman across the table, but Orlov's eyes were now riveted on the face of Chief Inspector Rostnikov.

"Were you aware that the guards on the front door, Officers Skitishvili and Romanov, were under observation all night by a series of military police officers?" asked Elena.

"No," said Orlov.

Terhekin shook his head no as well.

"Are you married?" she asked.

Both men answered yes.

"Children?"

"One boy, two years old," said Orlov.

"Girl, six months," said Terhekin.

"Do you have photographs?" Rostnikov suddenly asked.

Both officers fished their wallets out of their pockets and handed them to Rostnikov, who showed the photos to Hamilton and Elena Timofeyeva. Then Rostnikov nudged Hamilton, who pulled out his wallet, removed a photograph, and handed it to the officers across the table. The men nodded in approval. Terhekin gave a pained smile. Wallets and photos were returned. Rostnikov nodded at Elena to continue.

"In return for a full confession," she said, "including details on where the stolen items can now be found, we are prepared to recommend that you both be given letters of commendation for helping to relocate and protect treasures of great value to the state. Perhaps you both had a drink of something warm offered to you and you passed out. Perhaps you noticed some small detail that helped us trace the truck.

"If you refuse to cooperate," Elena went on, "you will be charged with conspiracy to defraud the Russian people and the theft of government property of extremely high value. You will be dishonorably dismissed from your service, tried, and found guilty. If you do not cooperate, you will spend the rest of your lives in prison."

She looked up from her notes and tried not to look uncomfortable. Why had Rostnikov asked to see the photographs of the young men's children? Elena knew enough of the system by now to know that each man would scramble within his own organization to make a deal or else they would both go to trial, insisting upon their innocence, and quite possibly get away with the crime. If, she thought, there was even a crime. As far as Elena was concerned, the treasures belonged to Natalya Dokorova.

"I would like to confer in private with Officer Terhekin," said Orlov.

"Unfortunately," said Rostnikov, "I have, as you may have noticed, a somewhat crippled leg that makes it difficult for me to move. If you would like to use the large closet in the corner or step across the room and whisper..."

"The closet," said Orlov, rising.

Terhekin rose more slowly, and the two men went to the closet behind Colonel Snitkonoy's ample desk. They closed the door.

"Well?" asked Rostnikov, standing and holding on to the back of his chair.

"Can you really offer them such a deal?" asked Hamilton.

"We can offer what we wish," answered Rostnikov. "However, I have little to deal with in exchange for the trust of criminals. So my word is good. It is my hope that a sufficient number of criminals and those in criminal investigation know this. Tell me, have you ever eaten alligator?"

"Alligator?" asked Hamilton.

"Yes," said Rostnikov.

"I have," said Elena. "In Florida."

"Did it taste like chicken? The Americans think everything tastes like chicken," said Rostnikov. "Rattlesnakes, alligators, iguanas."

"It tasted like fish," she said.

Rostnikov nodded and said, "I would like to taste these things—rattlesnakes, alligators, lizards. Americans eat everything."

"Not the heads of fish or the brains of lobsters," said Hamilton.

"I personally do not care for the heads of fish," said Rostnikov. "As for the brains of lobsters, I have never had the opportunity to try them."

The closet door opened and the two young officers stepped out. Terhekin looked particularly pale. Orlov stood straight and determined. They took their seats, and Orlov spoke. "We have done nothing. We have nothing to say. We wish to speak to our superior officers."

"Terhekin, you agree?" asked Rostnikov.

Terhekin, eyes moist, said, "*Da.*"

"You will bear with me," said Rostnikov. He opened a drawer in the desk in front of him. "I am not familiar with these new electronic devices."

Rostnikov pushed a button, and the machine emitted a scream of piercing terror. Hamilton reached over, pushed a button to stop the machine, and asked, "Which number?"

"I believe it is number two," said Rostnikov.

Hamilton's dark fingers danced on the keys. There was a whirring sound and then the sound of faint voices. Hamilton turned up the volume, and the five people in the room listened.

Terhekin: They know everything.

Orlov: They know nothing.

Terhekin: What difference does it make? They need to blame this on someone. If the Washtub decides to blame us, then it is we who will take the blame. You heard him.

Orlov: Bluffing.

Terhekin: And if not, we go to prison. I've heard what happens to police officers who go to prison. And how do we know the old woman will give our shares to our wives?

Orlov: She must, or we will talk. She knows that. On your salary, are you living like a man? Feeding your family enough meat?

Terhekin (laughing bitterly): Meat?

Orlov: If we talk, we go to jail.

Terhekin: But the Washtub said...

Orlov: I do not believe him, and even if I

believed him and we talked, it would be the end of our hopes for wealth. Every day we see men and women growing rich by extortion, murder, theft. This is a Russia of madness. You understand? (Pause) Good.

Everyone then heard the sound of a door opening and closing. Hamilton reached over to turn the machine off. Rostnikov nodded his thanks and pushed the drawer closed.

"Even the toilet stalls are wired," said Rostnikov. "Voice activated. Colonel Snitkonoy wants a full and complete record of every word spoken in this office. The colonel"—here Rostnikov turned to Hamilton—"is a great admirer of your Richard Nixon, who did the same thing. Our colonel, however, is hopeful of better results and eventually a book he can sell to the French or the Americans."

This was, in fact, the first Elena had heard of the hidden microphones. She began to go over in her mind all the conversations she had engaged in there. There were few, but was there anything compromising? A few weeks after she had joined the department, Major Gregorovich had strongly suggested that they work intimately together, but she had politely rejected him. Was there anything else?

"Gentlemen," Rostnikov said. "Do we arrest you, call the procurator's office, and wait for trial?"

Terhekin sat silent, looking at the floor. It was Orlov who spoke.

"We are each given commendations?"

"Lovely ones, complete with frames," said Rostnikov. "Provided—"

"A percentage of what is recovered?" asked Orlov.

Hamilton coughed and succeeded in suppressing a laugh.

"I am afraid that is not within my power," said Rostnikov. "It will have to be discussed with those above me."

"Two trucks," said Orlov. "The old woman made the arrangements. A garage near the Kazan church. That is all we know. You can raid all the garages near the Kazan church at the same time. We are the tax police; we do things like that all the time."

"We are grateful for the expert advice," said Rostnikov. "Inspector Timofeyeva, would you ask Natalya Dokorova to return."

Elena hurried to the outer door, opened it, and asked the waiting old woman to return. When she entered the room, still clutching the flower, she glanced at the two young men, who were definitely not looking at her.

"Another chair, Inspector Timofeyeva," said Rostnikov.

Elena brought another chair and placed it next to Orlov. The woman sat.

"I have nothing more to say," she said.

"Agent Hamilton, would you like to take the next step?" Rostnikov asked, easing back into his chair.

Hamilton, hands folded, looked at each person

across from him and in a soft, firm voice said, "Last night, Natalya Dokorova approached these two officers and asked them to conspire with her to steal her brother's collection of antiques and treasures. Insisting that she had a full legal right to her brother's possessions, Natalya Dokorova offered them a large sum of money, perhaps pending the sale of certain items. They talked, argued, and eventually agreed, allowing the old woman to go to a public telephone to make a call to someone with whom her brother had worked in the past. While they waited for the trucks, Natalya Dokorova, possibly with the aid of one of these two men, destroyed much of the old furniture in her house. The trucks eventually came, slowly and quietly. Sergeant Orlov went to the front of the building to be sure that the two men guarding the front door harbored no thoughts of returning the visit. This was reported by the two guards there. The loading was done quickly, perhaps carelessly but quietly. It was probably just before dawn when the trucks pulled away."

"Natalya Dokorova," Rostnikov said softly, his hands folded before him as well, "it is late. I am hungry. I want to see my wife and the two little girls we have taken in. Please give us the name and address of the garage, or I will have to be up all night raiding garages near the Kazan church."

The old woman looked angrily at the two officers who had betrayed her. She looked at her flower and flung it at Rostnikov, whose hand came up quickly to catch it. He placed it on the table before him.

"Natalya," Elena said gently. "Tell the chief inspector. This is a new Russia. You can get lawyers, people to help you, courts that will listen."

"Betrayer," said the old woman, looking at Elena. "I promised you cooperation and you have brought me to this."

"I believed you were innocent," Elena said.

"I am guilty only of moving my own possessions from one place to another safer place," the old woman said. "I did not feel my house was safe with all these people in uniforms yelling, threatening, watching. Not much of a crime."

"The address of the garage," said Rostnikov.

"Then I betray those who helped me," said the old woman.

"You simply hired them to bring trucks to your back door and haul away a large load of items," said Hamilton. "I doubt if they had any idea of what was taking place."

"That's right," said Natalya.

Orlov let out a deep sigh, and something that might have been a sob escaped from Terhekin. Natalya looked at Rostnikov, who was straightening the petals of the flower and ignoring the eyes of the old woman.

"All right," she said. "I'll tell you, but there are two conditions."

"Which are?" asked Elena.

"First, I talk to a lawyer, the best lawyer in all of Moscow," the old woman said.

"Second?" asked Elena.

The old woman stood and held out her hand toward Rostnikov. He returned the flower. She did not know the address of the garage, but she did know the name. She gave it to the three investigators sitting across from her.

"Pulcharia called me a name," screamed Sasha's mother the moment he entered his apartment. "But I have forgiven her."

Maya, dark, pretty, and showing no sign of having had two babies, brushed down her hair, moved to her husband, and kissed him softly. Maya and Sasha exchanged a brief look of mutual suffering.

"Would you like to know what she called me?" asked the wisp of a woman who was Sasha's mother, pulling herself away from the evening news on the television. She was sitting a few feet from the set so that there could be a compromise level of volume, but the television was still loud.

"I can think of nothing that would give me more satisfaction," said Sasha seriously, taking off his jacket and hanging it on a hook near the door.

"The sarcasm comes from his father's side," Lydia screamed.

The children in the other room had learned to live with their grandmother's shouting and snoring. They shared the bedroom with her.

Lydia's strident voice was a result of a deafness she refused to acknowledge. Each year it grew worse.

The table was set for Sasha—a cold plate of something that looked like sausage, a large piece of bread, and some slices of raw cucumber and onions.

"We have soup," Maya said, moving to the stove in the corner and turning it on. "We ate late."

"Is it warm?" Sasha threw his head back to clear the hair from in front of his eyes as he sat down at the table.

"Yes," said Maya.

"No need to heat it," he responded, tearing off a piece of bread. "I have to get a few hours' sleep. I'm replacing Zelach on a watch at midnight."

Maya sighed with deep resignation—her usual response to such announcements. She touched his hand.

"What am I? A block of wood? A stuffed chicken?" Lydia asked, moving to the table to sit in front of her son.

Maya walked immediately to turn off the television.

"I'd say a stuffed chicken," said Sasha. "If those are my only choices."

"You are not funny," shouted Lydia. "Not funny. Like your dead father. He thought he was funny too. I watch the children all day till Maya gets home from work. I expect respect."

Holding a forkful of sausage, Sasha looked seriously at his mother and said, "What did Pulcharia call you?"

"*Pahnohs*," Lydia belted out, folding her arms in indignation. "Diarrhea."

Sasha examined the bowl of dark, thin soup his wife had just placed beside his plate.

"Why?" asked Sasha.

"I told her she had to go to the toilet," said Lydia. "When she woke up from her nap while the baby and I were watching that show with the clown. I told her, 'Use the toilet.' She called me 'diarrhea.'"

"Maybe she was just telling you that she had…Can this conversation wait till I finish eating?"

"I know the difference between a child telling me she has a problem with her bowels and a child calling me a name," said Lydia, ignoring her son's request.

"She is three years old," said Sasha.

"No excuse. I never let you make excuses," said Lydia, looking at Maya. "I never let him make excuses. Just the truth. Am I right?"

Though Lydia was not within a kilometer of being correct, Sasha said, "My mother is right."

"And Maya refused to discipline her," Lydia went on, feeling a wave of triumph.

"I didn't think she had done anything that deserved discipline," said Maya, taking a seat at the small table.

"It is nice to be home," Sasha said, reaching out to touch his wife's hand. Maya's hands were soft. Maybe if he yawned a few times and reminded his mother that he had to get back to work in a few hours, his mother would retire to the bedroom with the children and read a book. Maybe he and Maya could pull out the sofa bed, turn out the lights, make love, and still have time for enough sleep.

"So, what are you going to do?" Lydia insisted.

"I'll beat her with a belt when I return in the morning," he said. "Or maybe I should get it over with and pull her out of bed now for the beating. She'll never forget it."

He tried the soup. Beans. Still warm. The soup was good. He dipped his bread in it.

"You will not strike that precious child," Lydia said indignantly. "I never laid a hand on you when you were a child. Neither did your father."

Sasha contemplated the selectivity of his mother's memory.

"I'll starve her for a week," said Sasha. "Maya, no food for Pulcharia for a week. Make a note."

"Stop," Lydia insisted. "You don't intend to do any of those things."

"Then, Mother, what shall I do? Maya, what is in this sausage?"

"I'm not sure," said Maya. "It's not bad, though."

Sasha agreed. He simply didn't like eating the unknown.

"Deprive her of…of television," Lydia said. "For two days."

Since Pulcharia seldom looked at television, Sasha agreed.

"I would, however, like to ask her why she called you a name," he said.

"*Pahnohs*," she reminded him as he continued to chew a piece of the unidentifiable sausage.

"I will ask her about this gross violation the moment I next see her," said Sasha. "Immediately after dinner I would like to get some sleep."

"You can sleep in the bedroom," Lydia said. "Maya can clean up, talk a little, watch the television. We'll wake you."

"I'm sure you will," said Sasha. "But I want to shave, get out of my clothes, shower, and go to sleep in here, with my wife, who will, as usual, have to get up early for work."

"You want to make love," Lydia said indignantly.

"That is a possibility," Sasha agreed, smiling at his wife.

"You take away my last crumb of dignity and you smile," said Lydia with an enormous sigh.

"You have my full and deep respect," said Sasha.

"I made the soup," Lydia said, looking at the bowl from which her son was drinking.

"Perfect," Sasha said.

Lydia talked. Sasha and Maya listened. When he was finished eating, Maya cleared the table. Lydia was on to one of her favorite subjects— Boris Yeltsin and his stooges who had succeeded in making things much worse instead of even a little better.

"I'm not saying I agree with Zhirinovsky," she said. "But he has a point. And Yeltsin is a drunk who doesn't know what he's doing. If it weren't for the Americans and their money, Yeltsin wouldn't be wearing those pressed suits and designer ties. You know where he would be?"

"No," said Sasha.

"In a little apartment with a big bottle," Lydia said triumphantly.

Sasha had argued with such observations before. This time he nodded and yawned.

"That's not a real yawn," his mother said. "That's a yawn that says, 'Mother, go to bed.' Fine. I have books. It's early, but I have books. You haven't asked me how I feel today."

"How do you feel today?"

"*Toot bahlyeet*, a little pain right here," she said, pointing to her stomach, "and a touch of *pahnohs*."

Sasha did not smile.

"A good reason to get into bed and get some rest," Sasha said, reaching over to touch his mother's thin arm. She put her hand on top of his and smiled.

After a shower and a shave, Sasha emerged in an oversized white American T-shirt that had a crude cartoon of a yellow-haired boy and words that Maya had told him meant "Don't Have a Cow."

The humor and meaning had always escaped Lydia, who finally retired to the bedroom with a thick paper-covered book. Maya was already in bed. She wore a blue and white long-sleeved nightgown tied at the neck. When the bedroom door was closed, she slipped out of her nightgown and let him see and touch her. Then she reached over and turned off the

177

lights. They made love to the sound of Lydia screeching a lullaby in the shower.

"Romantic," Sasha whispered.

"Funny," she whispered back.

He rolled her over onto her stomach and climbed gently on top of her from behind.

"All right?" he asked.

She lifted her buttocks and rose to her knees. In the shower Lydia squealed, "Never any soap in this house."

Emil Karpo sat at his desk eating a sandwich he had purchased at a stand near the Belorussia train station. The bread slices were thin, the pink and white sheet that passed for ham was even thinner, and there was barely the hint of butter. A bottle of water stood next to the sandwich, which lay on a sheet of paper.

Karpo stopped in his review of his notes from time to time to take a bite of sandwich and a drink of water. It was Thursday night, the night he would normally be with Mathilde. He continued his search. There were Igor Kuzens listed in the directory, and the MVD computer system had come up with a probable Igor Kuzen, a medicine hijacker, but he was in prison. The name had touched a memory in Karpo. He had seen it somewhere, written it somewhere, and now he was going methodically through his cross-index in search of a reference. All names listed in his books of notes were cross-indexed.

He couldn't find it.

Karpo sat back to finish his sandwich. There was a table lamp before him and a standing lamp in the corner. Mathilde had placed a painting of some people having a picnic on one wall, a painting of a huge red flower on another. She had found a patterned blanket for his cot and was on the verge of convincing him to buy a real bed. She had brought life to Emil Karpo. Communism had been his meaning, but Mathilde had brought life. Now she was dead. A stray bullet from an automatic weapon. The cross fire between two gangs fighting over what? Territory? Nuclear weapons?

Emil Karpo tried to summon anger, but he couldn't. It was an emotion he bore little of when he was a child and none when he became an adult. He was determined, relentless. He could feel regret at the enormous waste of human life he saw— a murdered child, a woman raped and left for dead, a young man with a meat hook through his body. He had seen this and much more, and it had made him determined to find whoever committed such atrocities.

Now Mathilde was dead and he wanted to feel different. It was Thursday. He wanted to feel angry, but all he could feel was empty. He had lost everything, everything but his work, and he was even beginning to wonder what the point was to that.

"Spelling," he said aloud, flipping through the index volume where each entry was clearly printed in his own precise hand. He was now going through the *T*'s, and that was where he found it.

Igor Tuzen. A single reference. July 1986. Questioned in relation to the beating and death of a woman who lived in the apartment next to his. The man had identified himself as a physicist. He'd claimed not to have heard the sound of a struggle on the night of the murder even though he had been home all night. The walls were not thick and the woman's struggle had been fierce. Tuzen maintained that he had been completely absorbed in his work and that furthermore a hockey game had been blaring on his television. Description of Igor Tuzen: age forty, height approximately five feet eight inches, weight 155 pounds. Thick dark brown hair and a pink, youthful face. Glasses with thick lenses. No nervousness. No signs of regret at the murder of his neighbor. No fear. Cooperative. Sorry that he couldn't help. Wore a smile all the time as if either the world constantly amused him or he were on the verge of idiocy.

Karpo noted the man's phone number and dialed. The person who answered said no one named Kuzen lived there. Karpo dialed the home of Paulinin. There was no answer. He called Paulinin's laboratory on the second lower level of Petrovka.

"What?" Paulinin answered.

"Karpo."

"I have no new information for you," said Paulinin. "What I have is a new corpse, a Gypsy woman, no obvious means of death. I have a theory."

"Do you know a physicist named Igor Kuzen?"

"Kuzen? Igor Kuzen." Long pause, then, "Yes, I'll find it. Igor Kuzen. Not a physicist. Science training. Wrote a few articles back five, ten years ago, discredited nonsense about the effects of nuclear explosions on plant life, changes in gene patterns, acquired characteristics that could be passed on. He was not completely wrong, just completely ignorant. I might be able to find the articles if you can wait."

"What happened to Kuzen?" Karpo asked.

"Went to work for a foreign pharmaceutical company," said Paulinin. "Started in research, moved quickly down to quality control. Last I heard of him."

"The foreign company?"

"Czech company. Jansco Pharmaceuticals. They make a poor brand of American Prozac. They call it Prinsco. Sells like mad now that everyone thinks he is mad. Can I get back to my corpse?"

"Thank you," said Karpo.

"You have a night open for dinner perhaps?" Paulinin ventured.

"Perhaps," said Karpo. "We do not eat in your laboratory."

"Out, wherever you say."

"Yes," said Karpo. "When I've finished with what I am working on."

Next he called the office of Jansco Pharmaceuticals just beyond the outer ring road. He got one of those answering machines and a number to call in case of emergency, which he dialed. A tired woman answered. Karpo asked her how he might find Igor Kuzen. She gave the phone to a man.

"What is this emergency that you have to find Kuzen?" the man asked with some irritation.

"Police," said Karpo.

"Doesn't surprise me," the man said. "I fired him more than eight months ago."

"Why?"

"Passing on formulas to the Chinese."

"Where does he live?"

"I'm at home right now. How am I supposed to remember where a former employee lives? I could check in the morning."

"I'll meet you at your office in one hour," said Karpo.

"It's nearly midnight," the man groaned.

"One hour."

"Just a moment," said the man.

The moment passed. Karpo could hear the woman who had answered the call complaining. The man came back on the phone.

"The last address I can find for Igor Kuzen is Two-thirty-four Lermontov Prospekt. Do you want the phone number?"

"No," said Karpo, and hung up.

He cleaned up the crumbs left from his dinner, drank the rest of the water, put on his jacket, then paused for a moment to look at the painting of the people in the park. He turned off the lights. He set three hairs he plucked from his head at exact markings in the door, where only he would notice. Should someone enter his apartment or try to during the night, the hairs would move, and even if the person was an expert, it would be difficult to find them and return them to their precise positions.

Karpo checked the pistol in the shoulder holster under his jacket, a Browning that held a thirteen-round clip, and went out into the night. Unlike so many others in the new democratic Russia, Emil Karpo was not afraid of the night. He had, however, begun to fear that he was afraid of being alone.

Chapter 9

Night

"What are you looking for?" the little girl asked.

It was well past her bedtime, but after dinner Sarah had told him the Karenskovs on the fourth floor had a badly leaking pipe under their bathroom sink.

Laura and her eight-year-old sister were both frail, with short dark brown hair. They looked nothing like their grandmother, who was in prison for shooting the manager of a government food shop. The grandmother had been raising the children since her daughter disappeared, leaving the brief message that she would return sometime, maybe. The girls' father was already long gone, and there were no aunts or uncles. The Rostnikovs had taken the girls in, and slowly, cautiously, the children had been coming out of their near-cata-tonic state. Now the eleven-year-old was express-ing a definite interest in Rostnikov's activities.

He was lying on his back under the Karenskovs' sink, his copper-colored tool kit on the floor be-side him. The girl, in her nightshirt, was kneeling.

"Searching for the leak," Rostnikov said.

"You are getting dirty," Laura said.

"The plumbing is old," he said. "It rusts, it leaks, it makes noises like the wind and machine guns. Hand me the pipe wrench, that big metal thing with jaws."

She found the wrench and offered it into the darkness below the sink. Rostnikov clamped, tugged, grunted, and pulled. Rust flaked over his face and he closed his eyes.

"No use," he said, sliding out awkwardly.

The girl smiled when he sat up. His face was covered with red rust. In his hand was a dirty length of piping.

"I amuse you?" he asked. "Good. Now hand me that piece of pipe. No, the smaller one."

She handed him a short section of plastic pip-ing he had brought with him.

"The pipes are all forty years old, and made from inferior galvanized steel," he said. "They are be-ginning to rust from inside. Small holes are de-veloping in the pipes. They can be patched with tape for a while, but eventually they will all have to be replaced, just like I am replacing this section."

The Karenskovs waited in the other room watching television. Rostnikov and the girl could

184

hear the cheerful voices of a man and woman on the television. Then the audience laughed.

"The plumbing in this building, like most of the buildings in Moscow, is similar to our government," Rostnikov said, putting down the rusted section of pipe and examining the tube of black plastic the girl had handed him. "It is rusty and rotten. Soon…leaks everywhere. The system is falling apart. It has to be replaced, but the cost is great. Do the new plumbers simply make repairs with plastic tubing?" He held up the plastic pipe section in his hand. "Or do they completely replace the entire system as they have promised but which they cannot afford to do?"

The girl listened, a look of intensity on her face.

"You don't understand, do you?" he asked, reaching out to touch her cheek.

"A little," she said.

When he removed his hand from her cheek, he saw that he had left a handprint of rust and dust. He put the two pieces of pipe side by side on the floor. The black plastic one was longer.

"Saw and clamp," he said, pointing at the tools.

The girl handed them to him and said, "It's like being a nurse, a little."

"A little," Rostnikov agreed with a smile. "You would like to be a doctor or a nurse?"

The girl considered this while Rostnikov turned his body, biting his lower lip to control the pain in his leg, and fixed the clamp and black piping together on the edge of the sink.

"No," she said. "I want to be a traffic director.

I'll have a uniform and stand in the street telling cars when to go and stop. Or I'll be up in one of those little traffic towers."

"A noble ambition," Rostnikov said as he stood up and started to cut the pipe to the same length as the rusty one he had removed. "Well within your grasp."

"You are a policeman," she said.

"I am," he answered, continuing to saw.

"You put my grandmother in jail."

It was the first time the girl had spoken of her grandmother, though both Sarah and Porfiry Petrovich had given the girls messages from her.

"I took her to the judges, who put her in jail," said Rostnikov without looking away from his sawing. "I am trying to get her out. You know what she did?"

"Yes," said the girl, also standing now and watching with interest as Rostnikov sawed. "She shot a mean man who wouldn't give her bread for me and my sister to eat."

"Basically correct," said Rostnikov as he sawed through the piece of plastic and the loose end fell to the floor.

The girl picked up the four-inch piece of black plastic and asked, "Can I keep this?"

"Yes," said Rostnikov, loosening the clamp and painfully beginning to make his way back under the sink.

"There may be things I can make with it," she said, turning it around in her hands.

"Now," he said, the top of his body hidden

under the sink, "hand me that small can of oil. The blue can."

She did so, and after a minute he handed it back out to her.

"Now the bigger can, the one that looks like a small drum."

She handed it to him. Moments later he handed it back out.

"Finally," he said, "the bottle. It is solvent. Handle it carefully, and if you feel brave enough, unscrew the top."

Slowly she unscrewed the top. The solvent smelled terrible. She handed it to him and listened to him grunt and turn. The girl looked at Rostnikov's withered leg and said, "Does your leg hurt all the time?"

"Almost all the time," he answered with another grunt from the darkness. "There."

Rostnikov, covered now with even more dirt and rust, eased out from beneath the sink and reached back under it to retrieve some rags, a spatula, and another small tool. He had to grip the sink with both hands in order to rise, and once he had risen he stood silently for two minutes coping with pain.

"The metal snake," he said, pointing to a drain auger, perhaps his most valued tool.

Laura handed it to him, and he began to drive the coiled metal serpent into the sink and through the new piece of plastic piping. She leaned over the sink to watch the metal coils disappear as Rostnikov pushed the device deeper and deeper into the piping. Finally it was as far as it would go. Rostnikov tugged, twisted, and pulled the metal snake carefully out of the pipe.

"Well, it is done," he said with satisfaction, holding out his right hand. The girl took the large hand and they shook on their success.

"Why do you like doing this?" the girl asked as they put the tools away and cleaned up the mess they had made.

"This is very simple. The work I do as a policeman is very complicated," he said.

"Why?"

"Because I must deal with people, and people are seldom simply good or bad. It is rare for a policeman to be able to fix a problem. One problem creates another one. It doesn't end, and when it does, the end is not simple and the system is not working any better. Does this make sense?"

"A little," she said. "It's like what happened to my grandmother."

"Yes," said Rostnikov. "When I fix plumbing, I search for the problem, find it, repair it, and receive the gratitude of those who live with the system. Like this leak."

He gathered his tools, took the girl's hand, and went out to report his success to the Karenskovs. They were young, in their early thirties perhaps, and she was pregnant. He worked in the Moscow office of Pizza Hut.

"Fixed," Rostnikov said. "But don't use it till morning."

"Thank you," said the husband, taking Rostnikov's dirty hand.

"Yes," said the pregnant wife. "Thank you."

"Please take this," the man said. "I know you won't take money."

Actually, Rostnikov was getting close to the point where he thought he might accept a few kopecks to replace equipment. Money was tight and his salary small. Combining his salary and that of Sarah, who had gone back to clerking at the music store, they could make it through each month, but there was nothing left over. Money was there to be had for a policeman, but Rostnikov had never considered selling himself. Once he took even a few kopecks from a suspect or a criminal, he would have sacrificed the very meaning of his commitment to the law. There was a line. He would never cross it.

However, he could accept the four pieces of paper young Karenskov handed to him.

On the way up to the apartment the girl asked, "What did he give you?"

Rostnikov reached into his pocket and handed the four pieces of paper to the child.

"What do they say?" she said. "They are in..."

"English," he said. "They say we can have four large pizzas free."

"Pizzas. Like on the television."

"Better," said Rostnikov. "Better."

When they opened the door to the Rostnikov apartment, Sarah was sitting at the table near the window drinking tea with Major Gregorovich, who was dressed in what appeared to be a new, dark gray business suit. Gregorovich stood, looked at Rostnikov and his toolbox with disapproval, and said, "Colonel Snitkonoy wishes to see you immediately." There was clear satisfaction in Gregorovich's tone.

"I'll wash up," Rostnikov said, moving toward the bedroom where the other child was sleeping.

"The colonel specifically said 'immediately,'" Gregorovich said.

Sarah shrugged and Rostnikov sighed. He let go of the girl's hand. "Then by all means let us go."

"Thank you for the tea," said Gregorovich.

"You are most welcome, Major," Sarah said.

"And the biscuit," he added.

"For that too," she said. She took Laura's hand.

"Don't wait up for me," Rostnikov said.

"I won't," Sarah said. "I have to be up early to get the girls ready for school."

Both Porfiry Petrovich and Sarah knew she would be awake when he returned.

"You have a car?" Rostnikov said as Gregorovich hurried down the hall.

"Of course," said the major.

"I'm afraid I will make the car a bit dirty," said Rostnikov.

"That can't be helped."

"Major, no matter what the urgency of this summons, I can walk no faster than I am now doing. So you will either go ahead and meet me or make an effort to match my pace."

Gregorovich slowed down, and Rostnikov

patted him on the back in thanks, leaving a large, dark handprint on the major's new suit.

Bakunin leaped at Elena before the door was fully open. Once the cat had been lean and the leap had been high and often. Now that Baku had grown old and heavy, his leaps came less frequently, and they fell far short of Elena's arms.

Anna Timofeyeva sat in her chair at the window, a book in her lap. She was fully dressed in a particularly hideous brown pair of slacks and an almost-matching long-sleeved blouse. She was a heavy woman with short gray hair and a look of suspicion that had come to dominate her face sometime before her career-ending heart attacks. She had begun as an assistant to one of the commissars of Leningrad in charge of shipping and manufacturing quotas. She had no background in law, no training for a position as procurator, but she had been rewarded with the position after almost twenty years of service in Leningrad, and she had taken to it with the same zeal with which she had hounded shippers and manufacturers. In her second ten-year term as procurator in Moscow her heart had reenacted the history of the Revolution. At first it complained and she ignored it. Then it protested and she pretended that she did not hear. Next it rebelled and she sought professional advice and was told to make peace with her heart. That, too, she ignored and continued to work fourteen-hour days and indulge in her only vice, cold tea. And then revolution—heart attack—and she had no choice but to capitulate. Now, at age fifty-seven, Anna had been retired for more than three years.

Elena walked over to her aunt's chair and gave the woman a kiss on her warm cheek. "Did you walk today?" Elena asked. She was carrying a small bag in one hand and her aunt's old briefcase in the other. She put them both down.

"Walk," Anna repeated. "I went out in the brisk, cool air and ran, ran like the wind. Neighbors gawked. Strangers marveled at the sight of a sack of potatoes in a blue sweat suit running through the streets."

"Did you walk?" Elena repeated, starting to unload the small bag of groceries.

It had taken Elena two hours and four visits to black marketeers to get the three cans of soup, two onions, four potatoes, one large yogurt, and a piece of meat that was purported by an earnest Latvian to be from the finest cattle raised on the great pampas of Argentina.

"I walked," Anna Timofeyeva said, starting to get up.

"Have you eaten?"

"We, Baku and I, had some bread, cheese, and tea. I think I have lost weight."

Elena nodded. Bakunin rubbed against her leg.

"I'll make something," said Elena.

"Yes," said Anna.

Having learned what little she knew of cooking from her busy mother, Elena was a poor cook. Her aunt was far worse, as they both knew—

indifferent to ingredients and seasonings, inclined to let things almost burn or else to serve them long before they were ready.

"You had a good day?" asked Elena, kicking off her shoes in the general direction of the front door.

"Mine was fine," said Anna. "For over three weeks now I've watched the skinny woman with the fat little boy steal small items from the other mothers in the courtyard. She is so good that she was probably a professional thief before she became a responsible mother."

Elena found a pot, rinsed it in the sink, opened a can of soup, and poured the soup into the pot. She filled the can with water from the tap. The water looked a bit browner than usual today. As she brought the soup almost to a boil, adding water slowly as well as the handiest of the spices and condiments on the counter, Elena sensed from her aunt's unusually prolonged silence that the older woman had something to say.

"Well?" asked Elena, her back to her aunt. She added a bit of the quickly diminishing contents of a jar of basil.

"Porfiry Petrovich called," Anna said.

Elena continued stirring and made no comment.

"He asked how I was doing and promised to visit soon," Anna went on. "He'll be here within the week. He is a man of his word."

Her back still turned to her aunt, Elena added pepper and laughed quietly.

"He also talked about you," Anna said.

"What did he say?"

"That you were angry and that he would discuss it with you soon. I volunteered to talk to you."

"I displayed no anger," Elena said, gripping her stirring spoon tightly and pushing Bakunin gently away with her foot.

"You do not hide your feelings well, Elena," Anna said.

"I'm working on it. I've had less than a year on the job."

"Work harder," said Anna. "It's something about an old woman and a theft of valuable antiques."

"He gave me the case," Elena said, now turning, spoon in her fist, voice reasonably calm and low. She had a tendency to raise her voice when excited.

"And then?" asked Anna as she turned on the second light in the room.

"Then he took it from me—called the old woman in, intimidated her, threatened security guards, and allowed me to ask a few prepared questions."

"He found the antiques and caught the thieves, with your help," Anna said, moving to the stove where the teapot was beginning to whistle gently. She removed the pot before it made the screeching sound that sent the cat hiding under the bed in the other room.

"Yes." Elena turned down the heat and reached for another spice. Their collection was not great, but her need to keep her hands occupied was more important at that moment than the resulting flavor of the soup.

"Had he waited for you to investigate, what would have happened?" asked Anna. She was in the process of preparing three cups of tea.

"Happened? I would have eventually won the woman's full confidence. She would—"

"By the time you won her confidence, where would these valuable books and antiques have been?"

Elena shrugged and continued to destroy the soup.

"They would be dispersed among collectors and dealers. The state would have nothing, and you would still be trying to earn the old woman's confidence."

"Perhaps," said Elena.

"Porfiry Petrovich has a great deal of pressure on him from those above," said Anna. "It was he who would be held responsible if the crime was not solved quickly."

"He could have talked to me," Elena said, looking at the dark, simmering soup and wondering for an instant what kind it was. She remembered and took it off the burner.

When she turned, she saw that her aunt had set the table, put out the tea, and sliced thick pieces of bread. Baku was in the third chair.

"He talked to me. I am talking to you. Your job is to do what Porfiry Petrovich tells you to do," said Anna, pouring cups of tea for all three of them.

"And if I don't like it?" asked Elena grimly. She sat down in her chair.

"Many times our Porfiry Petrovich did not agree with an order I gave him," said Anna with a smile, setting a cup of tea on Bakunin's chair.

"But he did what he was told," Elena said wearily.

"No, he did what he wanted to do if he could get away with it," said Anna. "And though I was often extremely angry with him, his way usually worked. There is no single right way to approach any case, and the pressures from above are always frantic and in conflict with one another."

"So," Elena said, pouring soup. "I should ignore what my superior officer tells me? Less than a year on the job, the only woman in the department, and I should ignore my superior officer?"

"No," said Anna. She held a spoon suspended in the air as she looked down suspiciously at the dark brew in the bowl before her. "You should do what he tells you. You should learn from him. I'd say you are a year or two away from defying him. Remember, however, when you do decide to defy him, do it quietly and be sure you are right, at least most of the time."

"I'll lose my job," Elena said, tasting the soup. It wasn't too bad.

"I don't think so," said Anna.

"Aunt Anna," said Elena, reaching for a piece of bread, "if you were back as a procurator and someone asked you to describe me, what would you say in your report? Be honest."

Anna continued to eat, glancing down at the cat to be sure he had made a reasonable attack on the tea. As she spoke, she poured a bowl of soup for Baku and blew on it.

"Five feet five inches tall. Weight, around one hundred forty pounds. Figure full but well proportioned. Fairly large breasts, firm. Hair a light brown, cut short. Eyes a very dark brown. Complexion excellent, skin rosy. Nose straight. Perhaps a touch of the Oriental in her quite-pretty face."

"Thank you," Elena said.

"It is not flattery. It is accuracy. You want more accuracy?"

"Why not?"

"The soup is edible but not very good."

"It is the price we pay for living together," said Elena. "Baku likes it."

"Baku's charm," said Anna, looking approvingly at the cat, who leaned over his bowl, "is his unpredictability. One morning he leaps into my lap and naps. Another morning he lurks and turns from me."

Elena looked up at her aunt and paused, spoon halfway to her mouth. "What do you mean?"

"Mean? Just what I said," said Anna, not quite ready to reattack the soup, and then she understood. Anna was well experienced in picking up the unexpected hint of reaction from a suspect.

"Who?" she asked.

"Who?" Elena repeated, drinking rather quickly and reaching for another slice of bread.

"The man who seems interested one day, indifferent the next," said Anna. "The one who makes you ask me questions about how you look."

"No one," said Elena.

"No one," said Anna.

"It does not interfere with my work," Elena said.

"I didn't claim that it did," said Anna. "It may, however, have contributed to your anger at Porfiry Petrovich."

"So," said Elena, banging her spoon on the table, "because you think I am interested in his son, you think I can't do my job. Because I am a love-starved woman—"

"The men are worse," said Anna. "But they have learned to hide it better."

"Now you are a psychiatrist," said Elena sarcastically.

"I am a former deputy procurator, the highest rank a woman has yet achieved in the Russian procurator's office, and likely to be the only one since the system is being torn apart. That is better than being a psychiatrist."

"I'm tired," said Elena.

"Go to bed. I'll do the dishes."

"If you like, I'll play a game of chess first," said Elena, standing.

"A good game of chess requires desire, mind, and heart," said Anna, starting to rise. "I don't think you could give me any of these tonight."

Elena had begun sleeping in the tiny bedroom while Anna and Baku slept on the sofa. It had been Anna's preference. She rose frequently during the night and read or listened to the radio or both. Besides, for reasons that were clear only to those who had built this one-story concrete building around a concrete courtyard, the bathroom was located not in the bedroom but in a corner of the slightly larger living room. Anna's visits to the bathroom had increased during the year in which her brother's daughter had lived with her.

Anna returned to her chair.

"Don't forget the exercises," Elena called, retrieving a long nightshirt from the closet.

"I will do sit-ups, push-ups, and knee bends," said Anna. "When we have enough money, you can buy me weights. Within a year I'll be stronger than Porfiry Petrovich."

"Just the sit-ups," called Elena. "Not the jokes."

"Thank you for acknowledging my attempt at humor," said Anna.

Baku jumped into her lap and purred as Anna petted him gently.

It was mad, Elena thought as she prepared for bed even though she wasn't tired. She would try to find something to read, something to distract her. Iosef Rostnikov had not called her in two weeks—two weeks and one day. He had pursued her. She had resisted. They had made love twice, both times very good. Emotionally volatile. Perhaps he had gone back to Trina. Elena had met Trina. She was a slim, very young, dark beauty who worked with him at the theater. And Trina had been nice.

Did Porfiry Petrovich know? Elena couldn't help remembering what it had been like in bed with Iosef, who looked more like his mother than his father. Iosef was light, taller than either of his parents. She wanted his bare chest next to hers, his mouth open on hers. She wanted him to call. She decided to lie in bed listing his deficiencies, but the effort failed.

Was he still attracted to her at all? She had picked up hints of Iosef's behavior with women from the odd comments and sly smiles of the actors and other people he worked with at the theater. She had gone twice to watch him direct rehearsals at the little theater that used to be a small church.

Tomorrow, she thought, *tomorrow I will stop this foolishness. Tomorrow I will indicate to the young bull of a sergeant who heads the morning squad that protects Petrovka that I will go to dinner with him.* He seemed nice enough, reasonably smart, certainly strong, decent-looking, unmarried. She turned out the lights and hoped that if she were to see the sergeant out of uniform, he would not be too hairy.

In the other room Anna turned on the radio. Her hearing was excellent and the music was low, but Elena could hear it through the thin door. She rolled over, found her rubber earplugs in the night-table drawer, and put them in.

The Gray Wolfhound sat in his office in full uniform, back straight, hands resting before him on his perfectly polished desk. He looked to Rostnikov as if he were posing for a portrait.

"Chief Inspector," the Wolfhound said, "you are filthy."

"Major Gregorovich said there was no time for me to wash and change."

Major Gregorovich stood at Rostnikov's side thoroughly enjoying this encounter.

"Major," said the colonel, "you are dismissed. Please wait outside."

Gregorovich nodded and marched out. The Wolfhound looked at the handprint on the major's back and turned to Rostnikov when Gregorovich had gone.

"Why are you so filthy?"

"I have been plumbing," said Rostnikov. "It is a hobby of mine."

"Plumbing?"

"Plumbing."

Thoughts of the rattling sound in his pipes at home came to the colonel, who shook them off. He had both an impression to make on the chief inspector and a problem to be addressed. He spoke in his measured baritone. "Emil Karpo, with your approval, is pursuing a gang that is dealing in stolen nuclear materials, materials they plan to sell to a foreign government."

"There may be nothing to it," said Rostnikov.

"But there may," Colonel Snitkonoy countered. "And I should have been informed."

"I planned to do so as soon as we had some solid evidence that there actually was a theft of nuclear materials."

The colonel rose from his chair and leaned forward, hands on the table, knuckles up. "It is essential that I be informed," he said.

"You have been informed," said Rostnikov.

"Yes, but not by you. By a foreign government, by the Americans, by the FBI."

"Hamilton," said Rostnikov.

"It was Hamilton's superior who reported it to me," said the colonel. "Agent Hamilton is now in charge of this investigation. He will work closely with you and Karpo. He is an expert in such matters. That is why he is here. Porfiry Petrovich, we cannot afford to insult the Americans at this crucial time when our government needs their financial support and investigative expertise. Is this all clear?"

"Perfectly," said Rostnikov.

"Consider yourself reprimanded," said the colonel sternly.

"Am I on unpaid leave?"

Snitkonoy shook his head. His mane of perfectly groomed white hair vibrated with annoyance. "You know and I know that you are too valuable for me to give you time off. I ask you to be more mindful of the delicacy of my position."

"I will endeavor to do so," said Rostnikov.

Snitkonoy sat again and looked at his chief investigator. "I have a pipe somewhere in my house that is making a terrible noise when I turn on a tap," said the colonel. "Can you fix that?"

"Yes," said Rostnikov.

"Wash up, get some sleep, and be back on the job in the morning. We'll talk tomorrow of my noisy pipe. Go."

Rostnikov moved to the door as quickly as his leg would permit.

"And send in Pankov as you leave."

An instant after Rostnikov had departed, the tiny mass of quivering nerves named Pankov entered the office.

"Rostnikov has left a trail of dirt in here. See to it that it is cleaned up before morning. Supervise it yourself."

"Yes, Colonel," said Pankov, knowing that there was no way he could find a custodian who would clean the office. It was Pankov who would do it. "Anything else?"

"Tell Major Gregorovich that he may go and that I say he has done a good job."

"Yes," said Pankov.

When he was gone, the colonel moved to the window to look out at the chill night sky. He looked down at the single flowering bush in the garden. In the broad beam of a streetlight it seemed to have far fewer flowers today.

Chapter 10

Footsteps

It was moments before midnight. The street was empty. Somewhere above him in one of the rooms of a building, someone coughed. Sasha couldn't tell if it was a man or a woman. The cough sounded decidedly unhealthy.

A new wind had come with the night. Sasha's hands were plunged into the pockets of his jacket. He hoped the police widow had coffee. It would be difficult to stay awake through the entire night. He had failed to get any sleep at home. After Lydia's shower, he and Maya had talked softly together, listening until Lydia began to snore. Then they waited to see if Pulcharia would come out to complain about her grandmother's snoring. They waited twenty minutes. The girl did not come out of the bedroom.

And then, in the near darkness, a lone candle lit for the occasion, they had made love a second time, something they had not done since well before the baby was born. Sasha had been filled with passion, which surprised him. His day had been long and he had to get up in a little while. Yet he had felt powerful, and she had met him with lust.

They took a long time, and then Maya wanted to talk some more. He couldn't simply turn his back on her and sleep.

"I think we should hire someone," she had said.

"We can't afford it," Sasha reminded her, his head turned to her. Candlelight flickered on his wife's dark face, and her breasts peeked over the blanket.

"I don't know how much longer I can live with her," Maya said softly. "I don't know how much longer the children can live with her."

"I understand," he said. "We can't afford someone to watch the children. And she would never speak to us again if we made her leave and hired a woman to stay with the children."

"You could convince her," said Maya. "Tell her how she could get back to work, have some privacy and freedom. Make it sound like we were doing it for her."

"She wouldn't believe it," he said.

"I know," said Maya, chewing on her thumb and trying to think of some new approach to keep her sanity and get rid of Lydia.

The discussion had continued for almost an hour and concluded with Sasha agreeing to go over their budget during the day and see what he could do. By the time they had finished the discussion, Sasha had to get up, get dressed, and relieve Zelach. Before he had reached the front door, Maya was breathing the sound of sleep. She was amazing. She could fall asleep in an instant and be up at the slightest sound from one of the children. Sasha had trouble getting to sleep but heard nothing once he got there.

And now he slouched wearily down the dark street, his steps a bit uneven, lost in thought of how he could get more money. The only way he could do so with little effort was to accept the bribes he was sometimes offered. These were usually bribes from petty criminals. On occasion he had been tempted, and twice he had accepted "gifts" from grateful shopkeepers whose stolen goods he had recovered. He could probably make a great deal of money by selling his services as an informant to one of the Moscow mafias. He could

205

imagine seriously considering an illegal act if the lives of Maya or the children were at stake. After all, what had the state become? Where, as Gorky's *Mother* shouted at the court, is justice?

Sasha had a sense that he was only a few doors from the house where Zelach was sitting at the window. He glanced across the street, not expecting to see the three boys, not expecting to see anything.

He was certainly not expecting the sudden, solid pain in his head, a pain that dropped Sasha to his knees. Had he suffered a stroke? He was a young man. But his father had died of a stroke. Another blow came, and this time with it came the taste of blood and the sound of soft voices.

"Again, Boris, again."

Sasha raised his arm and felt the next blow crack against his elbow. A figure appeared before him, the vague shape of a boy looking directly at him, judging how much more it would take to kill this stubborn victim.

"Again, Boris," the boy before him said.

Now, as he rolled back on the sidewalk, he tried to curl into a ball and find his gun under all of his clothes. He could see three children, all boys, one with a plank of wood in his hands, the one who had been in front of him with his hands plunged into his pockets, and the third, the youngest, advancing with a brick in his hands.

Sasha struggled to shout, and perhaps he did. He tried to get back onto his knees, certain that the boys meant to kill him. He blinked his eyes to clear away the blood and got up on one elbow, still groping for his gun. Above him the young one raised the brick over his head and looked down at Sasha with no sign of emotion. Sasha was certain that he could not get the gun out in time. His other thought was of Maya, who would be doomed now to live with Lydia forever.

Sasha closed his eyes. There was a scuffle of feet. The blow did not come, or perhaps Sasha was too numb to feel it. There was a greater scuffling and the grunt of a man, followed by the pained, high, angry groan of a child.

Sasha opened his eyes. A man, Zelach, was kicking at the boy with the wooden plank. The young one who had hovered over Sasha with a brick was huddled against the wall, brick gone. He was holding his head. Zelach's kick was true. He caught the boy in the stomach. The boy dropped the plank and fell to his knees. The last boy, the one who had ordered Boris to hit Sasha, had begun to run across the small street, toward the apartment building the two policemen had been watching. Zelach looked down at Sasha, who had finally managed to pull out his weapon. Sasha nodded, and Zelach took off after the fleeing boy, who had a good start.

The next few seconds were miraculous. The usually slouching, recently ill Zelach caught the boy before he got through the door to the apartment building. He grabbed him by the neck and turned him back across the street, where the two other boys nursed their wounds and showed no inclination to run.

Methodically Zelach handcuffed the boy he had caught to the one who had hit Sasha with the plank. Then Zelach held out his hand to Sasha, who in confusion started to hand him his gun.

"No, Sasha," Zelach said softly. "Your handcuffs. I'll get them."

Zelach reached under Sasha's jacket and removed the fallen policeman's handcuffs. A moment later the three boys were handcuffed in a circle around a lamppost.

"Are you all right?" asked Zelach, kneeling in front of Sasha.

"I don't know," said Sasha, but he was reasonably certain that the words came out so softly that Zelach couldn't hear them.

Zelach touched his partner's arm and said, "I'll be back in an instant."

Sasha tried to nod and looked at the boys, small, angry-faced children around a dark maypole. The two older ones glared at Sasha with hatred, and the oldest one said, "Why didn't you say you were a cop?"

Sasha didn't answer. He fumbled to put his weapon back in its holster and thought he succeeded. He felt himself passing out.

"The widow is calling for an ambulance," Zelach called, coming back to Sasha, who nodded, eyes closed.

"He's dying," said the oldest boy.

By now faces were appearing at windows. People looked out of their dark little caves at the sight below them.

Zelach rose, stepped to the three boys, and hit the oldest one with the back of his hand directly in the face. The boy's nose began to bleed, and blood appeared in his mouth, covering his teeth. He looked like a pale-faced vampire, and worst of all he did not cry. He did not even look angry. He simply glared into the face of the policeman, who considered hitting him again but changed his mind. The first blows he had struck against the children had been to protect Sasha. This blow had been in anger. Zelach had no blows left in him, and at this point he was sure they would do no good.

"Stay awake, Sasha Tkach," Zelach said, moving quickly toward his fallen friend. "I think I already hear the sound of a police van. Stay awake."

Sasha tried.

He failed.

Karpo made what proved to be the mistake of stopping at his office. It should have been safe. It was well after midnight. The lights were out in the Office of Special Investigation, but before his finger finished flipping the switch, Karpo knew that he was not alone, that someone had been sitting in the darkness.

The man was seated in Karpo's cubicle, at Karpo's desk. It was Hamilton, the FBI agent. He looked dressed for the day, suit pressed, clean-shaven, the faint smell of aftershave lotion on his face.

Karpo stood in front of the man, who handed him a sealed envelope. Karpo opened the envelope and read the message, which was signed by both Chief Inspector Rostnikov and Colonel Snitkonoy. The message was brief. Karpo was ordered to surrender to the FBI agent all the information he had gathered on the gang called the Beasts and possible nuclear-weapons dealers. He was then to follow all of Hamilton's orders in pursuit of the investigation. In short, he was working for the American on the search for Mathilde's killers.

Hamilton pointed to the seat next to the desk.

"Are you ordering me to sit?"

"No," said Hamilton. "Inviting you."

"I decline the invitation."

Hamilton nodded his head in acceptance, took a small tape recorder from his pocket, and said, "I understand you had a relationship with the woman who was murdered."

Karpo did not respond. He had not been asked a question and felt no willingness to cooperate, though he would do what Rostnikov ordered.

"I talked to the man whose thumbs you broke," said Hamilton. "I assume it was he who broke your finger."

Karpo said nothing.

"If he ever gets out of prison, he'll be coming after you."

Karpo didn't think the man would come out of prison alive, but still he said nothing.

"Assuming you do find some individual or individuals you think are responsible, what do you plan to do? Break their thumbs?"

"No," said Karpo, at near attention. "I plan to execute them."

Hamilton shook his head and said, "No. You will not execute them."

Karpo said nothing.

"You will not execute them," Hamilton repeated. "That is an order."

Karpo did not respond. He had little imagination, but he was suddenly aware of the fact that a Russian police officer was under the direct command of an American FBI agent, who was no longer the enemy but rather was now his superior.

Hamilton pushed a button on the tape recorder and said, "Tell me everything you know about this case."

It had been a bad day and was about to be a far worse night for Artiom Solovyov. A few weeks ago he had been an automobile mechanic with a small but successful business. He had, with Boris, his one assistant, catered to the newly rich, mostly the Chechen mafia and their associates, who referred him to others. Business was growing, and one of his customers, who looked something like an American Indian, told him that if Artiom ever needed particular auto parts, he could help him.

Artiom worked every day. He liked cars. Cars seemed to like him. At night he would go home, get out of his greasy overalls, shower, and change. Artiom liked to go out. He had a few favorite bars, knew a few women. Sometimes he just liked to stay home in his robe, feet bare, watching television. He had been a happy, slightly heavy, dark man with a weary, handsome face and a perpetual and not entirely assumed look of stupidity, the result of heredity principally but not exclusively. It was that very appearance of open, dark good looks and stupidity that made his customers trust him.

From time to time a female customer would catch his eye, give him a smile. Nothing had ever come of it. Nothing was meant to. And then *she* happened, Anna Porvinovich. He was completely unprepared.

He was taking a shower after work, singing an American song about purple skies, when he heard a loud knock at the door. He turned off the shower, threw on his robe, and stamped the water off his large feet onto the carpeted floor as he walked. He had checked his peephole first and could tell only that it was a woman. He opened the door and stepped back, trying to comb back his hair with his fingers.

"Mrs. Porvinovich," he said as she moved past him into the room.

She had been dressed, he remembered, in a red and white, very tight dress, and her mouth matched the red in the dress. She smelled like vanilla and something he did not recognize. She pushed the door closed behind her, surveyed the mess of a room, and turned to him. Standing only a few feet in front of him, she seemed a bit older than she had appeared earlier, when she'd stood a car-length away. In fact, Artiom was sure, she was almost certainly older than he, which instead of calming him, gave him an immediate erection.

She looked at the bump in his robe, smiled, and reached down to touch it. He stepped back and she followed.

"I see the way you look at me," she said.

Artiom said nothing.

"And you," she continued, "see the way I look at you."

"How did you find me?" he asked.

She shook her head as if he were a foolish little boy. Then she unzipped her dress and kicked off her shoes. She was magnificent. She removed her bra and panties and stepped forward to unwrap his robe.

She tasted of heat, vanilla, and smoke. They made love on the floor by the front door, and when they were through, she coaxed him back to life with her mouth and they did it again. She smiled and made soft cooing sounds during what turned out to be less than half an hour. And then she rose and began to dress. He got to his feet, vertiginous as a result of what had happened. She put on her shoes and kissed him, tickling his tongue with hers. Then she was gone.

Artiom picked up his robe, then looked at the door and around the room, wondering if he had imagined the miracle. Artiom was not a man of great imagination, and he took no drugs that could account for such a vivid vision. He still smelled her in the room and on his body. He did not even consider getting back into the shower.

A few days later she had appeared with her car at the garage. She had a noise, a loose muffler. She was dressed in stylish black, complete with a small hat. She smoked a long cigarette while he worked on the car and gave no hint of her visit to his apartment. When he finished, she thanked him, shook his hand, and paid in cash. That day she did not smell of vanilla but of something distant and bittersweet.

She reappeared at his apartment that very night. This time they made love on his bed, which, he reminded himself, badly needed clean sheets. She did not seem to mind the sheets. This time when they finished, she smoked her long cigarettes and they talked. Or rather she talked—about her life, her husband, his wealth, and her attraction to Artiom, who was strong and uncomplicated.

She could not tell him when she would next appear, so he had taken to staying home with his television and his bare feet. He had hired a woman to come in and straighten his room and clean his linens. He sat waiting. Four days passed before Anna Porvinovich reappeared, looking sad and running into his arms, pressing into him passionately.

Less than two weeks after she had first come to him, Artiom agreed to kidnap and murder her husband. She made suggestions about time and place, where they might take him, how to handle it, and though he had been more than a bit reluctant when she brought up the idea of kidnap and murder, she had been very convincing.

He easily obtained the weapons from one of his mafia customers, recruited his assistant, Boris, with promises of money, and imagined a life of wealth and leisure with Anna.

The kidnapping went reasonably well, and the plan seemed to be fine. But it had all quickly become very complicated when Porvinovich comprehended what had happened and who was responsible. Accepting Porvinovich's offer was out of the question. He had done this for Anna. But that was of small concern now that the police seemed to know what he had done. His simple visions were now of dark cells and sodomy and of weeping in the night. He hoped that he was not tried and executed for what he had done. Worse yet, Artiom had heard stories about how the police simply executed criminals in the street and put a cheap gun in the victim's hand to make it look as if he had resisted arrest.

All of this was on Artiom's mind as he put his key in the door of the apartment and wondered if there was anything he could take for his headache.

Something seemed wrong. Artiom closed the door. The light was on. Porvinovich sat in a chair across the room, half turned from the door. He did not acknowledge Artiom's arrival. Artiom looked at Boris, who was seated in his chair across the room. His mask had been removed, and he looked up at Artiom with a plea in his eyes.

For an instant Artiom stood before the door looking from man to man. Then he realized that his assistant did not have the weapon in his hands, on his lap, or on the floor beside him. He also realized that Boris's hands were behind his back.

Artiom froze. Boris let out a tiny sob. Porvinovich rose from his chair, the automatic weapon in his hands. He was smiling.

"You're late," Porvinovich said, his words slurred by his shattered, swollen face.

"Things…the police know…I came to release you."

Porvinovich smiled again.

"I'll ask you a question. You answer truthfully and briefly."

Artiom wet himself. He nodded.

"It was my wife's idea, wasn't it?"

"Yes," said Artiom. "All her idea."

"She made love to you a few times and you agreed to murder her husband," said Porvinovich.

The man bound on the chair sobbed a little louder.

"To kidnap you," said Artiom. "Not to murd—"

He was cut short by a sharp sound from the weapon in Porvinovich's hands. Artiom closed his eyes and then opened them, fairly certain that he had not been shot. He looked at Porvinovich, who nodded toward Boris, who was slumped forward, held up only by the cord that tied his hands behind him to the back of the chair. There was blood dripping from a wound in the man's chest and even more blood coming from the bent-over head of the man, who was surely dead.

"You killed him," said Artiom.

"You lied."

"I…"

"You were going to kill me. She told you to."

"Yes," said Artiom, unable to take his eyes from the bleeding dead man. "I've never killed anyone. She—"

"I believe you," said Porvinovich.

Artiom did not feel relieved.

"The neighbors," Artiom said desperately. "Some of them must have heard the shots."

"Two shots. A car backfiring. Light bulbs falling," said Porvinovich. "They will mind their own business. I assume she picked this place."

"Yes," said Artiom.

"Then it is unlikely that any neighbors here would report what may have been two gunshots. You agree?"

"I agree," said Artiom. "May I sit? I don't feel…"

Porvinovich pointed the barrel of his weapon at the chair he had stood up from. Artiom, wet and sick to his stomach, made his way to the chair and sat. Porvinovich stepped back half a dozen feet.

"Have you ever met my brother?" asked Porvinovich.

"No," said Artiom, gripping the sides of the chair to keep his hands from shaking.

"I've had all day to think about this, Solovyov," said Porvinovich. "All day. I am a smart man cursed with a scheming wife who cares as little for me as she does for you. I'm sure she cares even less about Yevgeniy."

"Yev—?"

"My brother, whom, I am now certain, she has helped nurse back from impotence. Without Yevgeniy, who is not smart—don't ask me why some genes pass to one child and not to another—she cannot handle the business. It is my belief that without me he cannot handle it either. If you had a reasonable amount of intellect, you would understand that you are not part of her future plans. My guess is that she has already arranged for your death within a very short time. And that she realizes she will have to do it herself. Yevgeniy is incapable of either complex thought or direct action."

Porvinovich paused. Artiom nodded.

"Do you want to know what happens next, Artiom Solovyov?"

Artiom wasn't sure that he did. He resisted the sudden, compelling urge to turn his head and look at his dead assistant.

"I'll tell you," said Porvinovich, leaning back against the wall. "I'm afraid the events of the day have made me temporarily insane, especially when I discovered that you had murdered my wife and brother."

"Your wife and…?"

"You just came in and told me that you had murdered my wife and brother," Porvinovich said. "I was enraged. I rushed at you, took you by surprise. You fired, killing your assistant. I wrenched the gun from you and you started toward me. I shot you."

"But your wife is not dead," said Artiom, looking into the purple face of madness.

"No," said Porvinovich, "but she soon will be."

This time there was a burst of fire from the weapon, not just two shots. Artiom's initial reaction was surprise and then relief that he had not been shot. Suddenly the pain came. In his stomach. He looked down. Three, maybe four holes bleeding as one.

"I'm dying?" Artiom asked.

"I certainly hope so," said Porvinovich, who fired once again.

This time Artiom felt nothing.

Elvira Chazova arrived just before the police ambulance. A neighbor, with what appeared to be sympathy, but was certainly satisfaction, had knocked at her door and told her that her boys were being arrested in the street right outside.

Elvira had grabbed the baby and run past the neighbor. From across the street she saw a man lying on the ground and another man kneeling next to him. The nosy widow from the first floor across the street stood in her doorway watching. Other eyes looked down from darkened rooms.

Her sons were in a circle, handcuffed around a lamppost.

"My babies," she screamed.

The slouching man on his knees rose and stepped toward her. Two men leaped from the ambulance and hurried to the fallen man.

Just before she reached her sons, Zelach stepped in front of her.

"They are bleeding," she moaned. "Look at them. Babies. You have beaten my babies."

The three boys looked at their mother, ashamed to have been caught. It was the baby in the woman's arms who began to cry.

"I must take care of my babies," she insisted.

"They are under arrest," Zelach said.

"My little ones?"

"Attempting to rob and murder a police officer," Zelach said.

"They wouldn't attack a police officer. They wouldn't hurt anyone," she said. "Won't someone help us?"

The baby cried. Sasha Tkach was put on a stretcher and carried to the ambulance. As the stretcher moved past the three handcuffed boys, they looked at the barely conscious policeman with vague curiosity.

At that moment a police car, one of the "new" BMWs, which already had over two hundred thousand kilometers on it, pulled up to the curb, lights flashing. Two young policemen got out of the car.

"Help me," Elvira Chazova cried, showing her screaming baby to the two officers, who registered no particular emotion.

"Those three," said Zelach as he handed the handcuff keys to the first officer to reach him. "Beating and attempted murder of a police officer. Don't let them run."

The officer nodded. The mother reached out an arm to stop him.

"My babies would never do such a thing. It was someone else. Wasn't it?"

"Someone else," said Alexei Chazov. "We were just coming home. We saw the man on the ground. We went to help him. Then this guy came out and started to beat us."

"That's right," said Boris and Mark.

The young policeman had unhandcuffed the Chazov boys and was leading them to the waiting car.

Elvira started toward the police car. Zelach stepped into her path.

"What will happen to my poor children?" she cried. "What will happen to me? There is no money."

"What will happen to my partner?" said Zelach.

The police car's doors closed. Zelach turned his back on the woman and motioned to the officer, who was driving the car. Zelach climbed into the backseat, muscling the boys over to give himself room. There was enough room for all of them. The brothers were small.

"Drop me at the hospital," Zelach said. "Then take these three to your lockup. I'll come by later to write a report."

The car started. The officer in the front seat who was not driving made a note on the pad snapped to his clipboard. Elvira Chazova appeared at the window of the police car and screamed over the sound of her infant, "Where are you taking my babies? Tell me. I have a right to know. This is a democracy now."

"This is a lunatic asylum now," the young policeman in the passenger seat said.

The police car pulled into the street. Elvira looked around. The widow had gone back inside. No faces were at the windows. No one came out and no one called down to her.

She stopped screaming and patted the baby gently on the head as she moved to the sidewalk across from her apartment building. The street lamps were not bright, but she could see the blood of the policeman on the stone wall and the concrete sidewalk. There was quite a bit of blood.

Elvira shook her head. The baby was crying much more quietly now. She had picked up the almost naked child and run with her into the cold night. Elvira moved back across the street whispering to the child to be quiet. She would put the baby to bed and then sleep for a few hours. The coming days and nights would be a hell for her. She needed her rest, if only a few hours.

This was a new world, she thought. There was always hope.

Yevgeniy Porvinovich lay on his brother's bed while his brother's wife went through the ritual of massaging and petting him to climax even though he was not capable of erection. Yevgeniy was especially unresponsive. Anna rubbed her bare breasts against his legs, moving upward, barely tickling. Yevgeniy, who had pronounced himself unable even to consider sex, groaned.

Anna Porvinovich was especially patient. It was

a small enough price to pay, and it was something she could stop doing completely when she was a grieving widow. Yevgeniy's principal interest in the plot to kill his brother was the business. He had a reasonable grasp of that business and, propped up by Anna, he was confident that he could handle it. Maybe he wouldn't be quite as successful as Alexei, but everything was already going, the deals were already in place with both the police and the mafia. There wouldn't be that much to do.

"You like that?" she asked in the darkness.

"Yes," he said.

Her breasts were hanging between his open legs now, and she felt a distinct firmness beginning in her brother-in-law.

"The police know," he said.

"They don't," she whispered. "Shhh."

"They know," he insisted, sitting up.

She sighed, turned on the lamp that was on the table next to the bed, and reached for her cigarettes. She patted his shoulder. Yevgeniy was terrible in the dark. In the light he was much worse. Now that he was beginning to whine, she began to alter her plans slightly. Yevgeniy would have to die. Perhaps an accident. Perhaps suicide because he could not consider living without his dear only brother. It would have to be soon. She couldn't tolerate him much longer.

She lit her cigarette with the gold lighter and looked at Yevgeniy, who looked quite frightened.

"It will be fine," she reassured him, but her thoughts were elsewhere.

She needed a man to run the business or to appear to do so. After a decent interval following the death of her husband and Yevgeniy, she would pick out a worthy successor, a younger successor, a younger, good-looking, not particularly bright successor, such as Artiom, who would be long dead by then. It would be preferable if the successor was married, so that she would not have to spend too much time with him playing games. She was growing tired of playing games.

"Sleep, Yevgeniy," she said, gently easing him back. "You'll feel better. I'll be right at your side."

He lay back and closed his eyes. To Anna he looked dead. She assumed that her husband was already dead. Her choice of men had been most unfortunate. Artiom Solovyov had proved less determined and capable than she had expected. He had certainly killed Alexei by now. She hoped that he was not fool enough to call her again.

She rose from her bed, put the cigarette between her teeth, slipped into her art deco green silk robe, and turned off the light. There was a bed in the next room. She would sleep there, with a door between her and Yevgeniy's inevitable snoring.

Chapter 11

Weary Men

Rostnikov had taken a cold shower well after midnight. It was not cold by choice. First he had undressed and dropped his clothes on a chair, being careful not to wake the girls. The water was no more than a halfhearted trickle, but Rostnikov was accustomed to that and to the hard, abrasive Chinese soap that did wonders for getting rid of grease, rust, and dirt but did nothing for the condition of one's skin.

Naked, leg aching, and not in one of his better moods after being dressed down by Colonel Snitkonoy, Porfiry Petrovich had crept as quietly as he could through the darkness and into bed. The blanket was cool, almost cold, the way he liked it. Sarah turned and asked dreamily, "What time is it?"

Rostnikov turned his head to look at the illuminated dial of the bedside clock and answered, "Nearly two."

"What did he want?" she asked, just barely awake. She moved into his arms.

"To tell me I had been a bad child, that I had kept secrets from my superior."

"Did you?" she asked.

"Keep secrets? Frequently. Gregorovich is an open microphone to Klamkin in the Ministry of the Interior. And who knows what our Wolfhound tells those to whom he must report and retain the illusion of comradeship?"

"The girls were afraid you were being taken away like their grandmother," Sarah said.

"I'll talk to them. I'll tell them I'm the police, the plumbing policeman, that no one takes me away, that I take people away, that...I must get some sleep."

"I was waiting for you," she said.

"I knew you would be," he said, hugging her to him. Her hair brushed his face. It had grown completely back since the surgery, which had almost taken her life and her wits.

"Tomorrow night," he said, gently rubbing her back in the darkness. "Tomorrow night we will make love. Disappointed?"

"Tomorrow night," she said, kissing his cheek. "You shaved."

"In the shower."

"Tomorrow night you may be more tired," she said, running a hand over his chest. "And why waste a perfectly good shave and a freshly scrubbed body?"

It had been months since Sarah had initiated any sexual contact—months of recovery. Twice over the past few weeks Rostnikov had touched her in the ways she knew meant that he wanted her. She had responded lovingly. But this was the first time she had initiated it. He could not refuse.

When he looked up at the clock later, it was nearly three. Then he slept until the phone woke him slightly after five. It was still dark. Rostnikov sat up and grabbed the receiver before the second ring. He listened, whispered, "Yes," and hung up. Ten minutes later he was dressed, his hair combed. The hardest part about dressing was getting a sock and shoe onto his left foot. Bending the deformed leg was agony. Usually Sarah did it for him, but during her long illness he had grown accustomed to the pain. By the dim bulb of a night-light near the bed the two girls shared, he found a jar of cold coffee and half of a large loaf of bread. He drank the coffee directly from the jar, finishing it. He ate some of the bread as he wrote a note to Sarah.

"You are back," came the voice of a little girl from the bed.

"Shhh," whispered Rostnikov. "Your sister is asleep."

"Did they take you where they took my grand-mother?"

"No," he whispered. "My colonel had an urgent plumbing problem. He needed the plumbing policeman."

The girl giggled.

"Go back to sleep," he whispered, moving toward the door, a large piece of bread in his hand. "There is school to attend, and I will be needing my plumber's apprentice to be well rested for emergencies."

She giggled again and put her head on the pillow.

There was a car waiting at the curb for Rostnikov. It was a small white Lada. The driver was a woman in full uniform and cap. Rostnikov climbed into the backseat and closed the door. The car pulled away into the gentle hint of sunrise.

"Have you eaten?" asked Rostnikov.

"Yes, Chief Inspector," she said. "I am on the night shift."

Rostnikov nodded and sat back to finish his bread, tearing off little pieces to make it last longer. He had drunk the cold coffee too quickly. Each bump in the street—there were many small and not-so-small holes—upset his stomach.

With the small amount of traffic so early in the morning, they reached the hospital in ten minutes.

"You may go," Rostnikov said, getting out of the car with the usual difficulty.

"I am on duty till nine," the driver said. "I have been assigned to you directly by order of Colonel Snitkonoy."

"Then," said Rostnikov, "I shall be down shortly."

He made his way to the desk. He knew several of the day- and night-shift people at the hospital. He had many occasions to come here, but the man on the desk this morning looked up without recognition. Rostnikov took out his identification card and said, "Tkach, what room?"

The man in white behind the desk looked up the room number. Rostnikov thanked him and moved down the hall to the elevator. There was a sign on it that read OUT OF ORDER.

Rostnikov sighed, found a stairway, and made his way painfully to the third floor. A nurse at the station at the end of the corridor looked up as he hobbled toward her. As softly as possible, to keep from waking the sleeping patients, he said, "Tkach."

She was very young, very thin, and very plain, with big glasses and a uniform at least a size too large. She gave him the room number and suggested he not stay long.

He smiled at her, found Tkach's room, and went

in. It was a double room, a luxury in a Moscow hospital. Even Sarah, when they were not sure if she would survive her tumor, had been in a room with three other women, one of whom moaned throughout the night.

Standing next to the first bed, the dawn now truly coming through the window, stood Colonel Snitkonoy, nearly at attention, his hands clasped behind his back. He looked impeccably clean, well pressed, and not the least bit tired, though he couldn't have gotten to bed much before Rostnikov.

"Colonel," Rostnikov said, softly moving to the opposite side of the bed and looking down at the sleeping Tkach. Sasha's head was covered with a turbanlike white bandage that showed a large red blotch of blood.

"Chief Inspector," said the Wolfhound quietly. "He has suffered a severe concussion and a thin crack in his skull. No blood appears to have leaked through the crack and there is no apparent brain damage. He has a jagged cut on his back that required forty-two stitches. The doctor, whom I know, assures me that he should be up and in pain within a day or two. He will probably be quite dizzy."

"What happened?" asked Rostnikov.

"The boys he was attempting to find found him. Officer Zelach apparently saved Inspector Tkach's life and apprehended the boys. In better days I would recommend Zelach for a medal. Now..." The Wolfhound looked down at the medals on his uniform. "I will give him a certificate of merit, framed and enclosed in glass."

"He will appreciate that," said Rostnikov. "Does Tkach's family know? His wife and mother?"

The colonel looked at his watch.

"When I was told that he would survive, I thought they should have a peaceful night of sleep. I will go to his home now and inform them," said the colonel, touching a stray hair just behind his left ear. "I will also inform them that you have already been here."

Although he was wearing his boots, the colonel managed to walk lightly and quietly out the door.

"Is he gone?" whispered Tkach, eyes still closed.

"Yes," Rostnikov answered.

"Good," Tkach said, opening his eyes.

He looked in the general direction of Rostnikov, found him, tried to turn his head, felt a swift pain, and closed his eyes again. "I didn't know what to say to him," said Tkach. "I couldn't carry on a conversation."

"That is understandable," said Rostnikov.

Tkach's arms were lying at his sides over the thin orange blanket that covered him. One hand moved toward his head. There was pain in Tkach's face. Rostnikov intercepted the hand and put it back at his side.

"My head," said Tkach.

"I'll ask a doctor to give you something for the pain," said Rostnikov, realizing that he was still holding the young man's hand.

"That would be welcome," said Tkach, eyes still closed. "Zelach just left. He saved my life."

"The colonel just told me."

Tkach tried to shake his head but found it impossibly painful, so he simply slumped back and licked his lips. "I think I should sleep now," he said. "I had little sleep last night."

"I'll be back later," said Rostnikov.

"No need," said Tkach dreamily.

"I'll be back," said Rostnikov, and then he left.

At the desk in the corridor he told the plain-looking nurse with the glasses that Tkach needed something for his pain. She said she would find a doctor.

It was dawn when Rostnikov hit the street. It was definitely cold, not as cold as it would be in a month, but it was certainly *Nahyahbr,* November, and cold enough for snow. This was Rostnikov's weather. His leg hurt less in the cold; it often went quite pleasingly numb for brief stretches in the winter.

He got in the car and checked his watch. It was a little after six, a very unreasonable hour for a social call. He gave the driver the address of the Porvinovich apartment building and leaned back to get a few minutes of rest as she pulled into the early-morning traffic.

Emil Karpo recognized the building on Vozdvishenka, the Street of the Exaltation of the Cross, which, along with the Noviy Arbat, New

Arbat, was still called by most Muscovites Kalinin Prospekt, in honor of Mikhail Kalinin, one of the few old Bolsheviks to survive the purges of Stalin and die an honored old man in 1946. The apartment building, a one-block walk from the Praga Restaurant, dated back to the turn of the century and therefore was much sturdier and well built than the skyscrapers that had come after the war against the Nazis. It had originally, though briefly, housed large apartments for those in the czar's ministries. Then, until recently, it had housed members of the president's cabinet and high-ranking members of the politburo, along with a sprinkling of bankers. Now it housed the newly rich and influential, men such as Igor Kuzen.

Hamilton had admired the building as they walked toward it from the FBI agent's dark Ford, which was parked quite illegally with the flap down, indicating that he was there on police business.

It was a few minutes after six in the morning.

There was a man on guard at the locked door. He was dressed in a dark suit and tie, and his battered face looked formidable. Karpo showed his identification card. Hamilton took out his FBI photo ID. The man with the battered face reluctantly opened the door.

"Igor Kuzen," said Hamilton.

The man was not accustomed to black men, particularly those who showed cards and acted with such confidence. The policeman with him was as chilling a pale specimen of humanity as he had ever seen, and he had seen a great many in his life.

"He is probably not yet up," the man said. "He seldom rises before eight or nine."

"Unfortunately," said Hamilton, "we will have to disturb his routine. His room number?"

The man with the battered face was confused. He looked back into the lobby, from which a large man emerged. The large man wore black pants and shoes and a white long-sleeved turtleneck shirt under his jacket. He was completely bald.

"Is there a problem, Georgi?" the man in the turtleneck asked.

He was big, very big, and Karpo could see that the backs of both his hands were tattooed.

"These men want to see Mr. Kuzen," the battered man said. "They are from the police."

This information did not appear to impress the big man.

"You will have to come back later," the man said. "Mr. Kuzen is not up yet. Give me your names and numbers and I will ask him to call you when he gets up."

"We would like to see him now," Hamilton said.

"Out of the question," said the big man, now standing directly in front of Hamilton.

"I'll have to ask you to step out of our way or be arrested for obstructing a criminal investigation," said Hamilton, meeting the man's eyes.

The big man smiled.

Hamilton's left leg shot out and came back behind the left knee of the big man, who started to crumple to the ground as he reached under his jacket. Hamilton's right hand brought the reaching hand backward, fingers almost touching the man's wrist. With his other hand Hamilton reached under the now-kneeling man's jacket and came up with a pistol, which he handed to Karpo, who stood watching without emotion.

"What room is Mr. Kuzen in?" Hamilton asked, releasing the fallen man's hand and straightening his tie.

The man with the battered face looked at the kneeling man, who gave him no help. The kneeling man was nursing a very sore knee and a very numb right hand.

"Sixty-three," said the battered man.

The big man in the white turtleneck with no gun tried to stand, but his left leg wouldn't cooperate.

"Impressive," said Karpo as the two men went to the open elevator, and the man with the battered face went to help the fallen giant.

"Thank you," said Hamilton, not knowing whether Karpo was capable of sarcasm. "What would you have done?"

"Sudden, quick palm to the bridge of his nose," Karpo said, getting on the elevator.

"You might have driven the broken bone into his brain," said Hamilton.

"It would be a possibility," Karpo agreed as the elevator doors closed.

The door to room 63 was opening just as they arrived. The man with the battered face had undoubtedly alerted Kuzen to the arrival of the unwanted visitors.

"It's early," said the drowsy man, standing in the doorway.

He was around fifty, a small man with a bit of a belly and thinning gray hair, which looked a bit morning-wild. He wore thick glasses and green pajamas, which were probably silk. He stepped back from the open door and invited the two men in.

"Georgi tells me you've hurt Karono," he said, closing the door.

Neither Hamilton nor Karpo said anything.

They were in a reception room with white walls and gold baseboards along the floor. A painting stood over an antique telephone table.

"This way," the man said, scratching his head and moving down the corridor to a room on his right. "You want coffee? Tea? Something to eat?"

"No," said Hamilton.

They followed the man into a huge room with a broad window looking out toward the city. The sun had risen over the roofs of the clearly visible towers of Saint Basil's.

The room was furnished with delicate, turn-of-the-century furniture that looked quite authentic to Karpo.

"I started coffee when Georgi's call woke me," the man said. "I need a cup to wake up."

"You are Igor Kuzen?" Hamilton asked.

"I am," he said. "And I'm much more impressive when I'm fully dressed. Have a seat. Excuse me for one moment only."

The two men continued to stand.

"Why do you do what you do?" Karpo asked, looking around at the furniture.

"Why do I...? To feed my family. Because I believe in preserving and protecting my government," said Hamilton.

"Capitalism?" Karpo asked, examining a cushioned chair with delicately carved ebony legs.

"Capitalism," Hamilton agreed. "Democracy."

"Capitalism and democracy seem to be destroying my country," said Karpo. "This chair is of museum quality."

"Why do you do this?" Hamilton asked.

"Because I believed in Communism," Karpo said. "I still believe in Communism. It was the weak, stupid, corrupt leaders who only gave lip service to our system who eventually destroyed the Soviet Union and betrayed Communism."

Karpo kept examining the furniture, knowing that he was conversing with the FBI agent primarily to help contain the urge he had to begin destroying everything in the room.

"So you work in the hope that Communism will return," said Hamilton, watching him.

"No," said Karpo. "If it returns, it will be the same or worse. It is too late. I continue my work because I know nothing else to do and I do it well. The sense of satisfaction has diminished, whereas crime has increased. I've become a garbage man cleaning polluted litter that never stops falling and may destroy me."

Since he did not know Karpo, Hamilton was not as amazed as his colleagues at the Department of Special Affairs would have been at Karpo's openness. Karpo found it easier today to talk to a stranger who was very much like him in many ways.

"And the woman?" asked Hamilton. "Mathilde Verson?"

Karpo turned to look at the FBI agent and this time said nothing. The question was not a welcome one. The tension was broken by the return of Igor Kuzen with a cup of coffee on a saucer. Both cup and saucer were patterned with flowers and looked very delicate. Kuzen had also taken the time to brush his hair and put on a robe that exactly matched his pajamas. He sat in one of the more erect pieces of antique furniture and began to drink his coffee.

"You don't want to sit?" he asked.

"No," said Hamilton.

"As you wish," said Kuzen.

"Aren't you curious about why we have come?" asked Hamilton.

"Yes," said Kuzen. "But I assume you will soon tell me. I saw you admiring the furniture."

"And the view," said Hamilton.

Kuzen smiled and took another sip of coffee.

"You are a scientist."

"Correct," said Kuzen.

"By appearances a wealthy scientist," said Hamilton.

"I am comfortable," admitted Kuzen, looking at Karpo, who definitely made him uneasy.

"You worked in a government office, at government wages," Hamilton said. "Fifty dollars a month, maybe a bit more."

"A bit more," Kuzen said. "I'm a good physicist."

"You worked in nuclear research," said Hamilton.

"Dismantling nuclear arms and disposal of nuclear waste," said Kuzen. "Beyond that, as your colleague will tell you, I am unable to comment."

"You quit," said Hamilton.

"To work in private industry," said Kuzen, finishing his coffee and setting cup and saucer on an ornate metal trivet on the table in front of him.

"Private industry seems to have recognized your expertise," Hamilton said, looking around the room.

"Capitalism has been good for me," Kuzen said, folding his hands.

"What company do you work for?" Hamilton said. "We couldn't find it in your files."

"I am a consultant to many companies," Kuzen said. "Both foreign and domestic."

"Do you know a Mikhail Sivak?" asked Karpo.

"I've met him," Kuzen said. "Hired him and some of his associates to transport goods for a company I do some work for."

"Do you know that Sivak is dead?" asked Hamilton.

"I was informed," said Kuzen, growing increasingly nervous at the hovering presence of the gaunt policeman in black.

"A shoot-out," said Karpo. "Rival gangs. A woman died in the cross fire."

"I'm sorry to hear that," said Kuzen, adjusting his glasses.

"Sivak was a member of a mafia," said Hamilton. "An organized gang composed mostly of former convicts, the Beasts, many of whom had served sentences at Correctional Labor Colony Nineteen."

"And?" Kuzen asked, looking at Hamilton.

"And members of this mafia can be identified by a prison tattoo, an eagle clutching a nuclear warhead," said Hamilton.

"I never noticed such a tattoo on Sivak or any of his friends," said Kuzen.

The two men had slowly inched forward and were looking almost directly down at Kuzen.

"The tattoos are generally in places that are not visible if the man is clothed," said Hamilton.

"Interesting," said Kuzen.

"Several years ago an attempt was made to smuggle nuclear material into Germany," said Hamilton. "Is that also interesting?"

"Yes," said Kuzen.

"You had heard about this attempt?" asked Hamilton.

Kuzen was definitely sweating now and was unwilling to wipe his forehead for two reasons. First, the policemen would see. Second, he might stain his silk robe or pajamas.

"Something. Vaguely," said Kuzen, "when I worked for the government."

"How secure are nuclear weapons in Russia?" asked Hamilton. "Your best guess."

"Not terribly secure," said Kuzen.

"Weapons depositories are guarded by a few untrained soldiers and a barbed-wire fence," said Hamilton.

"I know nothing about that," said Kuzen, looking up from man to man, sitting back as far as he could.

"How much of a problem would it be to steal fissionable material, perhaps even short-range warheads?"

"I couldn't begin to speculate," said Kuzen.

"The mafia for which you are working," said Karpo, "is already, with your help, in possession of nuclear material and planning the massive theft of nuclear weapons. These are to be shipped out of Russia with the help of Italian criminals and sold to North Korea, Iran, and China."

"Me?" Kuzen said, pointing to himself.

"You," said Hamilton. He wondered where Karpo had gotten his evidently accurate information.

"The woman who died in the cross fire between the two gangs was a particular friend of Inspector Karpo's," Hamilton said.

Kuzen looked up at the blank white face. The men standing before him looked like chess pieces—one black, one white, avenging knights who might strike at odd angles.

"Inspector Karpo has already visited with a member of the gang we are discussing with you," said Hamilton. "He has visited a prisoner named Voshenko. Do you know Voshenko?"

"Voshenko? Voshenko," Kuzen said, finding it impossible to control the trembling in his voice. "The name is—"

"Very big man," said Hamilton. "Bigger than the man downstairs whose knee I accidentally dislocated."

"Big man. Voshenko. Yes. Maybe," said Kuzen.

"Inspector Karpo broke both of his thumbs," said Hamilton. "It was an accident too. Accidents can happen to anyone. For example, I could walk in the other room, find myself a cup, and pour myself coffee. I might hear the crash of breaking glass, and when I returned to this room, I might find the window broken and you missing. Do you have a family, Igor Kuzen?" asked Hamilton.

"Wife, two daughters," he said, his voice breaking. "They...we live in a dacha outside of town."

"Business success forces you to live in this apartment most of the time?" said Hamilton.

"Yes," said Kuzen. "Listen, please, I know nothing of this gang business, or killings, or any theft of nuclear materials. I've done a few things that may not be strictly legal. Who really knows what is legal and what is not anymore? But killings, nuclear weapons. *Nyet*."

"I need a cup of coffee," Hamilton said.

Kuzen looked at the FBI agent in panic and reached for his sleeve. "No, please."

"I'm just going to get a cup of coffee," said Hamilton calmly, a smile on his face.

"They have no warheads, no weapons, yet," said Kuzen.

"Nuclear material?" asked Hamilton.

Kuzen shrugged.

"We have carefully examined your background, Kuzen," Hamilton said. "It is our conclusion that you do not have the requisite skills to assemble a functional nuclear weapon. How long will it be before the Beasts discover this?"

"You don't understand," said Kuzen. "They already know. I am only a decoy. I know enough to talk the language of nuclear weaponry with people sent by the North Koreans or the Iranians."

"So the Beasts have no plans to deliver real weapons?" asked Hamilton.

"Not yet," said Kuzen. "The German they killed in the café, Kirst. He figured out I was a fraud. He was going to tell the buyer and..." He shrugged.

"Why are you confessing so readily?" asked Hamilton.

"Because," said Kuzen, "if you leave without taking me with you, they will come and question me. I am not a man of great courage. They will assume that I have talked or might soon talk."

"We will have the names of all members of the mafia for whom you are working," said Karpo.

Kuzen laughed nervously.

"And," added Hamilton, "we will have your testimony and all information you possess about illegal activity."

Kuzen stopped laughing, tried to catch his breath, and said, "I will be a dead man. There is no place you could put me that would be safe. They would get to me in any prison."

"What about the United States?" asked Hamilton.

"I don't know," said Kuzen. "What do you mean?"

"I mean that you will testify against this mafia and I will arrange for you to have immediate political asylum in the United States. I can also arrange for you to find employment in our nuclear-disposal efforts."

"America?" Kuzen said. "My wife? Daughters? If they stay..."

"Your wife and daughters too," said Hamilton.

"This is all so fast," said Kuzen. "I need time to...You just walk into my home..." He pointed around the room at his possessions. "You take everything away."

"There will come a time," said Hamilton, "when your mafia will find your information too old and limited. Then they will buy themselves another expert and eliminate you. How can someone as intelligent as you are be so stupid as to not see this?"

"I..." Kuzen began, but he never finished.

The front door burst open. The bald man from the lobby came limping in with a gun in his right hand. Karpo and Hamilton drew their weapons as the limping man, his teeth clenched in either pain or a grin, began firing.

The bullet from Hamilton's weapon crumpled the man forward on his knees as the shot from

Karpo's gun hit the man in the forehead, jerking his head back.

"Are you hit?" asked Hamilton, moving cautiously toward the fallen killer without looking back at Karpo.

"No," said Karpo.

"How could he miss?" said Hamilton, kicking the weapon away from the dead man.

"He didn't," Karpo answered, looking down at Kuzen, whose beautiful silk robe and pajamas were drenched with blood. "He came to kill him first."

Hamilton looked at Kuzen's body and the delicate coffee cup and saucer, which were untouched. Then he felt himself beginning to tremble. He fought against it. He had never shot anyone before, had never had reason even to draw his weapon, and now he had almost been killed. If the dead man on the floor had chosen to, he could have killed Hamilton or Karpo or both of them.

Hamilton had assumed the dead man had been there to protect Kuzen. It was clear now that the dead man had been there to be sure that Kuzen did not talk to the police.

"There's a phone in the corner, near the window," said Hamilton. "Our assassin may have called for backup, or the doorman may be doing that right now. I suggest we do the same."

The FBI man was sure that he was not trembling. He was also still clutching his weapon in both hands, keeping his eyes toward the front of the apartment through which the killer had come. Karpo placed his weapon back in the holster under his jacket. He ignored Hamilton's suggestion.

"I suggest you call the police number," said Karpo. "They will attempt to tell you what district we are in. Armed officers will begin showing up within ten minutes of your call. Someone at the district will, by that time, have also placed a call to a member of the mafia responsible for this, if the doorman has not already done so. I am the ranking Russian officer on the scene. I suggest we search the apartment while we wait for help. When help arrives, evidence may disappear."

"You are a cynical bastard," said Hamilton admiringly.

"The recognition of reality in a world of political chaos is not cynicism but reason," said Karpo.

"Do you always quote Lenin?" asked Hamilton, putting his weapon away but keeping his jacket unbuttoned.

"Do you always recognize when someone is quoting Lenin?" asked Karpo, moving toward a room that looked like an office. The door was open and a computer sat on the desk in the room.

"Not always," said Hamilton. "But it's impressive when I do, isn't it?"

He paused at Kuzen's body, touched the man's neck for a pulse. He didn't find one, but he hadn't expected to. He moved to the telephone and made the call to the police for immediate backup, using Colonel Snitkonoy's name.

"Ten-minute search," said Hamilton, going to the front door and pushing it closed. The lock was now broken, but the door stayed closed.

"Ten minutes will be adequate," said Karpo, who was now out of Hamilton's sight.

Even though the man on the floor had a bullet hole in his forehead directly above his left eye, Hamilton knelt again to be sure he was dead. When he entered the office, Karpo was going through papers stashed in neat wooden cubbyholes on the table next to the desk. The walls of the room were filled with books. A stack of manila folders lay neatly on one side of the computer. On the other side were boxes of floppy disks.

"My computer skills are adequate, but not sophisticated," Karpo said, turning on the computer. "I assume you are well trained."

Hamilton moved behind the desk and examined the names of the files on the screen. Karpo continued a search of the contents of the envelopes and the cubbyholes.

"I doubt if he'd leave anything incriminating sitting on top of his desk," said Hamilton.

From where he sat, he could see both of the bodies in the next room. That was the way he liked it.

Karpo examined the cubbyholes. Each was marked by a small white tab in black ink. There seemed to be no order to the slots, not alphabetical, not by subject. There were fifteen slots with labels such as RELATIVES, MARKETS, CARTOONS, CATS, CLOTHING, PENSION.

"Orderly man," Hamilton said. "Files in order, indexed by subject, title, entry dates."

Hamilton opened a file at random and shook his head. "No wasted words, our Kuzen. Efficient."

In front of Karpo stood the less-than-orderly cubbyholes. He stared at them while the FBI agent hurried through the hard-disk files.

"Plenty of data here," said Hamilton. "Take hours to go through it. Everything looks like it's backed up and indexed on floppy. I'll double-check. Then I suggest we look at the backups when we have more time. We're down to seven minutes."

"I'll continue to look," said Karpo, going through a stack of letters and notes from the cubbyhole marked TAXES.

"It's your country," said Hamilton, racing through computer files.

"It was," said Karpo.

"We're not going to get this done in time," said Hamilton, lining up the backup disks and looking around the room.

"He wouldn't leave anything lying around," said Karpo.

"Then what are we looking for?" asked Hamilton as he switched off the computer. "There could be something on the hard disk or one of the floppies that can be opened with a code. The man was a scientist. An anal-retentive one. Look at this place. It looks as if a tcam of maids left five minutes ago. Except..."

They both looked at the mess of cubbyholes.

"A concession," said Hamilton.

Karpo shook his head no.

"Then what?" asked Hamilton. He stood up and felt more comfortable because he could get his gun out quickly.

"What if the disorder of these papers and the randomness of these slots is neither disorderly nor random?" said Karpo.

"Meaning?"

"If someone touched a shelf or looked at its contents when Kuzen wasn't here, he would come back and know it."

"Why would he care if...?" Hamilton began, and then stopped.

"Something is hidden," said Karpo.

He ran his fingers delicately along the wooden slats between the compartments. His touch was light, his eyes unblinking. Suddenly he stopped.

A piece of paper, the tiny corner of a newspaper or page of a book, fluttered to the table.

"Which one?" asked Hamilton.

"This," said Karpo, pointing to the cubbyhole marked BILLS.

If someone disturbed the papers even slightly, the seemingly random bit of paper would flutter to the table. The person who had disturbed the papers could ignore it, throw it away, pocket it, or try to return it to the sheaf of papers. But return it where, between which two sheets?

"A very cautious man," said Hamilton.

"His caution failed to save his life," said Karpo,

pulling out the stack of bills and handing half of them to the FBI agent.

Two minutes later they had examined the small pile.

"We can take them and check them," Hamilton said, adding the bills to the pile of floppy disks.

Karpo removed the sliding bottom of the now-empty cubbyhole. The bottom was a narrow slat of wood that fit into a slot, just like the rest of the open-faced shelves. There was nothing taped to the slat of wood, nothing taped to the back of the shelf.

"Two more minutes," Hamilton said, checking his watch.

Karpo ran his fingers around the edge of the slat of wood. When he was gently brushing one side of the slat, he stopped and examined it.

"How thin can a disk be?" he asked.

Hamilton shrugged. "Paper-thin. Why?"

"Our time is up," Karpo said, starting to slide the slat back into the wooden cabinet. "I'll call again. You can check the other rooms."

"Right," said Hamilton, moving toward the living room.

With one hand Karpo picked up the phone and dialed Petrovka. With the other he removed the slat again, found the spot he was seeking, and dug his thumbnail into the nearly paper-thin, one-inch-long slit of clay that had been painted the same color as the thin wood. He asked again for immediate support and hung up, listening for Hamilton's footsteps in the other room. Karpo quickly removed the clay and turned the slat of wood onto one side. A round, bright circle of metal fell into his palm. He pocketed the metal, slid the slat back in its slot, and returned the bills to the cubbyhole. He carefully gathered the bits of clay in his fingers and deposited them in another pocket.

Fifteen minutes later a quartet of police, in full uniform, weapons at the ready, were standing in the room over the bodies of the two dead men while a very black man in a very good suit and a tall, gaunt figure they recognized as Karpo the Vampire answered questions put to them by their officer, a young captain who was already losing hair and gaining weight. The young captain looked tired. The sight of the bodies barely drew his attention.

"Mafia," he said with a resigned sigh.

"Yes," said Hamilton, explaining who had killed whom less than half an hour earlier.

Kuzen's dead eyes were open. Karpo looked down at them. The dead man had lost his life and his secret.

Chapter 12

Lies

Arkady Zelach had a headache. He wasn't sure whether it was from his old injury, the fact that he had now gone a full twenty-four hours without sleep, or the presence of the screeching woman on whose shoulder a baby slept.

Colonel Snitkonoy himself had called to congratulate him on saving the life of Sasha Tkach and apprehending all three of the killer children. Porfiry Petrovich had done the same and told him to wrap up the paperwork and get home for some well-deserved sleep.

Zelach had already called his mother for the third time. He had called her the night before to say that he would be home slightly after midnight. Then he had called her to say that Sasha Tkach had been injured and that he would have to work at least a few more hours. After that Zelach went to the hospital to be sure Sasha was all right and then back to the district station where the three boys were being held. Their mother was waiting for him along with a skinny man with curly black hair and the face of a night animal with long teeth. The man's name, he was told, was Lermonov. Lermonov was a lawyer, a new and rising breed who knew there was no longer a viable written criminal justice code. Lermonov and others like him jumped in where the Parliament feared to walk. The new lawyers quoted precedent, old laws, new laws, invented laws. Each and every one of the hundreds of mafias had its own lawyer or two or three. Lermonov was sure he was on the way up, that some well-connected businessman or high-ranking mafia member would recognize his ability and move him into a position of power. Meanwhile he made the best of things, representing whoever called on his services, which he hawked with business cards inserted into the mail slots along the streets of the vast neighborhood in which the Chazovs and others who might get into trouble with the police lived. The five hundred cards had cost him nothing. They were the price of representing a printer named Kholkov, who had set up business in a Gorky Street basement with no permit from the police or the local mafia. Lermonov had simply made one small bribe to a police sergeant on Kholkov's behalf as well as the promise of an immediate substantial percentage of Kholkov's business for the mafia, which in turn promised to give Kholkov customers.

It was because of one of his cards that Elvira Chazova had called on him in his tiny apartment-office. He had taken on her cause immediately. He took on all causes immediately as long as there was a payment up front. Elvira, child in her arms, belly full, had pleaded with him to take on the legal protection of her children in the name of mercy and decency. Elvira was a fraud. Lermonov saw through her and demanded cash or goods. Elvira had given cash, and now Lermonov and his client sat across from Zelach in the large, echoing room. Zelach's head ached. He needed help. Paperwork and screaming mothers and insistent lawyers were beyond him. He sat quite still, back straight, and said little.

"The boys you are holding are completely innocent," Lermonov said. "In fact, they are heroes. Just before you came rushing out to attack them, Mrs. Chazova's boys had beaten off two older boys, who were attacking the policeman. The

Chazovas drove them away and were tending to the policeman when you came out and started to beat and handcuff them."

"No," said Zelach, determined to show no signs of wavering, which he accomplished by conjuring up the image of Tkach on the sidewalk and one of the boys about to strike him with a brick. "It was they."

Elvira Chazova wailed. The wail echoed off the walls of the interrogation room, which were badly in need of paint. The wail woke the baby in her arms, who began to cry.

Zelach fought the urge to cradle his head in his hands. His eyes met those of the lawyer.

"How can you be sure?" said the lawyer.

"I saw them standing over him. There were no others on the street. Sash...the fallen officer told me it was they who attacked him."

Lermonov sighed patiently and spoke over the crying and wailing.

"He was struck down from behind. He saw a trio of small boys armed with sticks and stones, small boys who had driven off his attackers. Heroes. They should get medals."

"They did it," Zelach repeated. "And they have done it before."

"The court will not agree," said Lermonov, rising. "I demand that you release the children into the custody of their mother. They are her sole support."

"No," Zelach repeated.

"You will lose your job over this," said

Lermonov, pointing a finger at the weary and confused detective.

"I am tired. I have a report to write and I don't want to talk to you anymore," said Zelach, unable now to keep his hand from moving to his throbbing forehead.

"This is—" Lermonov started but was cut off by Zelach, who suddenly rose, his chair falling backward to the floor.

"Out," he said. "Now. Both of you."

"Nazi," shouted Elvira Chazova. "Communist. Dog."

"Out," Zelach repeated, starting to move around the table.

Lermonov grabbed Elvira Chazova's arm and led her to the door as Zelach slouched forward. The baby screamed. Elvira Chazova pointed back at Zelach and cursed him. Lermonov said something, but Zelach couldn't understand him.

And then they were gone. Zelach's headache was still there, but his tormentors were no longer in his face. He waited a few minutes before he left the room in search of an aspirin.

Natalya Dokorova sat with her hands folded, a large shopping bag at her side, listening to the explanation of the woman in the suit who told her that there was no appeal beyond this office. The treasure her brother had accumulated would not be returned, and she would almost certainly receive compensation only in the form of an increase in her pension.

Natalya bewailed her fate and the evil being done to her brother's life's work, but the young woman behind the desk was unmoved.

"You may leave, Natalya Dokorova," the woman said. "When there is anything else, we will tell you."

Natalya rose, tired from her efforts, sure that she had lost. She picked up her shopping bag and said a silent "Thank God" as she went out the door. In four days she would be in Germany. A day later she would be in England. She had prepared for this day even before the death of her brother. She had removed a number of items from the treasure room—only things that could fit into her shopping bag—and she had moved them to the apartment of her cousin, who considered the items a clutter of junk.

For one of the things she carried in her shopping bag at the very moment an English dealer in rare objects had offered a small fortune. Natalya had contacted the man when he visited Moscow earlier this year. The man had expressed, with the help of a translator, his awareness that many valued items had been unearthed in the Ukraine, Estonia, and Russia, objects the Americans, Arabs, and Japanese would pay much for.

The manuscript in her shopping bag was, the man from London had said, probably the most valuable of all. She had left it in sight of her cousin after carefully creating a new cover page. The cover of the manuscript now read "*The History of the Kardovs* by Natalya Dokorova," a page that was certain to turn even the most curious examiner away.

The real cover page was buried in the many pages of manuscript that her brother had purchased from a woman who claimed that her mother had worked for the great Gogol just before his death. The woman's mother had told her that Gogol had thrown the manuscript into the fire just days before his death and had walked out of the room. The woman's mother had reached into the fire and rescued the manuscript. It had been singed slightly, but the woman had reasoned that something by Gogol might have some value. The woman had sold the manuscript to old Dokorov for the cost of a new wardrobe for her daughter.

Dokorov knew he had the real thing, but he had verified it by showing a single page of the manuscript to a professor of literature at Moscow State University. Dokorov had paid the man and told him it was the only page he had. The man had immediately pronounced it authentic.

"Do you realize what you have here?" the professor had said.

"No," Ivan had replied.

"The only remaining page of the manuscript for Gogol's sequel to *Dead Souls*. What do you plan to do with it?"

"Cherish it," Ivan had said. "My love of literature is greater than my love of life."

There were other items too—a small, almost priceless Chinese jar, which Natalya had filled with very cheap perfume, as she had its equally valued companion jar, which she would now retrieve if only the police had not found it. But the prize that she would present to the dealer in London was a slightly more-than-life-size jeweled Fabergé egg in which nestled a perfect miniature carousel that spun in a gentle circle when wound with a tiny key. She had sealed the lid of the egg with paste that could easily be removed and she had taken a sticker from the Dom Toy Shop and placed it on the egg. There were other items, too, just as well disguised.

Though she was a strong woman, the weight of her bag and the trials of the day had slowed her down by the time she reached her front door. The policewoman stood waiting.

"Let me help you," Elena said, taking the shopping bag from Natalya. "Can we speak? Just for a moment?"

Natalya nodded her head yes, exaggerating a tiredness she definitely did feel.

The house was almost bare now. Almost every item that might be worth something had been removed. There were now three wooden chairs and a small table painted green in the kitchen.

Elena followed the old woman and placed the bag on the table.

"Some tea?" Natalya said, sagging onto one of the chairs.

Elena pulled one of the other chairs forward and placed it directly before the woman. Then she sat and took one of Natalya's hands in hers.

"I am sorry, Natalya Dokorova," Elena said sincerely. "I told you I would help you and..."

Elena looked around.

Natalya put her free hand on the young woman's shoulder.

"It will be all right," the old woman said. "Come."

She rose, and Elena followed her to the small bathroom, where Natalya turned on the light. Toilet. Sink. Tiny tub. Medicine cabinet. Natalya opened the cabinet, reaching past the tube of Crest toothpaste to a small bottle nestled among a quintet of other small bottles.

"I would like you to have this," said Natalya.

"Thank you," said Elena with a smile.

"Don't worry too much. I shall be fine. But I must rest now."

Natalya walked Elena to the front door and opened it.

"Thank you for stopping by," said the old woman. "It was kind of you."

"And thank you for the gift," Elena said, stepping into the street. She looked down at the bottle in her hand. It was definitely Oriental, decorated with exquisite tiny flowers in a garden. The colors were vivid. Elena opened the top of the jar and smelled the cheap perfume. When she got back to Petrovka, she would empty the bottle, rinse it, and keep it on her desk as a paperweight.

In a rather odd way Anna Porvinovich reminded Porfiry Petrovich of Colonel Snitkonoy.

He watched her cross the room in her somber black knit dress. Her dark hair was brushed back, and not a hair was out of place. Her earrings were simple black onyx. She walked as if she were in some old movie—slowly, pensively, erect. She stood before him and allowed herself to be examined. She wore a knowing, worried smile.

She was, Rostnikov decided, a well-groomed Doberman, not a Wolfhound.

Yevgeniy Porvinovich had let the policeman in. Yevgeniy was wearing gray slacks and suspenders over his white shirt. He had immediately asked if the police had found his brother or identified the kidnappers. The man was a terrible actor. It was clear to Rostnikov that Yevgeniy wanted the answers to his questions to be negative. Rostnikov answered, "We think we know who the kidnapper is."

Yevgeniy had swayed slightly and barely managed to say, "Good," when Anna Porvinovich made her dramatic entrance and moved toward him without speaking. She motioned carelessly to the chair and sofa, and Rostnikov accepted, sitting down on one of the high chairs without too much awkwardness. Only when he was seated did she take her own place on the sofa. She checked her dress for wrinkles, smoothed out a nonexistent one, and draped one arm over the back of the sofa. Yevgeniy sat in the chair identical to the one in which Rostnikov was seated.

"Tea?" asked the woman.

"Tea," said Rostnikov. He had unbuttoned his jacket but not removed it. In a day or two he would have to start wearing a hat. When possible, he would wear his favorite hat, a brown cloth cap with a little brim and ear flaps. His wife said the cap made him look like a comedian in an American comedy. More often he wore a black fur hat, which Sarah had said made him look like a diplomat.

Yevgeniy hurried off to get the tea.

"You have news?" Anna asked.

"A theory," said Rostnikov. "Your husband was kidnapped by a man named Artiom Solovyov and an unidentified accomplice, probably his assistant in the garage."

"Artiom Solovyov," she repeated as if trying to place the name. "The big man where we have our car repaired?"

"Yes," said Rostnikov, opening his jacket a bit more. "You have trouble placing him yet you spoke to him on the phone yesterday."

"Ah," she said, reaching forward to remove a cigarette from the box on the table between them. "I remember now. So much has happened. Alexei...so much."

She toyed with the cigarette in her fingers and looked down at it pensively.

"We think you and Artiom Solovyov planned the kidnapping of your husband."

She looked up suddenly, wary, jaws slightly tensed. Not a dog, thought Rostnikov, a Siamese cat with red claws.

"You have no comment?" Rostnikov said.

"It is too absurd to reply to," she said, putting the cigarette between her lips.

The tremble was slight, ever so slight, but Rostnikov had been looking for it. She lit her cigarette, which gave her time to gather her defenses. She glared at him with a well-performed look of *How could you think such things of me?* Yevgeniy returned, carrying a tray on which were three cups, spoons, sugar and milk, and a white porcelain teapot. He walked slowly and carefully. He was halfway across the room when Rostnikov said, "I was just telling your sister-in-law that we believe she is responsible for the abduction of your brother. She and a garage mechanic named Solovyov."

Yevgeniy did not drop the tray, though he did stop rather suddenly, and the cups slid to one side of the tray. He looked at Anna.

"Put down the tray," she said calmly.

Yevgeniy did so.

"As I recall," she said, "you take sugar and milk."

"Yes," said Rostnikov.

"Sit, Yevgeniy," she said, preparing the tea for the policeman.

Yevgeniy sat, took a breath, and said, "Absurd."

"It depends on how you react to it," said Rostnikov, accepting the cup of tea from Anna Porvinovich. "When I first became a policeman, I was often struck by the absurdity of most of the crime I encountered. Gradually what used to seem absurd began to seem quite normal."

He sipped his tea and looked at Yevgeniy.

"We are not policemen," Yevgeniy said.

"I know," Rostnikov replied. "You are kidnappers and, possibly, accessories to murder."

"We…?" Yevgeniy said, looking at Anna again and getting no help.

"Yes," said Rostnikov, reaching over for another lump of sugar. The move did not please his withered left leg. It protested as Rostnikov sweetened his tea.

"The tea is a bit tepid," Anna said, taking a sip. "I'm sorry."

"It is excellent tea," he said.

"Do you plan to arrest us?" Anna Porvinovich asked calmly.

"Not yet, unless you would like to confess and tell us where your husband is?"

"I cannot do that," she said. "I do not know. I know nothing about Alexei's kidnapping."

"Well," said Rostnikov, finishing his tea. "We will get the information from Solovyov. I must go." He rose, holding the arm of the chair to get himself into a reasonably erect position.

"Is it particularly painful to have such a crippled leg?" Anna Porvinovich asked.

"Yes," said Rostnikov. "But my leg and I have come to an understanding. I no longer curse it and it minimally cooperates."

"When you walk," she said, "it looks as if you are in pain."

Rostnikov looked at the woman, who was smiling, a very slight, falsely sympathetic smile.

"Given the choice," he said, "I would prefer to live with pain than with guilt."

"You have no choice," she said, looking at his leg.

"I will return soon," said Rostnikov, buttoning his jacket. "Thank you for the tea and sympathy."

She remained seated, languidly holding her cup of tea in one hand, her cigarette in the other. Yevgeniy rose and moved ahead of Rostnikov to the door.

"I assure you, Inspector," Yevgeniy said, "we are distraught over what has happened to my brother. Anna and I had nothing to do with his kidnapping. We only wish him back. We will pay them anything. I'd give everything I have to see him walk through that door."

There was a click in the door in front of Yevgeniy and Porfiry Petrovich. The door opened, and standing there, a key in one hand, a pillow in the other, stood a man. The man was about six feet tall, perhaps a little shorter. He wore a badly rumpled suit without a tie. His hair was uncombed, and he had a day's growth of brown and gray stubble over his grotesquely distorted and swollen purple face.

"Alexei?" said Yevgeniy.

Still standing in the doorway, the man let the pillow drop to uncover the automatic weapon he carried. He said nothing, but pointed inside the apartment. Rostnikov and Yevgeniy backed up, and Alexei pocketed his key and closed the door.

"You," he said to Rostnikov, pointing the gun at him. "Who are you?"

"A policeman," said Rostnikov.

"Alexei, I'm so—"Yevgeniy began, but was

cut short by a sudden thrust of the weapon across his face.

"Shut up," said Alexei Porvinovich.

Yevgeniy's face was bleeding from a nasty slit across his nose and left cheek. He looked as if he was about to weep.

"Move," said Alexei.

Yevgeniy kept his hand across his face, trying to stop the bleeding. Rostnikov was at his side. They moved slowly into the big living room.

Anna turned and stood erect at the sight of her armed husband. She put down her cup and her cigarette.

"Pleased to see me?" asked Alexei.

She said nothing. Cool. Unafraid.

"Well, I am pleased to be back with my family," said Alexei with a horrible smile. "It has been a difficult night and day. Sit."

Anna sat, and Yevgeniy and Porfiry Petrovich went back to the same seats in which they had been sitting before. Alexei stood about three yards away from the trio, much too far for Rostnikov to attempt a leap, even if he were capable of such an action.

"Would you like to know what I have been up to since you last saw me?" Alexei said. "I spent a night of fear and the expectation that I would die. I spent the night knowing that my wife and brother had planned my murder. And then I devised a plan and got this gun from one of the fools who had taken me. I bound him and waited for your friend, Artiom.

Then we had a nice talk and I killed them both. I seem to be in a killing mood."

"You're crazy," said Yevgeniy, pressing a napkin to his cheek. The napkin was already dark red with blood.

"Precisely," said Alexei. "I am insane. I hope it is only temporary, that sometime after I kill you and Anna, my sanity will return. That happens sometimes, doesn't it, policeman?"

"Chief Inspector Porfiry Petrovich Rostnikov," Rostnikov said.

"Do you think I am out of my mind?" asked Alexei, his weapon pointed at his wife.

"Yes," said Rostnikov. "But it is complicated. You are crazed by what has happened to you, but you think you are not. You think you are only pretending to be insane so that you will not be held responsible for killing your wife and brother."

"Either way, I'm crazy," said Alexei with a grin.

"True," said Rostnikov, "but we have a strange judicial system. I have seen demonstrably mad killers sentenced to death or prison and quite lucid murderers declared insane."

"But did they go through what I've gone through?" Alexei shouted.

"My wife and I are caring for two young girls," said Rostnikov, unbuttoning his jacket. "Their grandmother, with whom they were living, could barely feed them. She shot a food-store manager, killed him, and sat down on a little stool. What she had gone through had driven her quite mad. She is now in prison and will probably spend the rest of her life there. Would you like another example?"

"No," said Alexei. "I still intend to kill these two."

"Alexei," said his wife, "I am sorry."

"Sorry," Alexei said with an animallike snort. "You expect me to believe that?"

"No," she said. "You misunderstand. I am sorry you got away. I am sorry that fool Artiom didn't kill you. I'm sorry the plan didn't work, such a simple plan and such fools to deal with. I sometimes wonder why I get involved with men who are fools."

"Am I a fool, Anna?" Alexei asked as his brother reached for a fresh napkin and began to sob.

"A clever fool," she said, folding her arms.

"Are you afraid, Anna?" asked Alexei.

"No," she said. "I know that is what you want, and perhaps you deserve it, but I am not afraid. I'm weary of all of you."

She turned her back on her husband and walked to the window.

"Was I so bad to you?" Alexei shouted.

"Yes," she said softly, closing her eyes.

"How?" he demanded. "What did I do that deserved my murder?"

She shrugged and said, "Little things, big things. I'm not going to give you a long list. The way you laugh, snore, gloat. The business stories you tell over and over. Your pitiful sex. There's much more. What difference does it make? You are going to kill me soon."

"If you put down the gun," said Rostnikov, "I

will arrest them both for your kidnapping. When they come out of prison, they will be old. They will have missed life while you are free to start a new life without them. Isn't that better than killing them?"

"Is it?" asked Alexei.

"Yes," said Yevgeniy eagerly.

Anna, her back still turned, shrugged.

"I do not want to live in a prison," she said. "I would prefer to die now in my own home."

Alexei shook his head and ran his fingers across the growth of beard on his mask of pain. "I deserve satisfaction," he said. "I deserve having you try to talk me out of killing you. I deserve to have you sobbing like Yevgeniy when I kill you."

Yevgeniy was leaning stiffly back in his now-blood-splattered chair. He looked at Rostnikov for help.

"I will give you no satisfaction," she said, looking out the window.

"Take them," Alexei Porvinovich said, lowering his gun and his head. "Take them now."

He sat on the sofa, a bit dazed, the weapon in his lap.

Rostnikov rose, using both arms of the chair, and said, "Yevgeniy Porvinovich, Anna Porvinovich, I arrest you for the crime of kidnapping and attempted murder. Other charges may be brought following an investigation." Rostnikov went around the table and reached for the weapon on Alexei Porvinovich's lap. Alexei did nothing to stop him. He looked straight ahead.

Anna turned from the window and said, "The cloth coat, Yevgeniy. The fur would be stolen by the police, and you might bleed on it."

"I need a doctor," Yevgeniy said.

"You'll get one," said Rostnikov. "Let's go."

They moved forward.

"Where are the two dead men?" Rostnikov asked.

Alexei told him.

"I'll be back. Have some tea. Get some sleep," Rostnikov said.

Alexei nodded, reached for Anna's lipstick-stained cup, and drank what was left.

In the hallway Rostnikov dropped the gun to his side and walked behind the two prisoners. Yevgeniy held a napkin to his wound and looked as if he would fall over.

"I doubt if either of us will go to jail," Anna Porvinovich said to Yevgeniy. "Stop weeping. If we do have to spend time in prison, I doubt it will be for very long. There are people to bribe and men to reason with. Isn't that true, Inspector?"

"Probably," said Rostnikov, wondering how he was going to get the two of them to the closest district station. He had not wanted to call for a police car from the apartment. He had wanted to get them out quickly in case Alexei changed his mind and went for a weapon.

"We worked well together," Anna said, turning to look at him with a smile.

"Let us say, your performance was excellent,"

Rostnikov said. "Deprive the poor victim of his satisfaction."

"While you," she said, "promise him a punishment for those who have harmed him, a punishment you cannot deliver."

"We were wonderful," said Rostnikov.

Anna smiled at his irony. It was a smile of perfect white teeth. Rostnikov felt that she was a rare combination of seductiveness and intelligence, with more than a touch of madness.

"When we are safely wherever you are taking us," she said, "I would like to make a few phone calls. And I would like you to come back and arrest Alexei for threatening to kill me. Yevgeniy and I had nothing to do with Alexei's kidnapping. You have no witnesses now that this Solovyov is dead, no witnesses but my vindictive and deluded husband."

They were in the elevator now. Yevgeniy, his face bloodred, leaned back until his head bounced against the wall.

Anna continued. "Perhaps this Artiom made up a story about my involvement in his crime. He made certain suggestions—certain advances toward me—which I rejected. He may have taken Alexei out of revenge and told him I was involved in order to torture my poor husband."

"You are probably the most dangerous woman I have ever met," said Rostnikov.

"Not the most dangerous person?" she asked, meeting his eyes.

"The most dangerous person I have known

senselessly murdered at least forty-two people," said Rostnikov.

"If I thought it would do any good, I would seduce you," she said as the elevator doors opened on the ground level.

This time Yevgeniy purposely banged the back of his head on the wall.

"No good at all," Rostnikov confirmed.

They stepped outside the building. A cab sat free only a few feet away. The driver looked at the trio, particularly the box-shaped man with the machine gun and the man with the bloody face, and sped off down the street.

"What now?" asked Anna.

"We find a phone," said Rostnikov.

She was now near enough that Rostnikov could smell her. He hoped she would move away. He hoped she would stop talking. He hoped there was a phone nearby.

Chapter 13

Night

Karpo knew little about computers, which was why he sat in his small office reading the manuals that he had obtained from Colonel Snitkonoy's little Pankov, who had a computer on his desk. There were many people he could ask about how to insert the disk and read it, but this he would not do.

He read, alone at first. Then Elena Timofeyeva returned and passed his office on the way to hers. She had a little bottle in her hand. He looked up as she paused.

"May I?" he asked, nodding at her hand.

"Yes," she said, handing the bottle to him. "I'm very sorry about Mathilde. My aunt asked me to send her sympathy, and if you are willing to tolerate our cooking, we would like to invite you for dinner on a day—"

"Where did you get this?" he interrupted.

"The bottle? From Natalya Dokorova."

Karpo continued to examine the bottle.

"What did she tell you about it?"

"Nothing," said Elena. "The perfume is a small gift for my trying to help her. Would you like the bottle?"

"No," he said, handing it back to her. "May I suggest that you take very good care of that bottle."

Elena took the bottle back. She looked at Karpo's face for a moment, then looked carefully at the bottle for the first time.

"You mean...?"

"I mean it is something you should take care of," he said.

Elena was suddenly afraid that she would drop the little bottle. She tucked it deeply into her pocket.

"Thank you," she said.

For a moment Elena considered leaving, but she had the feeling that Karpo had something more to say.

"How knowledgeable are you about computers?"

"I've had two courses on their use," she answered, wondering where this was leading. "I would say that I am reasonably knowledgeable."

Karpo pointed to the shining little metal circle on his empty desk. Elena had barely noticed it before.

"Can you put this on a computer so that I can read it?" he asked.

"Yes," she said.

"I would prefer that only I see the contents," he said.

"Of course."

Karpo handed her the circle and said, "How long?"

"If I can find what I need, you should have a readable disk in less than an hour. However, the information on the disk may be locked. If you like, I can check. There are things I can do to open it, but I would have to look at the information at least minimally to do this."

Karpo nodded and said, "One hour."

"Approximately," she said, feeling the bottle in her pocket.

"Thank you," he said. "Dinner with you and Anna Timofeyeva would be welcome."

Elena nodded and smiled. Her heart was beating quickly, and she wondered what she should do with the bottle, whether or not to tell her aunt, whether it was possible to get it appraised without having it stolen, whether it was her duty to turn it in to her superiors. At the moment she wasn't the slightest bit curious about what might be on Karpo's disk.

When Rostnikov finished turning his prisoners over to the district station and telling them the charges, he gave the solemn, overweight major in charge the address where he could find two bodies.

"Not in my district," the major said.

"You have my authority, direct from Petrovka, direct from the Office of Special Investigation, direct from Colonel Snitkonoy, to go to the apartment, examine the scene, and take care of the bodies. If you prefer, you may call the head of that district and have him check the apartment. As mad as it seems," Rostnikov said wearily, "you might consider working together."

The major nodded, making it clear that "working together" with another district would be out of the question. The major, Rostnikov decided, would risk the enmity of the director of the district where the apartment was located and take on the investigation himself. Scoring points with Petrovka and the Wolfhound's department would be worth a bit of additional tension between the districts.

From the district station Rostnikov then made a call to the cousin of his wife. Sarah's cousin was a surgeon, and they were close. With some difficulty Rostnikov reached the cousin and asked him for the name of a good psychologist. The cousin came up with two names of people who were trying to make the practice of therapy acceptable in the new democratic Russia. Rostnikov tracked down one of the therapists and told him about Porvinovich.

"I suggest you go there immediately," said Rostnikov, giving the man the address after telling him the story.

"It will be difficult to go now," the man said.

"Porvinovich is a wealthy man," said Rostnikov.

"I am on my way," the man said.

Rostnikov then called Alexei Porvinovich's apartment. The phone rang twenty-two times before Porvinovich picked it up without speaking. Rostnikov said that someone was on the way to help him.

"I'll take care of the situation with the two dead men," he said. "The condition is that you talk to the person who is coming to see you."

No answer.

"I need an answer now," said Rostnikov.

"*Da*," Porvinovich said, and hung up the phone.

Rostnikov called the hospital and discovered from a surly nurse that Sasha Tkach was now sleeping and that, considering his injuries, he was recovering amazingly well.

That was it. It was getting late, and his leg was telling him to get home, get something to eat, and go to bed. He would do his full weight workout when he woke up. Rostnikov put a little pressure on the major, who assigned one of the district police cars to drive the chief inspector home. The driver was not a talker, for which Rostnikov was truly grateful.

The six flights up the stairs of his apartment building on Krasikov Street were especially difficult this night. He was supposed to make the leg work, to walk as much as he could, to climb stairs. Tonight his leg, like a suddenly petulant child, refused to cooperate. By the time Rostnikov reached his door, jacket and hat over his arms, he was exhausted. He inserted the key, went in, and found himself facing a quartet of females—the two little girls, who, he thought, should have been in school by now until he realized that school was over; Sarah, who looked particularly relieved to see him; and Lydia Tkach, aflame with rage.

"Porfiry Petrovich Rostnikov," Lydia shouted, pointing a finger at him. "I denounce you."

Over the years he had known her, Rostnikov had noted that she shouted more and more as she grew deafer. One was then required to respond in a shout. But Lydia Tkach refused to acknowledge her hearing loss.

"I stand denounced," Rostnikov said, wearily hanging his coat on the rack near the door.

"My son, my only child," Lydia said, advancing on Rostnikov. "He is in a hospital, fighting for his life."

"I just talked to the hospital. He is doing fine."

"Fine?" Lydia shouted. She turned to Sarah and repeated her questioning indictment. "'Fine,' he says. Head broken. All beaten up. He could have been killed."

Rostnikov took her hand. She pulled it away.

"Porfiry," Sarah said. "I'll heat you something."

"Girls," said Rostnikov. "Go into the other room and pretend you are doing homework. You can listen from there."

The girls moved to him for a hug. He picked each girl up, gave her an enormous hug, and put her down. The girls scurried off to the bedroom. He sat down at the table where a half loaf of bread lay next to his plate. Sarah put her hands on his shoulders and massaged gently after he sat. Lydia took the seat across from him. Rostnikov cut a slice of bread and began to eat.

"We talked," Lydia said. "You promised. Do you remember?"

"We talked," Rostnikov said, "but I could not make the promise you asked of me. How can I promise that a policeman will not be hurt while performing his duty?"

"You said," Lydia continued, "that you would talk to him about quitting, about finding other work. There are many opportunities now for people with Sasha's talent."

"Legal opportunities?" Rostnikov asked. "Or opportunities that might be more dangerous than being a policeman?"

"Office. Ministry," Lydia said.

"Sasha won't accept that, even if I could get him transferred to an office job. He wants to be a policeman. He is an excellent policeman. Who knows, he might be king of all policemen when he reaches our age."

"Don't mock me," Lydia said. "My hearing may be going, but nothing is wrong with my mind."

Progress, Rostnikov thought. *She finally admits that she has a hearing loss.* He touched his wife's hand. Sarah touched his cheek and moved away to get him some food.

"I'll eat after our guest has left," Rostnikov said in a normal voice.

"I understand," said Sarah, sitting.

Sarah looked tired. Maybe it was too soon after her recovery to go back to work even if it was only part-time.

"So," demanded Lydia. "What will you do?"

"I have spoken to Sasha," shouted Rostnikov. "He is a grown man with a wife and two children. I cannot order him to quit for a safer job if he does not want to do so."

"You can fire him," Lydia said.

"I will not."

Lydia glared at Rostnikov and rose from her chair, pointing a finger at him.

"I denounce you," she said.

"You already did that," Rostnikov replied, also rising.

"Then I...I..." Lydia said, her voice dropping just a decibel.

Rostnikov moved around the table and stood in front of Lydia, who continued to glare at him.

Rostnikov opened his arms, and Lydia Tkach immediately stepped into his embrace and began to cry.

"Inspector Tkach," said the policeman, standing at Sasha's bedside, "are these the three children who assaulted you?"

The policeman was decidedly uncomfortable, for, in fact, the man lying in bed was his superior officer. But Yuri Pokov had survived for almost fifty years by simply doing what he was told—no more, no less. Such an attitude had earned him little opportunity for promotion and even less possibility of criticism. He resisted the urge to run his hand across his newly shaven head.

In the hall outside the hospital room people were waiting, including the lawyer Elvira Chazova had hired. Things were getting too complicated for Yuri Pokov, who considered himself a simple man. Now there were lawyers, trials for people who in the past would simply have been beaten and sent on their way, complaints of mistreatment, orders to be civil to civilians.

Sasha, his head still swathed in bandages and wearing a pair of his own shorts and a T-shirt, sat up leaning on one arm and looked at the three boys at the side of his bed. "No," said Sasha. "They are not." He slumped back onto the pillow and closed his eyes.

"Are you certain?" asked Yuri Pokov. "Please look again." Sasha opened his eyes. These boys were older than the ones who had attacked him. These boys were taller and heavier.

"I can have them put on their caps," said Pokov.

"No," said Sasha. "These are not them."

Yuri nodded, and ushered the three boys out into the hall. He had promised each of them one hundred kopecks, which his superior, Sergeant Knitsov, had authorized.

"Well?" demanded Lermonov, the lawyer.

"He said they were not the boys who attacked him," said Pokov.

Pokov looked around at the sizable gathering of people in the hall and wished that Sergeant Knitsov had taken this on himself. Pokov paid the three boys who had just left Sasha's room and motioned for the next three boys. He opened the door and led the boys into the room. Sasha's head was back on the pillow, his arm covering his face.

It was a rare sunny day for the season, and the shades were up. Outside the temperature had fallen to 20 degrees Fahrenheit.

"These?" asked Pokov.

Sasha turned, blinked, tried to focus. He definitely had difficulty focusing since the blow to his head. He immediately pointed to Alexei Chazov.

"That one. Not the other two," he said.

Alexei Chazov paused as the others turned. He glared at Sasha as he was guided out by Yuri Pokov.

The next three boys included Boris and Mark Chazov and a boy Yuri's sergeant had promised to set free on a pickpocketing charge if he went to the hospital and cooperated. The boy had agreed. The sergeant had been planning to let the boy go anyway.

"Those two," Sasha said, pointing at Boris and Mark. "Not the other one."

Boris smiled before turning. Mark looked around the room. Yuri Pokov wondered if he was getting that thing in his stomach again, the problem he had had five years ago. It certainly felt like it. Maybe it was just being in the hospital.

"Positive identification," said Pokov to the lawyer.

"I wish to speak to him," Lermonov said.

Yuri Pokov shook his head and let the boys stand in the hall. He was not afraid that they would bolt. Where was there to hide? Besides, an armed, uniformed officer stood a dozen feet from them, looking bored enough to shoot the children or even the lawyer if they caused him any trouble.

Pokov went back into the hospital room. This time Sasha did not move his arm from his face.

"Lawyer wants to see you," said Pokov.

"No," said Sasha.

Pokov nodded and went back into the hall, closing the door softly and turning to Lermonov to shake his head.

The three Chazov brothers had separated themselves from the other boys and were leaning against the wall.

"These boys are innocent," said Lermonov.

"I'm certain of it," said Pokov, looking at the Chazovs. Pokov did not like children even when they weren't criminals who attacked policemen and murdered drunks.

"I must speak to the arresting officer," Lermonov insisted.

"Inspector Tkach does not wish to speak to you," said Pokov. "We leave."

"But…" Lermonov said.

Pokov pointed at the armed policeman.

"My orders are to return these prisoners to custody and to comply with the wishes of Inspector Tkach. He does not wish to speak to you."

"So it shall be," said Lermonov with a shrug, motioning for the three boys to follow the others. "So it shall be."

Sasha had a string of visitors during the day, some of whom he vaguely remembered the next day. He was sure Maya came and kissed him and said something as she held his hand. He was sure she cried. He was absolutely sure his mother came but did not say a word. That was impossible, but Sasha was certain that it was true. Rostnikov seemed to have suddenly appeared, looking down at him. When Sasha opened his eyes, Rostnikov said nothing. He only smiled. Sasha awakened sometime after dark to find Zelach sitting on a chair next to his bed, hands folded on his lap, looking at him.

"Go home, Zelach. Get some sleep. I'll be fine," Sasha muttered dryly.

Zelach stood. "I could use a drink of water," Sasha said, and Zelach gratefully accepted the job. He left the room and came back with a pitcher of water and a glass.

Sometime later, when the lights were dim and the other patients in the small ward were asleep, Elena Timofeyeva came to his side. He looked up at her. In her hand was a single flower. She placed it in the glass of water.

"Rostnikov gave it to me," she said. "It came from the bush in the courtyard. He said he admires its ability to continue to bloom when other trees and bushes have gone winter bare and gray."

Sasha nodded.

Elena felt uneasy. She and Sasha had been partners, but they had never really worked well together. He was too volatile, ready to take offense, brooding over domestic problems, certainly more than a bit of what the Americans called sexist. She did not dislike him. On the contrary, she felt something for him and his constant struggle to find ways to accept the world in which he had found himself. He was boyishly good-looking, even as he lay pale with a white bandage wrapped awkwardly around his head.

"Can I get you anything?" she asked.

Sasha indicated no.

"The doctor says you are improving rapidly."

Sasha tried to smile. It came out as a pained grimace.

At that moment the door opened and another visitor entered, moved through the shadows, and stood next to the bed a foot from Elena. The new visitor looked at her, but Elena looked away.

"I'll tell you the truth, Tkach," Iosef Rostnikov said, leaning over to whisper. "You look like a dolt with a dunce cap."

Sasha grinned.

Iosef was taller than his father and built like a soccer player, with strong legs, a lean body, and good, broad shoulders. From his mother he had a handsome face and reddish-brown hair. He was wearing a scarf and jacket over his jeans and a red and black flannel shirt.

Iosef held Sasha's arm with his right hand. His grip was firm. Sasha reached over to touch the reassuring hand of his boss's son.

"Your show?" asked Sasha.

"My show," Iosef said with a sigh, turning to look at Elena. "What can I say? It will open in three days. It will close three days after that for lack of an audience. I am cursed to be out of accord with the public taste. I write a play about Afghanistan. No one comes. I write a tragedy. No one cries. I write a comedy and I'm confident no one will laugh. I am fast becoming convinced that a life in the theater is not for me."

"If it's still playing when I get out of here," said Sasha dryly, "Maya and I will come. I promise we will laugh, at least politely."

"It is too late," Iosef said. "I have already applied to join the police. No one wants to be a policeman anymore, so it's easy to get in. Besides, I think it is in my genes."

Sasha smiled again and closed his eyes. Iosef loosened his grip and patted the policeman's shoulder gently.

"I'll be back," said Iosef.

Iosef turned, looked at Elena, and invited her with a nod to leave with him. She followed him through the door and into the corridor.

"Good night, Iosef," she said, extending her right hand.

He took it and held it. "Forgive me," he said.

"For what?"

"For not calling," he answered.

"You owed me no call," she said.

He was looking directly down into her eyes. In the light of the corridor she could see that he had lost weight.

"I have little excuse for not making the call I did not owe you," he said with a smile. "I've been working long hours on the play—writing, directing, building sets, begging for props and money, learning my lines, making decisions."

"You owed me no call," she said. "You owe me no apology."

"You are definitely upset with me and uneasy in my presence," he said.

"No," she said.

"You hide it well," he said. "But I know acting when I see it. I know two things. First, how to shoot all kinds of weapons, because I was a soldier, and second, I know when people are acting, because I have been an actor. I have three great hopes. Would you like to hear them?"

Elena shrugged. They had stopped walking and were facing each other not far from the elevator. Their voices were low. A man pushing an empty gurney and softly humming something that sounded like Mozart moved past them.

"I hope that I make a better policeman than I did a soldier, playwright, or actor," he said. "That's one. Two, I hope my parents stay well and safe."

"And third?" she asked, pushing aside a strand of hair that had fallen across her cheek.

"Third," he said, "and most difficult to achieve, I hope that you will marry me."

Elena shook her head as if she were dealing with a comic who had told one too many for the evening.

"We went out three times," she said.

"Four," he corrected. "I'm counting the birthday party."

"Four," she conceded. "We went out four times. We got...close. And then for almost a month I hear nothing from you. And now a marriage proposal?"

"It is odd, isn't it?" Iosef said. "But that doesn't make it any the less sincere."

"You need a shave," Elena responded.

Iosef touched his cheek and said, "I loved you from the second I saw you at the birthday party at my parents' apartment. You walked across the room, ate a cracker, pushed a strand of hair from your face the way you did just now, and I loved you."

"Are you mad, Iosef?"

"No," he said. "I have gone without sleep for two days and I am probably a bit strange, but that does not alter the fact that I wish to marry you."

"Get some sleep," she said, stepping into the elevator, which had finally arrived and opened its doors.

A fat woman carrying a tray of medicine stepped out, and Elena moved around her to enter the elevator. Iosef jumped into the elevator just as the doors began to close. They both faced forward, not looking at each other.

"Will you come to the opening of the show Friday?" he asked.

"Perhaps," she said. "Perhaps not."

"We can go out afterward for some coffee," he said. "If you like, I promise not to propose again that night."

"Iosef," she said as the elevator slowly descended. "You do not know enough about me. I don't know enough about you. If it weren't that I know your parents, I would think you a lunatic."

"I spent three long years in the army being quite mad and killing people who struck me as being equally mad," he said. "Sanity is gradually coming back to me. Slowly, yes, but coming back. Come to the show."

The elevator door opened. A man and two women got on. They were arguing about someone named Eichen.

"I'll come," Elena said.

Iosef and Elena got off the elevator. She started to move across the small lobby of the hospital. A formidable-looking woman in her fifties sat behind the reception desk watching. Iosef took Elena's hand and stopped her. She turned and looked at him.

"My approach may be ill advised, coming as it does from an exhausted fool," he said, "but my words are sincere. My feelings are sincere. The only thing standing in the way of all this is what you think of me."

"I'm still considering that," Elena said, aware of the eyes of the receptionist.

"Good," he said. "How are you getting home?"

"Metro," she answered.

"I have a friend's car," he said.

Elena nodded her acceptance. There was much for her to think about. She had been depressed at his long period of inattention. Now his approach was bold and he spoke of marriage. Elena didn't know what she thought of marriage. She was fairly certain she didn't want it, not now. There was much for her to think about.

Chapter 14

Justice

The man who had been following Karpo for two days was very good. There were many reasons why Karpo might be followed, but the most likely one was that the man was connected to the information on the computer disk Karpo carried in his pocket and the printout of that disk he carried in his hand. Karpo guessed that the man had been in military intelligence, the KGB, or the Ministry of the Interior central office. He also guessed that the man was now working for the mafia that had been responsible for the death of Mathilde Verson.

The man had been waiting when Karpo came out of Petrovka early in the morning. He was across Petrovka Street talking to a street vendor and drinking something from a paper cup. The man was wearing a blue pea jacket and a dark knit cap. He did not look at Karpo. When Karpo got to the metro station, he did not see the man, but he was certain that he was there.

When Karpo got off at the Oktyabrskaya station, he spotted the man among the throng of morning workers hurrying to jobs in the district. Karpo walked down Dmitrov Street past the French Embassy at Number 43. The French had kept the original Igumnov House, a late eighteenth-century red-brick building, and in the 1980s erected a modern building beside it. Moscow, like the French Embassy, is a bizarre contrast of periods, a splatter of old architecture, new construction, and crumbling Soviet concrete. Karpo knew every street.

He walked slowly to the statue of Georgi Dmitrov, a hero of the Bulgarian workers' union. Dmitrov stood above him, supposedly calling on his audience to join the now-dead Revolution. When he was a young policeman, in his early twenties, Karpo had been at the unveiling of this statue. It had been one of the many affirmations in his life that the Revolution, in spite of its failures and the corruption of its bureaucrats, would succeed—tall, passionate, solid. No one but tourists paid any attention to the statue now.

Karpo turned down *Ulitsa Bolshaya Polyank*, Big Plank Street, and crossed the *Maly Kamenniy Most*, the Small Stone Bridge, over the *Obvodny* Canal, the twisting canal. The man had to be well behind Karpo now, and there were few people crossing the bridge. The man had no choice, if he were not to lose his quarry, but to cross the bridge as well.

Karpo looked toward the *Udarnik* Cinema, the hard worker cinema, on his left and then entered the square on his right, moving directly to a garden facing Lavrushinsky Lane. There was a bench under the statue of the artist Ilya Repin. Karpo sat and for the first time looked directly at the man who was following him. The man was a good fifty yards away, pretending to read a book after he checked his watch and looked down the street for an imaginary ride. When the man did glance in Karpo's direction, he saw the pale policeman in black staring at him. The man pretended not to notice and returned to his book. When next he glanced at the man on the bench, Karpo was motioning for him to come.

The man's confusion was brief. He was a professional. He had been in the KGB and had spent hundreds of hours following people. He tucked the book under his arm and walked over to Karpo on the bench. The man paused in front of the detective and then sat.

"What are you reading?" Karpo asked.

"A bad book about some fools who hijack a train in Germany," said the man. He was at least fifty and had a stocky build and a flat, blocky face.

"You have something to say to me?" the man said, standing in front of Karpo.

"I have something to say to the man or men

who employ your services," said Karpo. "I wish to make a trade with them."

Karpo took the printout of the disk out of his cloth bag and handed it to the man, who took it and read the first page. When he was done, he handed it back to Karpo.

"It was prepared by Igor Kuzen, who was murdered yesterday," Karpo said.

The man nodded in understanding and left in search of a phone. He returned five minutes later and sat next to Karpo.

"A car will be here in about five minutes," he said.

Karpo nodded. No more was said even after a black Buick with darkly tinted windows pulled up to the curb. Karpo followed the man and got into the backseat. The driver did not turn around. He had a tattoo of a green snake encircling his neck.

The car pulled up in front of the Sofia Restaurant across from the Pekin Hotel. On the sidewalk, in spite of the temperature, a man was playing the accordion while another man joined him with a violin. They had a single cap laid out for contributions. Karpo and the man who had followed him got out of the car. The car pulled away.

The musical duo was playing an old Russian dance. Six people stood around watching and listening. The man who had followed Karpo went to the restaurant, opened the door, and stood back so that Karpo could enter. There were no waiters, no settings on the tables. The restaurant would not open for hours. At the rear of the room, lighted at the moment by one small track

of lights, a man sat at a table smoking and looking at Karpo.

The man who had followed him motioned for
Karpo to go to the rear of the restaurant. Karpo
walked toward the man at the table. The man who
had followed him did not go with the detective.

When he approached the table, the seated man
pointed to the chair across from him. Karpo sat
and placed the printout on the table.

"Drink?" asked the man, leaning forward. "Coffee, tea, juice, a little Baileys?"

"No," said Karpo.

The man across from him was dressed like a
businessman—well-pressed suit with a colorful
Italian tie. He was a big man, a broad man, with a
pleasant, slightly pink face and long hair that was
tied in a ponytail. He smoked assiduously, pausing only to drink from what looked like a large
mug of tea. When the man reached for the mug,
Karpo saw the tattoos that crept down his arms
and the backs of both hands.

"Do you know who I am?" the man asked.

"I presume you are Lev Semionov," said Karpo.

"And how did you arrive at this assumption?"
asked Semionov.

Karpo looked at the thick computer printout.
Semionov reached for it, placed it before him on
the table, and began to read. His name was at the
top. He stopped reading after a page and began
to flip through the rest of the pages. He did this
quickly and then pushed the printout back to
Karpo.

"I've read it," said Semionov. "It seems that Igor Kuzen, the late Igor Kuzen, fooled me after all. He said that he had this disk and that he had sent a copy to a friend with instructions to mail it to the minister of the interior himself if Kuzen didn't call for three days. He did not, of course, give us the name of this friend. It took us five days to find everyone Kuzen had been close to since he was a boy. On the fifth day we found Katerina Molensaya, a cousin of Kuzen's in Minsk. She confessed almost immediately and turned over her disk. She died of the shock and a bullet."

"We also erased Kuzen's file on his hard drive," Semionov said. "But it appears there was still another copy. There may even be more."

"What happened three days ago—the killing on the street?" asked Karpo.

"Well," said the man, "as you know from reading this report of Kuzen's, we have no nuclear weapons or material. We have already received vast amounts of money from North Korea to deliver weapons and material we do not have and do not yet know if we can get."

"What happened Tuesday morning?" asked Karpo.

Semionov laughed, a small, bitter laugh. "The German worked for the North Koreans. Actually, he was a middleman, a counterpart of our Igor Kuzen, but much, much better. I could see on his face after he met with Kuzen that the German knew we had nothing. We followed him to the café where he met the prostitute, and we killed him before he could pass on information about the inadequacies of our famous scientist. I regret that your friend was killed, but…look, it's early. I've ordered a little something to eat."

"The bullets that killed Mathilde Verson did not come from the gun found near the body of Mikhail Sivak," Karpo said.

"The other gun," Semionov said with a shrug.

"There was no other weapon found at the scene except that of the dead German," said Karpo.

A man came to the table bearing a tray of rolls, butter, a coffeepot, and two cups. He placed the tray on the table and left immediately.

"I have no explanation," said Semionov.

"One more question," Karpo said as Semionov poured a cup of coffee. "Why are you telling me this?"

"Ah," said Semionov, putting down his cigarette. "I am confident that you did make copies of the disk, which includes information not only on our nuclear deception but on the crimes of all but a few of our more important members. Killing a policeman at this point will accomplish nothing. You have a list of names. A list of names means nothing."

Semionov handed a full cup to Karpo, who took it. Semionov's hand remained out. Karpo gave him the copy of the disk.

"See?" said Semionov, pocketing the disk. "If this were your only copy, you would not have handed it over so readily."

"And now?" asked Karpo.

"And now?" Semionov poured himself coffee. "We will have to find ways to neutralize this information."

Karpo nodded. "Bribes? Blackmail? Threats?"

"Actually," said Semionov, "you have done us a great favor. You have bought us some time to act instead of surprising us with a series of arrests. Or letting our North Korean partners find out before we do. Have a roll. Fresh. Smell them."

Semionov himself smelled one of the rolls, tore it open, and slathered it with butter. He offered it to Karpo, who declined it.

"She would be alive if you had not murdered the German," Karpo said.

"Oh, yes, I see your point," said Semionov, popping the roll into his mouth and chewing for a few moments. "But there is little more you can do. You've turned in the disk. Are you going to start killing us all? There are more than eighty of us," he said, tapping the printout in front of him. "And you don't even have the most important names. Kuzen didn't know them. Look at it this way. Had your system not fallen, we could not exist. If we did not exist, your…What was her name?"

"Mathilde Verson."

"Mathilde Verson," Semionov acknowledged with a wave of his hand, "would be alive today. Blame Yeltsin. Go shoot Yeltsin. Or if your fucking Revolution had not been corrupted by lunatics like Stalin and the fat thieves and alcoholics who followed him, there would have been no need to overthrow Communism. Go dig up Stalin, and Brezhnev, and…You see my point?"

"I see," said Karpo. "Everyone is responsible."

Semionov nodded in agreement, chewing amiably. "Now, I'm sorry," he said, "but I've got a lot of work to do to try to contain this. I'm not fool enough to offer you money or to threaten you. You've studied me. I've learned a bit about you."

"Responsibility rests with the one who commits the act and the one who orders it," said Karpo.

"Is that a quote?" asked Semionov, reaching for a second roll.

"Lenin," said Karpo.

Semionov shook his head sadly. "Yes, I heard you were one of those. When I was in prison, I read Lenin, Marx, Engels, Gorky, Dostoyevsky, Tolstoy, Gogol, Molière, Shakespeare, Nietzsche. I read. I thought. And you know what I concluded?"

"I do not," said Karpo.

Semionov waved the fresh roll in front of Karpo. "I concluded that I had no power, but that power was essential to me. It was as important as the blood that flowed through my veins. I concluded that life is short and meaningless and that killing neither damned me nor made me feel remorse. I concluded that all that would satisfy me was power. Not women, not a big house, not food. Only power. To tell people to act and have them obey without question. There is nothing more worthwhile in life. All else is lies to keep the system working."

"Though they could not express it so well," said Karpo, "that is just what most of the criminals we question believe."

"Yes," said Semionov with a smile. "But they do not understand why they want this or how this need has pervaded human history. I understand."

"And therefore," said Karpo, "you are far more dangerous."

"Precisely," said Semionov.

They sat silently for a few moments while Semionov ate and drank and thought and looked across the table at the rigid detective.

"I've changed my mind about you," said Semionov. "I think I shall have to have you killed. I think you are determined to kill me. Am I right?"

"You are right," said Karpo.

"There are tribes, those of New Guinea, who believe that you take on the power of the warrior you kill, especially if you eat his heart and liver. Perhaps I will eat your heart and liver, though I think they will be rather bitter. Leave now. You are depressing me."

Karpo turned and found himself facing the man who had followed him. The man was shaking his head no.

"You know what that shake means?" asked Semionov. "It means no one but Panushkin has followed you. And of this, Panushkin is certain, for it would mean his life if he were not."

Semionov placed a gun on the table, a gun that had probably rested in his lap during their entire conversation.

Karpo slowly put his hand to the lapel of his jacket and turned it over. A metal pin about the size of a kopeck was attached to the back of the lapel.

Semionov smiled and shook his head.

"Hubris," he said. "That feeling of power that makes you miss things. Who is on the other end of what we have been saying?"

"Does it matter?" asked Karpo.

Semionov shrugged, lit a fresh cigarette, and said, "If this is still private, we still have room to negotiate."

"There was never room to negotiate," said Karpo.

The door to the restaurant opened behind Karpo. The man who had followed him turned quickly, and two men came out of the darkness near the kitchen. Semionov sat patiently.

"We've got it," said Craig Hamilton evenly.

The men who had come out of the darkness raised their hands above their heads. Karpo turned to face the FBI agent and six heavily armed plain-clothesmen.

"Karpo," Hamilton cried suddenly, looking past Karpo at Semionov.

Karpo's gun was out and he turned in a crouch, aiming at Semionov and firing. The gun still sat in front of the startled gangster, who had started to reach for it when Karpo's bullet tore into his chest.

The hands of the other gangsters went up even higher.

"He was reaching for the gun," said Hamilton behind Karpo.

Semionov had bounced back against his chair and then slumped forward, overturning coffee, rolls, butter, and a full ashtray. Hamilton, an automatic weapon in one hand, moved forward quickly to the table and touched Semionov's neck.

"Dead," he said.

Karpo put his gun away under his jacket and looked at the FBI man, who said, "He was definitely going for the weapon."

There was no surge of power for Karpo. No sense of justice. No particular feeling. A man was dead. Mathilde was dead. Karpo turned, brushed past the man who had followed him less than an hour earlier, and walked to the door of the restaurant and out into the early winter.

There were twenty-seven criminal hearings set that day for this room in the House of Justice. That meant that the hearing boards had about fifteen minutes to decide if each case should go to trial. Eleven of the cases involved murder. The early cases would be heard by a board of three judges, none of whom was professionally trained in the law. By the afternoon wear and tear reduced the number of judges to one or two. The room was barely larger than a closet.

The eighth hearing took place slightly before noon. It was held before a panel of two men and one woman. The men were both around sixty. One was stoop-shouldered and tall. The other was short and thin and sat reasonably erect. The woman was much younger, perhaps as young as thirty or thirty-five. She was wearing a suit not much different from her colleagues, who sat on each side of her. Though he could not see her clearly, Sasha thought she was good-looking, dark, and a bit too thin for his taste.

Sasha's mouth was dry. Upon advice from the Procurator's Office, he had dressed but not changed the bandage on his head. There was a distinct patch of blood, and it was evident to anyone who looked his way that the nice-looking young man with the bandage was having trouble focusing.

"Are you all right?" asked Zelach, who sat next to him in the hearing room full of police and the accused.

"No," said Sasha, "but I will make it."

Two cases were called after Sasha arrived. Both were taken care of quickly. Two resulted in the accused being turned over for trial on cases of assault and vehicle theft. The third, a girl accused of theft and prostitution, was allowed to go because there was no evidence other than the testimony of the policeman. The victim had refused to appear. In the old days the word of a policeman would have been enough. Times had changed.

The Chazovs were called forward. They were wearing identical heavy brown trousers, white shirts, and plain brown sweaters. Their hair had been cut and they stood in a row, heads up facing the woman behind the bench. Their faces were clean. Behind the three boys stood the lawyer Lermonov and Elvira Chazova, apparently pregnant and carrying a small, sleeping child in her arms.

"Witnesses?" the woman justice called, looking at the complaint that lay in front of her. Her colleagues did the same with little interest or enthusiasm.

"Two," the man with the stooped shoulders said. "Officers Zelach and Tkach."

"Step forward," the woman said.

Zelach helped Sasha forward next to the three boys, who kept their eyes focused on the judges.

"Speak," the woman said.

"May I sit?" Sasha asked.

The justice nodded, and Zelach brought a chair forward.

"Thank you. We were staking out the apartment building of the Chazov boys. We had reason to believe they had murdered and robbed a man two…no, three days ago. We also had reason to believe they had robbed and murdered others."

The justices looked at the Chazovs and their mother and then back at the policeman.

"My partner was watching from an apartment across the street," Sasha went on dryly. "It was midnight and I was coming to relieve him. As I was about to enter the apartment building where he was watching from the window, I was attacked by these three." He pointed at the Chazov boys.

"You saw this?" asked the woman behind the table.

"I saw two of the boys in front of me. The other hit me with something. I turned. The boy was holding a piece of wood. It was covered with blood, my blood. Then something hit me again. I tried to turn and pull out my gun, but I went down and was unconscious for a minute or so."

"So," said the woman, "you did not actually see the boy hit you?"

"There was no one else there but the boy holding a piece of bloody wood."

"And then?"

"When I opened my eyes, the boys were handcuffed around a lamppost, and I thought I heard an ambulance coming."

"Officer Zelach, precisely what did you see and do?"

Zelach tried not to shift his weight from foot to foot as he met the eyes of the three justices behind the bench. It took a great deal of effort, but he managed. He also managed to look extremely nervous.

"I heard voices outside the window where I was watching for the Chazovs to return. I heard Inspector Tkach's voice. I ran out as quickly as I could. That boy..."

Zelach pointed at Boris.

"That boy held a rock in his hand and was about to bring it down on the head of Inspector Tkach, who was lying on the ground. That other boy held the piece of bloody wood in his hand."

"Did you see anyone else but your partner and the three boys?" asked the woman.

"No," said Zelach.

"And what did you do?" she asked.

"I...I knocked them down. I hit them. I hand-cuffed them to the lamppost."

The full courtroom sat restlessly, thinking about their own cases, trying to determine if there was some pattern, something they should say, some way they should act.

"Officer Zelach," said the stooped man. "You are a big man. Much bigger than these boys. Why did you have to hit them to subdue them? Each boy has bruises, even the little one."

"I was trying to protect Sasha Tkach," Zelach said.

"But," said the small justice, who was sitting erect and pointing a pencil at Zelach, "they were not beating Inspector Tkach when you arrived?"

"No," said Zelach. "But I could see they were going to hit him again."

"So you beat and kicked them?" asked the woman.

"I..." Zelach stammered.

"You were not just protecting your partner," said the woman. "You were taking out your anger on the boys who you believed had injured him?"

"I...They had almost killed Sasha Tkach. I was—"

"Angry? Out of control?" asked the woman. "Did you ask the boys what had happened before you started beating and kicking them?"

"No," said Zelach.

"Alexei Chazov," the woman said, turning her eyes to the tallest and oldest of the three accused.

"Did you and your brothers beat Inspector Tkach?"

"No," said Alexei, firmly shaking his head.

"Who did?" asked the stoop-shouldered justice.

"Two older boys," said Alexei. "Boys I've never seen. We saw them hitting this man from behind and we ran over to help. I hit one of the boys with a piece of wood, made him bleed. My brother Boris picked up a rock and threatened to throw it at them. The two boys ducked into the building right behind us. Then the big policeman came out and started to hit and kick us. We tried to tell him about the two boys who had gone into the building. We thought he might still be able to catch them, but he wouldn't listen."

"Mark Chazov," asked the woman justice, "is this what happened?"

"Yes," said the youngest and smallest brother, whose face had been scrubbed almost sore.

Lermonov patted Mark on the shoulder, and Sasha, through his dizziness, was sure he had seen nearly imperceptible nods exchanged between the lawyer and the woman justice.

"Any other witnesses? Any more evidence?" asked the woman justice.

"We are poor but good people," said Elvira Chazova, rocking her sleeping child. "That policeman would be dead if my boys hadn't run to help him. They took on killers bigger than they were. Instead of thanks they get beaten and put on trial."

"This is not a trial," the woman justice said.

"This is a hearing to determine if there should be a trial."

The woman turned to the other justices, and each spoke in her ear. She wrote on the declaration before her and then looked up.

"There is insufficient reason to hold these children for the attack on Inspector Tkach," she said. "There will be a notice of reprimand placed in the file of Officer Zelach for his thoughtless attack on these children. There is some reason to believe that these children actually saved the inspector's life. Instead of trying to get them incarcerated, he should be thanking them."

Sasha's eyes may have betrayed him, but he thought he saw another instant of eye contact between the woman justice and the lawyer.

"Your Honor," Sasha said, standing. "These are the boys who beat me. These are the boys who murdered a man only a day before. To let them—"

"The case has been presented and a decision made. You are out of order, Inspector, but court will overlook this because of your exertion. Alexei, Boris, and Mark Chazov are free to go," the woman went on. "The justices strongly recommend that their mother enforce a curfew of ten o'clock for her sons to keep them from further trouble."

"I will," said Elvira sincerely.

"Next," said the justice.

Zelach looked down at Sasha in Sasha tried to focus on the Chazovs as him. Each boy had a touch of a smile

304

Zelach looked down at Sasha in confusion. Sasha tried to focus on the Chazovs as they passed him. Each boy had a touch of a smile on his face.

The lawyer grinned and the mother paused, baby in her arms, to whisper something to Sasha.

The justices were reading the summary of the next case as Zelach helped Sasha to his feet.

"What did she say?" asked Zelach, looking at the retreating back of Elvira Chazova.

"She told me my home address," said Sasha.

The twenty-first of that day's hearing took place late in the afternoon. This one was much shorter, and there was but one justice and only a handful of people in the hearing room.

The single justice was a stout, bullish man in his forties with a short military haircut. He wore a brown suit and a tie that did not come close to matching.

Anna Porvinovich and Yevgeniy Porvinovich stood to the right of the table. Anna's dark eyes caught those of the justice and he looked away. Rostnikov stood to the left of the table with Alexei Porvinovich, who, with the help of the therapist and drugs prescribed by Sarah's doctor cousin, had managed to approach a semblance of composure. He was immaculately dressed and his hair perfectly trimmed. His face had an overall discolored puffiness, and his broken jaw had been wired shut so that he could only speak between his teeth like a poor ventriloquist.

"The wrong people are standing before me accused of a crime," said the judge. "Facts. Two men kidnap Alexei Porvinovich from the street and take him to an apartment. The two men work in the garage where the Porvinoviches take their automobile for repair. One of the two men, according to the distraught victim, claims that the kidnapping was planned by the victim's wife and brother and that he was the wife's lover. Was the kidnapper lying, perhaps to torment his victim? We do not know. Did the victim create a fantasy of his betrayal by his automobile mechanic, his brother, and his wife? This, too, we do not know. It has been known to happen to distraught victims who fear for their lives. We have only the victim's word for all of this, since he managed to disarm one of the kidnappers, shoot him, and, by his own words, calmly or not so calmly wait till the other kidnapper returned and then shoot him. His next action was to return home in a state of near madness. Had not a police inspector been present, he may well have murdered his wife and brother. What we have here is an unfortunate situation. It is my understanding that Alexei Porvinovich is under psychiatric care, which he certainly needs. There is no case here. All persons who are part of this unfortunate circumstance are free to go."

Alexei Porvinovich laughed through his teeth as his wife and brother walked past him and Rostnikov.

"Porvinovich," Rostnikov whispered.

Porvinovich could not stop laughing.

Rostnikov took his arm.

"You see how well they have learned from me," Porvinovich said, trying to control his laughter, his lips barely moving. "They've bribed the right people."

The justice looked up from his papers and glared at Porvinovich.

"Clear the hearing room," the justice said.

Rostnikov led Porvinovich from the room.

"You promised me justice," said Porvinovich.

"I was wrong," said Rostnikov.

"I could have shot them, but you stopped me," said Porvinovich.

Rostnikov had turned the tape of Mrs. Porvinovich's conversation with Artiom Solovyov over to the justice's office the day before. He had also indicated that both he and the FBI man were prepared to testify. The justice had made no mention of the tape and did not ask for Rostnikov's or Hamilton's testimony.

It was difficult to escape Porvinovich's accusation of bribery, but, to give the judge his due, he may simply have felt that there was not a sufficient case to bring to trial and that Rostnikov's and Hamilton's testimony and the tape would simply further clog the already confused judicial system.

In the corridor outside the hearing room Anna Porvinovich stood waiting. Yevgeniy stood nervously on her right. A tall, good-looking man with teeth as perfect as those of an American movie star stood on her left. Rostnikov thought she looked especially beautiful in her triumph.

"Alexei Porvinovich," the good-looking man said. "You have two days to remove your belongings from the apartment in which you and your wife have resided. She will meanwhile move to a hotel that will be billed to you. Anna Ivanovna

Porvinovich has filed papers of divorce, and we have obtained a court order that does not permit you to come within one hundred yards of your wife or your brother."

The man handed a confused Porvinovich a substantial folder full of papers.

"Do you understand?" asked the man.

Alexei looked at his wife, whose face revealed nothing. His brother looked down.

Alexei began to laugh again and held up the folder.

The good-looking man guided Anna through the crowd with Yevgeniy a few paces behind.

People looked at the laughing Alexei, but no one stopped.

"Alexei Porvinovich," Rostnikov said firmly.

"Ah," said Porvinovich, his eyes wet with tears of laughter. "First she tries to kill me and then she takes everything away from me. I've always underestimated her."

"Let's go," said Rostnikov, leading Porvinovich toward the door of the building. "We'll get some tea and talk about Russian irony. It should take us a century or two."

"It won't do them any good," said Porvinovich, controlling his laughter.

"Why?" asked Rostnikov, wishing they could sit somewhere, anywhere.

"Because I plan to have them killed," Porvinovich whispered.

And Rostnikov knew that, madness or no madness, the man meant what he was saying.

The twenty-seventh case of the day was heard by the stoop-shouldered justice, who could now barely keep his eyes open. Neither lawyers nor litigants had approached the justice in an attempt to secure a favorable decision. They were poor people quarreling over who had started the fight that resulted in both of them being arrested for assaulting the other. The women screamed at each other before the justice, who checked his watch and decided the day of work had ended. He told the women, both of whom were well over sixty, that since their injuries seemed more or less equal and that it was impossible to determine what the battle was about, there would be no trial recommendation and that they were ordered not to speak to each other again or come within one hundred yards of each other. Though the two women were sisters and lived across the hall from each other, they nodded obediently and left the courtroom quickly.

The justice stood up. Outside the closed courtroom door he could hear the two women arguing as they moved away. The few remaining spectators left. The justice took off his glasses and leaned forward to look at the handwritten decisions of the day. Of the twenty-seven hearings, twenty-two had been dismissed. Four had resulted in pleas of guilt and one, a lunatic who had run amok with a butcher knife in Red Square seeking out foreigners, had been turned over for trial.

At a nearby coffee stand, Rostnikov pushed a

cup of something hot and dark to Porvinovich, who drank in thirsty, angry gulps.

"In the 1860s," Rostnikov said, guiding Porvinovich away from the stand so that others could make their purchases of hot water with the hint of tea or coffee, "Czar Nicholas the First freed the serfs and reformed the courts. No longer were decisions simply handed down by judges who were themselves on the fringes of nobility. There were juries of different sizes with now-free and illiterate serfs and merchants pulled from offices, street markets, and shops. The trials were mad. Jurors screamed out questions about the defendant's family and political beliefs. Spectators often howled or laughed, and the judges carefully guided the juries when possible to the correct decision."

Porvinovich seemed to be paying no attention, but Rostnikov went on.

"The system eventually collapsed of its own corruption, to be replaced by a judicial system equally corrupt, and later by the Soviet system, which seemed to return to that of the 1860s. Now...It's part of a cycle. You were born in the wrong century, Alexei Porvinovich."

"I should have bribed the justice more than they did," said Porvinovich.

"You got away with murder," Rostnikov said.

"Execution, retribution," said Porvinovich wildly. "But where was justice?"

Rostnikov knew the answer, but he was not about to give it to this man who could not listen.

Chapter 15

Family

"Would you like another piece?" Sarah asked the girls.

Both nodded yes. Rostnikov motioned to the waiter in the ridiculous Pizza Hut uniform. The waiter approached.

"How much do I have left on my coupons?"

"Enough for two more pizzas," the waiter said. "And a Pepsi."

"Fine," said Rostnikov, looking at Hamilton, who had expertly disposed of two slices.

The waiter hurried off. The girls were chewing on crusts and nudging each other. At the end of the table Elena and Iosef were consuming the last of their pizza and talking quietly. Elena was smiling as if she had a secret.

"We must save a piece for Anna Timofeyeva," said Sarah.

Rostnikov had hoped there would be enough to bring a free American pizza to Tkach's family, but that was clearly not to be. He would have to buy one.

Sarah nodded and touched her husband's hand. They had invited, even urged, Karpo to join them, but he had refused, as had Zelach and his mother.

They had come very early, before the Americans, French, Germans, and recently wealthy criminals had descended on the popular restaurant, but now the room was starting to fill, and the waiters were looking around for tables.

"I ordered a pizza for Inspector Tkach's family," said Hamilton. "Compliments of the United States government."

"Thank you," said Rostnikov.

"I talked to my wife and kids this morning," said Hamilton. "They sounded like they were on another planet."

"America is another planet," said Sarah. "I've tried to get Porfiry Petrovich to go there, but…it's too late now. This is our planet."

The next two pizzas came. The waiter put one on each end of the table. Rostnikov reached over, felt the pain in his leg, and took another slice.

Emil Karpo sat in the chair next to Paulinin's desk. They were drinking strong coffee that Paulinin had brewed and poured into two cups that had been used for who-knows-what. Paulinin took a sip, wiped his hands on his dirty lab coat, and looked down at a sheet of notes.

"The ballistics people were right for a change," he said. "The bullets that killed her did not come from the gun in the hands of the dead man with the tattoos. His was state-of-the-art. The one that killed her…"

Karpo sipped his coffee.

"You sure you want me to go on?" asked Paulinin.

Karpo nodded.

"The dolts who did the autopsy didn't even check the bullets," Paulinin said. "Sloppy. They were better in the days of the czars. They had some pride. No second weapon was found?"

"No," said Karpo. "None was found in the hands or near the bodies of any of the dead."

Paulinin shrugged.

"You took care of…" Karpo began.

"You will have the ashes in a few days," said Paulinin.

Karpo nodded.

"Would you like to see a double kidney?" Paulinin asked. "I just—"

Karpo shook his head no.

Something bubbled gently in the darkness of the laboratory on the second level below the ground floor. Something creaked. And certainly something smelled. There were many smells.

"When did you last eat, Karpo?" Paulinin asked.

Karpo looked at the little man with some interest. Paulinin was definitely concerned about him.

"I'll eat later," said Karpo.

"I have half a chicken, a cabbage, and an almost full bottle of wine in my room," said Paulinin.

"I need no favors," Karpo said.

"But I do," said Paulinin. "I am tired. I am hungry, and yours is the only company I enjoy. Come, we'll eat chicken and I'll tell you about the most interesting bodies I have worked on."

"Who could resist such an offer?" Karpo said.

"You are developing a sense of humor in your depression," said Paulinin.

It was in the rear of her closet. Irina Smetenova

had not opened the bag since she had brought it back to her apartment. The dog had sniffed at the closet door, and Irina remembered the single orange she had placed in the bag. An orange, two potatoes, which were probably growing green little plants by now, and a jar of preserves.

Irina had a weak back, crippled knees, a small pension, and a hungry dog. Her life was an endless round of painful trips to the park with Dolgi and then the trips to the shops to buy what she could. She dealt little with her neighbors, who regarded her with the same suspicion with which she regarded them. Hers was not a good neighborhood, and it was getting worse all the time. Sofia Workovna, who lived on the ground floor, had been broken into and beaten up by two men. Her purse and television had been taken, along with her knives and forks and a few little inexpensive curios the old woman had collected. It was no longer a good neighborhood.

Irina moved to the closet, and Dolgi followed, wagging his tail.

These were troubled times, and there was no one to turn to. Irina's only child was a mother herself now with a grown daughter off in Estonia. Irina's sister was long dead. There were only herself and Dolgi.

So, when she had heard the gunshots across the street while heading for the park, she had fallen to her knees and pulled her dog into her arms. She had watched in fascination as the bald, tattooed man fired into the restaurant window. She saw the woman with the red hair jerk and fall forward. She saw the man next to her fire some kind of weapon out the window. She saw the tattooed man jerk back as he was shot, and the car drive off with a screech, its windows smashed by wild shots from the man in the café.

The shooting stopped. People got up. Many hurried away, not wanting to be witnesses. Some moved forward slowly. Irina had crossed the street holding her dog in one arm and her shopping bag in the other.

Irina had knelt next to the tattooed man in the street, who was not yet quite dead. He tried to speak and then closed his eyes, his head dropping to the left. Irina picked up the gun and put it into her shopping bag. Her knees ached as she stood. Dolgi whimpered at the smell of death.

Irina turned to the woman with the red hair, but knew she was dead.

And then the sound of a police car somewhere far off sent the looters flying through the broken windows and door.

Irina had joined the crowd by the time the police arrived—an old woman clutching her dog and her shopping bag.

Now, two days later, she opened her closet and pulled out the shopping bag. The orange was pungent and rotting. The potatoes were soft but still edible, and the gun was still shining and much lighter than one would have expected. She had picked it up without thought and now she held it in fear and some sense of excitement. Dolgi whimpered and ran to the ancient couch.

Irina held it the way she had seen them do on television. It did not feel bad. In fact, it felt very good, very comforting. Her door was sturdy. If robbers tried to break in, they would not beat her as they had Sofia Workovna, nor would they hurt Dolgi and steal her things. She was no longer a helpless old woman with crippled knees. She would sleep with the weapon next to her small bed in the corner. She would sleep less frightened than she had in many, many months.

Emil Karpo returned to his apartment around midnight. Paulinin had become quite drunk and insisted on recounting many of his most difficult cases. He even gave small hints about a father still living, a sister with two or three children, and years clerking behind the counter at the family's pharmacy in Minsk. Finally he had fallen asleep and Karpo had left. He had drunk nothing alcoholic, nor had he any desire to do so. Then he had walked the three miles to his apartment in the swirling wind and the first real snowfall of winter.

At his door Karpo paused. The hairs were out of place. Someone had entered his apartment. He took his gun from its holster and quickly went to the end of the hall, where he flicked the switch that sent the hallway into darkness. He made his way along the wall to his door, knowing that it would be awkward to insert the key and open the door with his broken finger, but he had to keep the gun in his right hand and ready.

He opened the door as quietly as he could and entered the one-room apartment in a crouch.

The small light on the desk was on. The room was empty. Karpo locked the door behind him with the interior bolts and moved to the desk. There was a note under the light. Still holding the gun, Karpo picked up the note and read it: "Emil, please excuse the intrusion. Sarah and I thought you should have it." The note was signed "Porfiry Petrovich." Karpo put his gun back in the holster and wondered what "it" was. He turned on the remaining lights in the room and immediately saw the painting hanging on the wall across from his bed. It was the only space that was not occupied by Mathilde's paintings, and now it held one more.

Karpo took off his jacket and holster and sat on his bed looking at the painting that Mathilde had given the Rostnikovs. In the foreground the figure of a woman reclined, looking up a grassy hill away from the viewer, her red hair billowing in a gentle wind. At the top of the grassy hill stood a small house. Karpo looked at the woman and joined her in looking up the hill at the house. He sat looking for perhaps an hour before he lay back, fully clothed, and fell asleep. For the first time since he was a small child, he slept with the lights on.